THE INDIGENT
Book of Aniyas

ISBN: 978-1-955228-08-4

Printed in the United States of America

Thank you dad. I love you.

THE INDIGENT
Book of Aniyas

ANECE ROCHELL

Beautiful Minds
Publishing

TABLE OF CONTENTS

Introduction 1

Chapter One 2
Welcome to My World

Chapter Two 11
Growing Pains

Chapter Three 23
A House Divided

Chapter Four 31
A Mother's Love

Chapter Five 42
Unlikely Pairing

Chapter Six 50
Deceptive Appearances

Chapter Seven 56
The Radiant Ones

Chapter Eight 61
Friends to Foes

Chapter Nine..70
Build, Destroy, Rebuild

Chapter Ten..79
Secrets Revealed

Chapter Eleven...93
Chastis of Doom

Chapter Twelve 103
The Source Bearer

Chapter Thirteen 115
The Rebellion

Chapter Fourteen 127
The Lost One

Chapter Fifteen 136
Training Day

Chapter Sixteen 145
No Going Back

Chapter Seventeen 155
The True Story

Chapter Eighteen 164
The Extraordinary Assessment of Valor

Chapter Nineteen 183
Shine Bright

Chapter Twenty 190
Rise Up!

About the Author 212

INTRODUCTION

Can you imagine a world with no crime or hatred? Just peace, joy and happiness, a planet where everyone loves and supports one another. I can, and I hope for it daily, but the reality is, we don't live in that world. Does it seem like every time you turn on your television or look down at your phone, it's another senseless act of violence, another protest, another life gone too soon? It most definitely feels that way to me.

I also feel that there are solutions to some of these unfortunate situations, and we can make this world a better place if we come together in love.

I started this trilogy back in 2018, and I'm elated to bring you the first book, which will touch on a few of the issues I just mentioned. Grab a snack and prepare for a journey of action and adventure. Also prepare to shed a few tears, laugh, and you might even feel the impulse to get up and bust out your best dance moves, but most importantly prepare to be hopeful and empowered.

CHAPTER ONE

Welcome to My World

While sitting in my sleeping chamber, I stared out the window at the glorious trees that stood before me. The trees were towering and vibrant. Purple, orange, fuchsia, and green were the colors of the leaves that swayed to the rhythm of the wind's whispers, and I swayed with them. My body began to swirl, twirl, and move, becoming lost in the melody that played in my head. I was free to be me behind these four walls, but outside of these walls was a different story.

There was no dancing allowed beyond my sleeping chamber. If Mother caught me, I would be punished. My mother always told me that dancing was wicked, and Emperor Kadar was not pleased with such things. Emperor Kadar never seemed to be pleased with anything. How could something that made me feel so happy and free be wicked?

"Aniyas!" Mother called. Her voice stopped my movements.

"Yes mother!"

"Get dressed for chastis and hurry up!" she yelled.

We attend chastis once a week, sometimes twice a week, to worship the Leading Light. I did not completely understand what I was worshiping, but it pleased Mother and I wanted to make her happy. Emperor Kadar led us in worship. Kadar was our connection to the Leading Light, and he enforced the rules given to us by the Leading Light via the Pathway. The Leading Light is our divine power, and the Pathway is a book used as our spiritual guide. It seems more like a book of rules if you ask me, but if we do not follow those rules there will be consequences. No one had ever seen the Leading Light, but Kadar assured us that the Light was real, and he was the way to the Light. Mother held on to Kadar's every word without question, but I questioned everything.

After I bathed, I donned my dress and hooded robe. The robes are mandatory for chastis. I went downstairs, sat in a chair, and Mother began to comb my hair. Even though I was old enough to comb my own hair, my mother insisted. Getting my hair combed was like slow torture. Mother used a heating wand on my hair to straighten it. She also made me keep my hair pulled back in a bun. I did not like my hair straight or pulled back. My hair was made to be big, loose, and free!

"Do I have to get my hair straightened?" I complained.

"Yes, you do!"

I already knew the answer to my question, but it never stopped me from asking. I also didn't like covering my hair. At academia it was not mandatory to cover our hair, but Emperor Kadar commanded that our hair be covered during chastis and when we were outside performing daily duties. Mother adhered to Kadar's commands. Meesa always followed the rules.

Who is Meesa? Meesa is my mother, and she is a complicated woman. Meesa is well-spoken, but she is also shy and quiet. Mother has a terrible temper, and her mean streaks are frightening. Meesa can also be cold and distant at times. She does not show affection, and I have never seen her cry. Mother is an introvert, so chastis is really the only place she goes. At home Mother seemed miserable, but at chastis she was always in a pleasant mood.

Mother is short in stature, and she has gained a few extra pounds over the years. But in her heyday, she was curvy with the perfect figure. Meesa's eyes are small and slanted. Her cheek bones are high and pronounced, and she has full lips. Mother never wears makeup because it is forbidden in the Pathway, but she does not need it anyway because her skin is flawless. Meesa's hair is so thick and full many people would envy it, but she keeps it straightened. Mother is a beautiful woman, but I am not sure she realizes it. Meesa always cooks, she educated us when we were small, and taught us to be well mannered. We are always well groomed, and Mother adorns us in the latest garbs. From the outside looking in, Meesa is the perfect mother, and we are the perfect family.

Landis and Landon walked into the kitchen turning their noses up at me. I stuck out my tongue and wiggled my head at them.

"Be still!" yelled Mother, as she struck my head with the comb. Landis smirked at me, while Landon giggled. In return, I rolled my eyes. Landis and Landon are my older twin brothers. The twins are the male versions of our mother. They resemble her, and they inherited Meesa's short stature. Landis and Landon were never that fond of me. When I was younger, I tried to follow my brothers everywhere because I loved them dearly. Landis and Landon did not see it that way, I was just their annoying little sister. Despite all my efforts, the twins still shunned me.

Landis and Landon were two years old when Mother met Father. Meesa and Father married after six months of dating, and ten months later I was born. The twins were not pleased with my arrival. As we grew older, I avoided Landis and Landon at all costs. It was necessary because we all had horrible tempers, and sometimes our arguments led to physical altercations.

"Good morning boys," said Mother, with a smile.

"Good morning Mother," the twins replied. Meesa favored the twins over me. Mother never expressed those exact words, but her actions showed it.

Adrielle walked into the kitchen. He is the kindest human I have ever met, and we are fortunate to have him as a father. He is a handsome man with a larger-than-life personality, and Father is extremely friendly. Adrielle is tall with wavy jet-black hair. He has round eyes and a full well-groomed beard. My father's looks and personality attracted people to him, especially women. I ran a great deal of errands with Adrielle when I was younger. Women would approach Father smiling and flirting, but I made sure to announce he was married.

A few years ago, Ms. Saunders strutted up to Father while we were making fruit deliveries. She was batting her eyelashes, flipping her hair, and giggling for no reason as they conversed. Very politely, I grabbed Adrielle's hand, looked Ms. Saunders in her eyes and said, "We have to go Father. Mother, your wife is waiting for us." Giving Ms. Saunders a fake smile, I pulled Adrielle away and walked off.

Father is a hardworking man, and he never complains about anything. Our family is far from rich, but we always have everything we need. Adrielle is not as strict about following the rules as Mother is, but chastis is an important part of Father's life as well. Adrielle did not agree with all of Emperor Kadar's actions, but he believes in the Leading Light and the Pathway.

"Hey moo-moo," said Father as he kissed my forehead. Father said good morning to Mother and the twins. Adrielle tried to kiss Meesa, but she turned away. Father walked out of the kitchen with disappointment in his eyes. Mother rarely accepts Adrielle's affection, and I do not understand why.

We were all ready to leave for chastis. Using vehicles is forbidden on chastis days, so everyone walks. I do not understand why we must walk, and no one can give me a good explanation. It is a sacred day Meesa would say, whatever that meant. What made this day so sacred that we couldn't drive? I have always been an inquisitive child and that annoys Mother. Meesa becomes even more annoyed when she does not have the answers to my questions. Mother's go to line is, because I said so. Father finds my curiosity amusing, and he tries to answer my questions to the best of his ability.

As we were walking, I saw my best friend Mara. Mara is a cute girl. She is slim and short in stature. She has light skin, a thin nose, thin lips, and long wavy hair. She is the societal standard of beauty, so, many people consider her to be beautiful. Mara is my best friend, but we are complete opposites. Mara is a girly girl, and I jump off my car port for fun.

When we were younger, Mara was the only girl in our province that would play with me. The other girls said I was too rough. It was not my intention to be rough, but growing up with two brothers and spending most of my time with Father, I developed some of their characteristics.

Mara lives with her grandparents because her parents had gone missing many years ago. She was a baby when they disappeared, so she does not remember them. Unfortunately, Mara's parents are presumed dead.

"Hi Mara!" I waved eagerly.

"Hey Aniyas!" she shouted back. I asked Mother if I could walk with Mara, but her answer was no. Folding my arms, I pouted like a toddler.

Walking into chastis, the elites and regime were standing in front by the platform. The regime rules the land and creates our laws. The laws that apply to us, do not apply to the elites. Elites are mean, snobbish, rude, and cruel. Emperor Kadar and the regime favor the elites for a couple of reasons, one reason being, they are wealthy. There are three rankings in our power structure and of course the elites top the list. The elites must wear all white. The colors we wear are not by choice, they are enforced by the regime to distinguish between the rankings. Attending chastis was also enforced upon all citizens by law. If we did not attend chastis, there would be dire consequences.

My family is in the middle of the power structure, we are known as conventionals. We are not rich, but we are not necessarily poor. The regime forced us to wear the color gray. At the bottom of the barrow are the indigents. Indigents are impoverished, and society treats them horribly. Indigents wear the color black because black is seen as the color of dishonor. The indigents are only allowed to be in the company of elites during chastis. Indigents and conventionals are allowed to intermingle, and some conventionals are allowed to associate with the elites, but the indigents cannot intermingle with the elites at all. Even though conventionals are ranked higher than the indigents, we are still looked down upon by the elites. Unfortunately, there are conventionals that also look down upon indigents, and Meesa is one of them.

Mother, many other conventionals, and some indigents long to be accepted by the elites, and I just do not understand why. I would never beg to be in the presence of a group of individuals that did not want to be around me. Meesa does not like me talking to indigents, but I find them to be much better people than elites.

Indigents are smart, creative, beautiful, artistic, and for the most part good people. I do not understand how they are at the bottom of our power structure. Keir is my good friend, and he is an indigent. Mother does not approve of me associating with Keir, but I talk to him anyway.

Keir is exceedingly intelligent, and like his father, he is tall, dark, and handsome. Keir's father has a kind soul, and his mother is kind too. Taking after his parents in that way, Keir was always nice to me. Mother instructs me to come straight home after academia, but some days I visit Keir. I lie and tell Meesa I am going to the information center to do homework. The information center is connected to our academia, so Mother feels comfortable with me being there. As an indigent, Keir and his family live in the quarters. The quarters are hut-like buildings that are connected. Their dwelling place is small, but it is the homiest, most loving place I have ever been in.

Spotting Keir at chastis, I began to wave. He waved back. Once Mother realized who I was waving at she grabbed my hand, pulled it down, and frowned. We took our seats, and Meesa whispered in my ear, "Why are you so interested in that indigent? You need to become friends with an elite, like that nice young man Chase."

I turned my head and rolled my eyes in disgust. There is nothing nice about Chase, he is a piece of work! Chase Edgerton is the most arrogant human being I have ever met, most likely because his family is the wealthiest of all the elites. You would think with all the coins his family has acquired, Chase would be happy, but he is a mean unpleasant bully. I hate his guts!

Mara and I are two of the few conventionals that attend academia with the elites. We were labeled as gifted, so we are allowed to attend their educational institution. Well, after years of protesting and begging, a few of the gifted conventionals were granted access to their institutions. I dislike Edgerton with a passion! Edgerton is the name of our academia, which was founded by Chase's great-great-great-grandfather. One day at lunch, Chase tripped a new novice. The novices' lunch went flying in the air, and the novice crashed hard onto the floor. Everyone began to laugh, but I did not think it was funny. I went and helped the novice off the floor and gave Chase the evil eye. Chase was not punished for what he did. Chase never gets punished because that is the privilege of being an elite.

All I heard was blah, blah, blah, as Emperor Kadar spoke. I am tired of hearing the same rules and what we cannot do every week. The songs we sing are dry, and there is no emotion put into anything. We cannot clap or sway. We cannot play instruments like the drum and guitar. All we have is a harp and piano, and they are played with no soul at all.

Chastis is boring and there are things I do not understand about it, like when the collection salver comes out. Every family must walk to the collection salver and pay a chastis tax, no matter how rich or poor they are. We collect a substantial amount of coins at chastis, but there are still poverty-stricken people everywhere. Emperor Kadar and the regime should help the indigents with these coins, but they do not. Instead, they force the indigents to give what little they have, and if they cannot pay their chastis tax they are disciplined.

Two months ago, an indigent family did not have their chastis tax. The father tried to explain why he could not pay that day, but Emperor Kadar disregarded his explanation. Kadar made the family kneel before him, kiss his boots, and beg for forgiveness. I did not see that family at chastis again until a month after that degrading day, and they looked awful. Even the young boy and girl of that family looked as if they had been through anguish. All these variables made me dislike chastis and Emperor Kadar. I only pretend to like chastis to make Meesa happy. My mother is a difficult woman to please, and I wanted nothing more but for her to like me. She loves chastis, so I thought maybe if I pretended to like something she loved, it would make her love and like me too.

After six, long, excruciating hours, chastis was finally over. The elites entered and left chastis through the front door. The conventionals and indigents must enter and leave through the back door. I was searching all around for Keir, but I did not see him.

"Let's go Aniyas!" called Mother. As we walked back to our dwelling place, Mara skipped beside me.

"Hey!" I yelled, as I hugged Mara.

Mara looked at me with a twinkle in her eye. "Did you see Chase? He looked so handsome today."

"Yuck!" I responded. Mara has had a crush on Chase since pre-academia. She was obsessed.

Mara continued to talk about Chase, and I wanted to vomit.

"Did you see Keir on your way out?" I asked, while changing the subject.

"Nope, I didn't see your boyfriend!"

"He is not my boyfriend! We are just friends!" I shouted.

"Aniyas and Keir sitting in a tree k-i-s-s-i-n-g!" Mara taunted.

"Stop it, Mara!" I pleaded, as I tried not to smile. She did not stop. Mara sang that song to me all the way home.

When we arrived at our dwelling place, I ran upstairs, changed my garbs, and let my hair down. Sitting on my bed, I began to daydream. A tap on my window startled me back to reality.

"Keir! What are you doing here?" I questioned, as I opened the window.

"I'm here to see you of course. I didn't get a chance to talk to you at stupid chastis, so I stopped by," said Keir.

"You know if Meesa sees you we are going to have a serious problem."

"You are worth any problem, beautiful." I blushed. Keir was aware that my mother was not fond of him. Adrielle on the other hand, loves Keir. As I chatted with Keir, I feared Mother would catch us. I wish he could stay longer, but it was time for him to go.

Walking downstairs, I asked Meesa for permission to go outside. "As long as you stay in the courtyard," she replied. Mother is overprotective. I am not allowed to go outside of our courtyard, besides chastis, academia, and the information center.

Stepping outside, I looked around and breathed in the fresh air. A gentle breeze caressed my face. Gardash is a lovely place. Gardash is the name of the province we reside in. While gazing at the beauty of our province and all the vibrant colors that surrounded me, I looked down at my gray garbs and became disheartened.

Even though Meesa dressed us well, I despised the fact we could only wear gray. I want to dress how I feel. My personality is colorful, and my garbs should reflect that. One day I will be free of all these rules and this place, mark my words!

CHAPTER TWO

Growing Pains

"Again!" yelled Adrielle, as the twins awaited their turn. Father is kind, but he is tough during training. "Again!" Father yelled, over and over.

It was the next day, and we were being trained. Adrielle has been training us in combat since we were small children. Father does not trust the regime or the elites and believes we should be prepared for anything.

"Take five and get ready to spar," said Adrielle.

"Get ready to get knocked out!" yelled Landis.

"Yeah whatever!" I replied.

I looked at myself in the mirror as I prepared to spar, admiring my warrior physique. I am five feet nine inches tall. My body is athletic and curvy, and my skin is brown like Adrielle's. My eyes are large and shaped like almonds, and I have Meesa's cheekbones. Father blessed me with his broad nose and round face, and my lips are full like my mother's. I was not the standard of beauty that our society created, but many people still considered me to be beautiful.

Landis stood up to spar against me. When we were younger, the twins defeated me in sparring most of the time and rarely showed mercy. As we grew older, I grew taller, faster, and stronger than both Landis and London. Those physical traits made the twins dislike me even more. As we were sparring, Landis struck me in my nose and drew blood. While I was wiping the blood from my nose, he smirked. While gloating, Landis did not see the two-piece combination and foot sweep coming. He crashed to the floor. I landed on top of Landis, ready to strike.

Father grabbed my arm, pulled me up, and stated, "That's enough for the day." I used to fear the twins when I was younger, but now I have no fear of them, or any human being alive.

After I stopped the bleeding from my nose, I went outside to help Adrielle in the garden. Gardening was one of my favorite things to do. Father was planting my favorite fruit, cherpinals. Cherpinals are a cross between pineapples and cherries, and they are delicious! Mother and Father taught us how to grow our own food because they want us to be self-sufficient. "If they feed you, that means they can starve you," Father would say.

"Hi moo-moo, what was that in training?" Father asked.

"What was what?"

"You lost your temper while you were sparring with your brother. When you lose your temper, you lose control, which also means you lose your wit. You must stay in control of your emotions, so you can logically think of your next move. Do you understand?" asked Father.

"Yes, I understand."

"Good, thank you for coming out to assist me, but I would like you to go meditate on what I just said," said Father.

I was annoyed, but I went back into our dwelling place without saying another word to him.

Walking into my sleeping chamber, I locked the door. I sat on the floor with my legs crossed trying to meditate on Father's words, but my mind began to wonder. Staying focused on one thought was difficult for me. Adrielle informed me meditation could improve my concentration. Closing my eyes, I took a deep breath in through my nose and out through my mouth repeatedly. My thoughts were focused on the words, *you are in control.*

My head began to throb, I became dizzy, and the room felt like it was spinning. Keeping my eyes closed, I tried to remain focused. The spinning feeling became too intense, I fell over and my elbow crashed onto the floor.

"What are you doing up there Aniyas?" questioned Mother.

I hopped off the floor and yelled, "Nothing Mother, I just tripped over my shoe!" There are things you must lie to Meesa about, and this is one of them.

Mother does not believe in meditation, only because meditation was outlawed by Emperor Kadar and the regime. Kadar believes meditation is an evil practice, and he says it can lead to insanity. By law, if you are caught meditating you will be placed in the House of Correction. I have heard dreadful stories about that place, but I am not afraid to go. Meditation is one of the issues Father does not agree with Mother or Emperor Kadar on. Adrielle believes meditation is a wonderful practice, and he encourages me to implement it into my daily schedule. Father would never steer me wrong. So, I vow to make meditation a priority and to practice every day.

Skipping into the kitchen, I saw Mother setting the table. Was it dinner time already? Wow! I had been in a meditative state for hours and did not realize it.

"Come help me set the table young lady," Meesa instructed. Grabbing the plates from her hand, I placed them on the table. The food looked and smelled scrumptious. Meesa is an excellent cook.

"Boys, come eat!" Mother shouted. Landis, Landon, and Father came and sat at the table.

Here in Gardash chores are the duty of women and girls. Women are taught to serve and cater to men. Meesa had no problem following the dwelling place chores, but when it came to catering to Father she did not. Adrielle does not enforce the rules that were created for girls and women. Father does his own laundry, irons his own clothes, and he even cooks and washes dishes sometimes. Mother is to serve Adrielle his food first, the boys, me, and then herself, but Father always made sure we were served before him. He insists that his children should always be fed first.

We are not allowed to talk during dinner. Meesa said we would choke on our food if we did. The silence was always a little awkward at the table. Looking over at Adrielle, I saw him smiling at the twins. Father never refers to Landis and Landon as his bonus sons, he always refers to them as his sons. Even though Adrielle has been in the twins' lives for years, is supportive, does and will do anything for them, they still do not give him the respect he deserves. Father stepped up in every way when their biological father did not, so I could not understand why the twins did not appreciate him more. Adrielle is a good man and good to them. Mother lacks appreciation for Adrielle, maybe that's where Landis and Landon get it from. As we ate in silence, I stared at Father with hurt in my heart, thinking he did not feel loved and appreciated in his own home.

After dinner, I washed the dishes and headed to my sleeping chamber. I read for an hour, showered, and prepared for bed.

"Get out, get out now!" screamed Mother.

Running down the stairs, I tripped over my own foot trying to see what was taking place. Landis and Landon were right behind me. Mother and Father were arguing.

"Calm down Meesa, calm down!" Father said as he tried to touch Mother's arm.

"Do not touch me, Adrielle!" Mother snarled.

The twins tried to calm her down too, but to no avail. Meesa continued to yell and started to throw things around the living space. I did not know what they were fighting about, but Mother was extremely upset.

"Mother what is wrong?" I asked.

Meesa looked me in my eyes and then looked at Father and said, "I told you to get out, and take her with you!"

As she pointed at me, my heart sank. It was one thing to have an argument with your husband and ask him to leave, but to tell him to take your only daughter, I did not understand. What had I done?

"If you do not get out tonight, I will kill you both!" Meesa yelled. My jaws dropped when I heard those words come from my mother's mouth. Why would she want to harm us?

"Get out and I never want to see your faces again!" screamed Meesa. Mother had outbursts all the time, but her words cut deep this time around.

With defeat in his eyes, Adrielle looked at Meesa and said, "We will go." I was always unsure if Meesa loved me or not, but this night I was sure she did not.

There was a loud knock at the door, Landon ran to open it. It was Aunt Rachelle; she is Mother's sister. Landon called her over to help with Meesa. Mother was still yelling and throwing things. Aunt Rachelle said, "Come on Meesa, it's okay. Come with me." Mother looked at Aunt Rachelle and continued on her rampage. Aunt Rachelle had no choice but to grab Meesa and drag her out of our home. Landis and Landon followed them out of the door.

Father looked at me and said, "I guess I will start searching for our new dwelling place tomorrow."

"Okay," I replied. Adrielle walked up the stairs, went into his sleeping chamber, and closed the door. What was wrong with Meesa? Why did she treat me this way? My heart was filled with hurt, and my head was full of confusion. I went to my sleeping chamber and cried myself to sleep.

Waking up in the morning, I sauntered to the washroom and looked in the mirror. My eyes were red as fire, and they were swollen. "I look dreadful," I thought to myself.

"Are you getting ready for academia, kiddo?" Father asked.

"Yes, I am," I replied.

"Okay, breakfast is on the table," said Adrielle.

After dressing, I went downstairs and sat at the table, but I could not eat anything.

"Are you going to eat?" asked Father, as he walked into the kitchen.

"No, I'm not hungry this morning."

"Well let's get you to academia then." We walked to the car and drove off.

"Are you okay?" asked Father.

"I'm fine," I said, knowing that I was not.

"I'm not sure when your mother will return, but I will be out late looking for a new dwelling place. When you are dismissed from academia, go straight to Mara's home," Adrielle ordered.

I was waiting for Father to say more. I thought maybe he would try to discuss what happened in our home last night. We never talked about our issues because our issues were swept under the rug in this family.

"We are here. Have a good day at academia. Be strong, and I love you," said Adrielle. That was one thing Mother and Father had in common, my parents always encouraged us to be strong and taught us to never cry. I was tired of being strong. I wanted to jump into his arms, but I just said, "I love you too."

A zombie, that's what I felt like as I walked through the corridors of academia. The extreme feeling of sadness was still consuming me, as I replayed the words Meesa spoke last night.

"Hey Aniyas!" Mara yelled from down the corridor, as she ran towards me.

"Hi," I replied dryly.

"Whoa, what is wrong with you?" asked Mara.

I was typically cheerful and energetic when I saw Mara, so she knew something was wrong. I revealed everything that transpired in my dwelling place last night. Tears started to form in my eyes, so I hurried into the washroom and ran into a stall. Crying was a form of weakness, and I did not want anyone to see me cry, including Mara.

Mara ran after me.

"Aniyas are you okay?" she asked.

"I'm fine," I replied, as I tried to hide the tremble in my voice. "Can I please come to your dwelling place after academia until my father returns home?"

"Of course you can!" Mara said with concern.

"Thank you so much Mara. You can go ahead to lecture hall. I will be there shortly."

"Okay, I love you," said Mara.

"I love you back."

As soon as I heard the door shut, I walked out of the washroom stall. Looking in the mirror, I took a deep breath and wiped the tears flowing from my eyes. Mara always told me she loved me, unlike my mother. I can't remember a time when I heard Meesa say those words to me.

"Get it together Aniyas, be strong, be strong!" I said to myself. Taking another deep breath, I swallowed my tears, stood tall, and pranced out the washroom with my head held high.

As I walked into the lecture hall, I saw an unfamiliar face. She was a beautiful girl, and her skin was dark as midnight. Her eyes were slanted, and she had two long thick French braids. I smiled at her as I sat in my seat. She smiled back. Our academia master, Ms. Cohen raised her hand and all the novices sat down in silence.

"Good morning, all. We have a new novice with us today. Her name is Allura," said Ms. Cohen, as she pointed at the unfamiliar face. "You all give her a warm welcome. Aniyas I would like you to be her escort for the day, you two have most of the same lecture halls."

"Yes Ms. Cohen," I replied. It was great to see a new face around here, especially a face that resembled mine.

Some time went by, and I was hoping Ms. Cohen's lecture hall was almost over. I became a little anxious when I had to sit for extended periods of time. The chime finally sounded, and it was time to go to the next lecture hall. Jumping out of my seat, I went over and introduced myself to Allura.

"Hi, I'm Aniyas, nice to meet you."

"Hello, I'm Allura, and nice to meet you too."

Allura stood up to shake my hand, and to my pleasant surprise she was tall like me. I was the tallest girl at our academia, I was also taller than a lot of the boys in our academia.

"You're very pretty," I said to Allura.

"Thank you and so are you," Allura said as she smiled.

Mara walked up and introduced herself to Allura.

"Where are you from?" asked Mara.

"I'm from the province of Ratlin. I moved here with my mom about a week ago." I had heard of Ratlin before, but it was far away. The distance made me wonder why they moved all the way to Gardash. I just met the girl, so I wasn't going to pry into her business, just yet.

After two more lecture halls it was time for lunch. Lunch was my favorite part of academia. I love food and I eat like a full-grown man. Lunches at Edgerton are always fantastic, they serve their novices' nothing but the best. As we walked into the dining hall, we passed Rebecca Hawthorne. I saw her stick her nose up at us out the corner of my eye. Rebecca Hawthorne is a popular mean girl, and she has two mindless minions named Kelsey and

Amber that kiss her behind. About a month ago I got into a heated argument with Rebecca, and I almost punched her lights out, but the lunch guardian stopped me. I didn't know why at the time, but Rebecca disliked me.

When I had that argument with Rebecca, we were both sent to our novice advisor's chamber. Mrs. Forte is her name, and I really like her. Mrs. Forte called me into her chambers to speak with me first.

"So, what seems to be the problem?" Mrs. Forte asked. I informed her that Rebecca was always starting fights with me for no apparent reason. Mrs. Forte said, "I'm going to let you in on a little secret but keep this between us. Rebecca might be jealous of you."

"Jealous of me?" I laughed.

"Yes, jealous of you," Mrs. Forte replied.

I could not wrap my head around the fact that Rebecca Hawthorne could be jealous of me. Rebecca was popular, all the boys liked her, and her family was rich. Why would she be jealous of me? I was just a conventional.

Mrs. Forte continued to explain, "You are a beautiful girl Aniyas. Not only are you beautiful, but you are also confident, one of the smartest novices in academia, you are tall like a model, you dress well, and you already have your womanly shape. Those are attributes that a lot of girls envy."

"Womanly shape, but Rebecca has the largest breasts I have ever seen," I said.

Mrs. Forte giggled, "But with you it is a little different, your entire body has curves." I never thought about it like that, but I guess she was right. Never in my life had I experienced feelings of jealousy or envy towards another girl, but now I knew why Rebecca and some of the other girls did not like me.

While eating lunch, we got to know Allura a little better. I really liked Allura. She was nice, funny, and goofy like me. "This might be the start of another beautiful friendship," I thought to myself. Mara is always unsure about new people; I could tell she was still trying to feel Allura out. As we chatted, I felt Rebecca burning a hole through the side of my face, but I just ignored her.

Chase walked into the dining hall, and Rebecca skipped right over to him. She jumped into his arms, and they embraced. Chase was the most popular boy in our academia, and Rebecca was the most popular girl, so I guess it was only right that they were an item. Mara looked at the happy couple and rolled her eyes. Mara was still crushing on Chase. Chase even flirted with Mara at times, but then again Chase flirted with everyone.

Lunch was over and we all exited the dining hall. We walked past Rebecca, Chase, Tweedledee, and Tweedledum. Chase smiled at us, and Rebecca saw him.

I then heard Rebecca say, "Oh, I see we have two giraffes in academia now."

Her minions giggled.

"This troll is so obsessed with me," I responded, and kept walking. Allura and Mara laughed. Chase giggled a little as well. Rebecca frowned and gave Chase the death stare.

"Who was that girl, and why was she so rude?" asked Allura.

"That was Rebecca Hawthorne and her two minions Amber and Kelsey. Rebecca is a popular, mean, rude, snob! We've been feuding ever since I stepped in Edgerton, "I explained.

Allura looked at me and said, "Well she does not want these problems!" Mara and I laughed as we walked to our next lecture hall.

The academia day had finally ended, and it was time to go home. My heart began to race thinking about what happened at our dwelling place last night. I was not looking forward to seeing Mother later. As we walked out of academia, Mara and I exchanged numbers with Allura and said goodbye. I was quiet on the walk home. Mara must have read my energy because she didn't say much either. We walked past Ms. Saunders' dwelling place. Ms. Saunders had the most beautiful, large, sunflowers planted in her courtyard. Looking at the sunflowers, I got a bright idea.

Turning towards Mara I asked, "Would you like to make sunflower seeds?" as I glanced at Ms. Saunders sunflowers.

"Indeed, I would," said Mara, with an evil grin.

I checked to see if I saw Ms. Saunders' car in the driveway, and it was gone.

"She is not home. On the count of three, we run, snatch the sunflower, and run to your dwelling place, okay?" I explained to Mara.

"Let's go!" Mara mouthed. I glanced around to see if anyone was watching.

"One, two, three," and we were off.

Mara ran slow, so I made sure to stay at her pace so we could grab the sunflower together. When we reached the sunflower and pulled it down, I tucked the sunflower under my arm and ran towards Mara's dwelling place.

"Go, go, go!" I shouted. We both began to laugh. As we were running, Mara tripped and fell.

"Get up Mara, get up!" I yelled, as we chuckled even harder. Mara picked herself up, and we ran into her courtyard. She unlocked the door via her keypad. We entered her home. The door closed behind us, as we fell out crying from tears of laughter.

We picked all the seeds from the sunflower, washed them, salted them, baked them, and ate them. The seeds were oh so delicious. Mara's grandparents were never home, so she was by herself most of the time.

"Where are your grandparents?" I questioned.

"Well, even though they are married, my grandfather does not live here. He has his own dwelling place, and my grandmother is over there a lot," said Mara.

I wonder why Mara never told me this before. A married couple that did not live together, I had never heard of that before, but to each their own.

Time flew by as we talked, laughed, and ate almost everything in Mara's ice chest.

"Let's go for a walk," Mara insisted. It was dark out, Meesa would never let me go out after dark. Even though it was almost curfew, I agreed to go. As we walked, the stars were illuminating the sky. I looked up and made a heartfelt wish. We turned the corner, and I almost had a heart attack. Mother was marching straight towards us. I stopped dead in my tracks.

"Aniyas, come here right now!" yelled Meesa.

I looked at Mara with fear in my eyes. At that moment I realized, I still did fear one human, and her name was Meesa.

Mara looked at me and said, "Don't go Aniyas, just come back with me!"

Mother charged towards me, grabbed my collar, and was practically dragging me towards our home. Mara chased after us. Mother turned around without letting my collar go, looked at Mara and yelled, "Stop following us child and go home right now!"

Mara looked at me and I looked back at her. I could not talk because Meesa was holding my collar so tight it was choking me. I gave Mara a look and Mara whimpered, "Yes Mrs. Nguvu," as she started walking back to her dwelling place.

Mother dragged me into our home. As she let go of my collar, she shoved me, and I fell to the floor. I quickly stood back up.

"I've been looking all over for you Aniyas! Where were you? Why didn't you come home?" Meesa shouted.

I stood there confused, because just last night she said she never wanted to see my face again. Mother locked the doors to the kitchen from both sides and went over to stand by the knives. A lump formed in my throat. Meesa had hit and whooped me several times before, and I never once thought to strike her back. But if she tried to harm me with a knife, I was ready to protect myself.

I knew Father was not home, so I called out for Landis and Landon. The twins did not respond. I don't know why I called out for them anyway, it's not like they would have helped me. Landis and Landon would have held me down, while Mother sliced away.

"They are not home," Mother replied.

I stood there staring at Meesa as she put her hand on the counter next to the knives. "She is really about to kill me or at least she is about to try!" I thought to myself. My breathing became heavy. Meesa took a step towards me, with this deranged look in her eyes. I shuffled backwards into the corner of the kitchen, preparing myself for what was to come.

There was a rattle on the kitchen doorknob.

"Why is the door locked?" I heard Father say. Adrielle's voice startled Meesa, and it was as if she snapped out of a trance. Mother went and unlocked the door. Adrielle walked in. I was backed in the corner and breathing heavily.

"What is going on in here?" questioned Father.

"Aniyas didn't come home from academia, and I was worried sick. I found her not that long ago, wandering the rows with Mara. I made her come home," Mother explained.

"I told Aniyas to go straight to Mara's dwelling place after academia, while I searched for a new home," Father replied. I was nervous to see what would happen next.

Meesa gazed at Adrielle and the waterworks began. "Are those tears?" I thought to myself, in shock.

"Somewhere to live? So, you're leaving me? Fine, if you want to leave me, just go!" cried Mother. Meesa always did this, she was very manipulative. Father would fall for Mother's tricks every time, but this was the first time I'd seen her cry with the antics. Mother collapsed to the floor. Adrielle rushed over to Meesa and helped her up.

"It's okay Meesa, stop crying. We are not going anywhere," Father assured Mother. Adrielle assisted Meesa to their sleeping chamber. Mother looked back at me with this conniving look in her eyes. I did not tell Father that Meesa dragged me into our dwelling place, locked the doors, and stood right next to the knives. I was not sure if Mother would have harmed me if Adrielle had not arrived, but I was sure I did not trust her.

CHAPTER THREE

A House Divided

There had always been tension in our dwelling place, but now the line was clearly drawn. After the kitchen incident, the blinders that covered my eyes were gone. I was tired of Meesa treating me like a stepchild when I came from her flesh. I was tired of her taking Landis and Landon on outings while leaving me at home. I was tired of being one of the brightest novices in our academia, receiving award after award and Mother not acknowledging my achievements. Mother obviously did not love or like me, so I no longer liked or respected her. When Meesa took her anger out on me by yelling and screaming, I returned her energy. If only Adrielle would stop her from saying mean and hurtful things to me, but he didn't. Father tried to calm Mother down when she had her outburst, but he never confronts the root of the problem. Adrielle had no backbone, and I didn't like it one bit.

My resentment towards Father began to grow. Why wasn't he protecting me from this mad woman? I love Adrielle and I know he loves me unconditionally, but Father is weak and that is something I will never be. Long gone were the days I dreamed of a happy home. Long gone were the days I longed for a mother that would hold my hand through life, a mother that would rub my head and tell me everything would be okay, a mother that would love and nurture me. I had come to the realization that Meesa was incapable of those actions and that would never be my reality.

As I sat and ate dinner alone, I remembered the times we all ate together. Mother had stopped calling us down for family dinner. Meesa still prepared our meals, but we all ate at different times. Landis and Landon were rarely home, and that was a good thing. Between working to provide for the family and all his extracurricular activities, Adrielle wasn't home much anymore. When Father was home, he would stay in the cellar until it was time for bed. The time I spent with Adrielle had decreased drastically. I had never spent much time with my mother, and these days I tried to avoid her. Meesa always wanted to fight, so I locked myself away in my sleeping chamber. Feeling alone and unhappy in our dwelling place, I began to spend most of my time meditating.

Slowly but surely, the more I practiced the better I became at controlling my thoughts. One day while meditating, my mind began to play tricks on me. "Did I just levitate?" I asked myself. No, it was just my imagination, or was it?

Father walked in as I was finishing my dinner.

"Hey kiddo! How are you? How was your day?" he asked.

"I'm good, it was good." I replied.

Adrielle washed his hands, went to the stove, and fixed his plate. Father began to tell me about his day. While Adrielle was talking, Meesa walked into the kitchen. Without uttering a word, Mother grabbed a glass from the cabinet, walked over to the ice chest, and poured apple juice into it.

"Hello dear," said Father.

"Hi," Mother replied dryly. Adrielle sighed deeply. Without looking Father's way, Meesa went back upstairs to their sleeping chamber. Adrielle raised his left eyebrow as he watched Mother walk away. My parents rarely spoke these days and when they did their words were few.

While glaring at Father as he ate his dinner, I wondered if my parents ever had a good relationship.

"Do they love each other? Are they in love? Have they ever been in love? When was the last time I saw my parents be affectionate towards one another?" were the thoughts swirling in my head. Oh wait, around six months ago while Mother was washing the dishes, Father embraced her and kissed her neck. Mother giggled but said, "Stop it, Adrielle." Mother then removed Father's hand from her waist and walked into our living space. I noticed a pattern with Meesa. Every time Adrielle tried to show her affection, she pushed him away. Was Mother always like this? Did she not like being touched? Maybe that's why Meesa never hugged or kissed me, maybe she doesn't know how to show or receive love.

Father must have noticed I was deep in thought.

"What is on your mind?" asked Adrielle.

"Do you love Mother?"

With a puzzled look on his face, Father answered, "Of course I do."

"Do you think she loves you?"

"Yes, your mother loves me," he replied. "Where are these questions coming from?"

Gazing up at the ceiling, I vented, "You barely speak to one another, you don't kiss and hug, you don't go on dates, you don't laugh together, and I never hear you tell each other I love you."

Father looked at me with a hint of sadness in his eyes.

"Honey, we love each other, and we used to have great times together. Sometimes in marriage, as the years go by things change."

"Well, they haven't changed for the better," I mumbled. I almost asked Adrielle if he was happy, but I already knew the answer to that question. After my conversation with Father and thinking about how my parents interacted, I came to one conclusion. I did not want a marriage like Meesa's and Adrielle's, matter of fact, I don't think I want to be married at all.

Suddenly, Allura crossed my mind. Earlier today at academia she asked if I could come to her dwelling place for a sleepover tonight. We didn't have academia in the morning, so it would be perfect! I already knew Meesa would say no, but I told Allura I would ask anyway. Mother never tried to talk to me, spend time with me, or take me anywhere outside of chastis, so I did not understand why she kept me locked away in our dwelling place. The furthest I could go was our courtyard or across the row to Mara's courtyard. I'd known Mara since pre-academia and Mother still would not let me go inside her home. Mara was allowed to sleep over at our dwelling place, but of course I could not stay the night at her home. I was too old for this treatment. Meesa had no idea what it felt like to be a prisoner inside your own home. I was a captive, but it was time to break free.

"Father," I said with a smile.

"I know that look, what do you want Aniyas?" asked Adrielle.

"Why do I have to want something?"

Father looked at me, tilted his head, and raised his left eyebrow.

"Well, since you asked, can I go to a sleepover at Allura's tonight, until Saturday?"

"The new girl at your academia? Now you know you must ask your mother for permission."

"Why do I have to ask her when I'm asking you?" I sighed.

"You know she does not like you staying the night in someone else's home."

"I know, I know but I never get to go anywhere. I am a teenager for crying out loud. It's not fair!" I left the table.

"Listen honey, I know you want to go, but you still have to get your mother's permission," stressed Father.

I turned my head and rolled my eyes as far back as they could go, and then I got a bright idea.

"How about you ask Mother for me? She likes you better than me, so she might tell you yes," I stated.

"Now, Aniyas," Father replied.

"Please, please, please dad!" I begged.

With a deep sigh Father said, "Okay Aniyas."

"Thank you, thank you, thank you!" I said as I jumped up and down. I skipped over to Adrielle and gave him a big hug.

I anxiously tiptoed up the stairs behind Father, as quiet as a mouse until I tripped on the fifth stair and hit my big toe. I could be a little clumsy at times. Adrielle entered their sleeping chamber door, while I listened close by.

"Hey dear, how are you?" I heard Father say to Mother.

"I'm fine," Meesa responded, without asking Adrielle how he was doing.

"Aniyas has been doing very well at academia, how about we give her a little reward," Father said.

"Why would we reward her for what she's supposed to do?" Mother responded.

"Here we go," I thought to myself.

Meesa never praised or rewarded me for my achievements, she barely ever acknowledged when I did well. Father then asked Mother if I could go to Allura's for a couple of nights.

"I don't know that girl or her mother, no she cannot," said Meesa.

"Come on honey, let her go. She never gets to go anywhere," Adrielle responded.

Mother raised her voice, "Oh I see now, Aniyas sent you in here to do her dirty work, to pit me and you against each other! I see what she's doing, I see!"

"What are you talking about Meesa?" questioned Father.

"Is she serious?" I said to myself. I was now convinced that my mother was psychotic.

My intent was not for my parents to get into an argument, but here we are. Meesa was doing what she usually does, thee most. She was yelling and screaming while the meek Adrielle tried to calm her down. Mother had been going at it for a while now, saying a lot of things that had nothing to do with the issue at hand.

"Ever since she was born, ever since she was born, I've had to deal with this, ever since she was born!" snapped Meesa.

"Ever since I was born?" I repeated aloud, as I began to cry. "Did my mother not want me? Was I a mistake? Did she wish I weren't born?" were the thoughts running through my head. Meesa had hurt my feelings deeply, once again.

Mother was still going on and on, but I couldn't make out anymore of her words because I was sitting on the top step crying. They must have heard me, because both of my parents stepped out into the hallway where I was.

"Why are you out here crying? You are the one who started all this confusion!" Meesa screamed. Mother lunged at me and pushed my head into the railing of the staircase. Adrielle grabbed my mother around her waist and pulled her away from me. Mother was flailing her arms and kicking her legs in the air, trying to reach me. Father forced Meesa back into their sleeping chamber and closed the door.

"Get off of me, get off me!" Mother yelled.

"Calm down, stop Meesa, stop it!" Adrielle replied. My head had hit the edge of the railing hard, and my head was pounding. I tried to stand up, but I lost my balance and stumbled into the washroom. What was happening to me?

Holding on to the washroom vanity, I regained my balance. I closed the door and stood behind it. Tears were still falling down my face, and Meesa was still screaming. It might have only been a couple of minutes, but it seemed as if I was in the washroom for an eternity before I heard silence.

There was a knock on the door, and I heard Adrielle's voice ask, "Are you okay?"

I exited the washroom. Father touched my shoulder and said, "Stop crying and be strong."

"Really, really, is that all you're going to say?" I thought to myself. This toxic cycle was getting old.

I was so tired of hearing the words, be strong. "How about telling your wife she's acting like a mad woman, and she needs to get it together!" I said to myself, but the only word I could muster up was okay. I walked to my sleeping chamber, closed the door, and locked it behind me. What had I done to my mother for her to hate me so much? Was I perfect? No, but overall, I was a good child. I guess it was my total existence she despised. After all, Meesa did say she had to deal with this, whatever this was, ever since I was born.

My head was killing me. I've had headaches before but this one took the cake. Touching the back of my head, I felt something wet. I looked at my hand and it was blood. I had hit my head much harder than I thought.

"Oh well!" I said aloud. I've had bruises, welts, scrapes, cuts, and broken bones before, between my mother, my brothers, and being an adventurous child, this was nothing new. I would patch myself up in a minute, but right now I did not want to move. Mother might hear me, break my door down, and attack me again. That lady is insane!

Sitting on the floor in my sleeping chamber, I replayed Meesa's words. I tried to cease the thoughts, but I could not. Overthinking is a huge issue of mine. I would and could dwell on the same negative thoughts forever. There were many nights I cried myself to sleep wondering why Meesa and the twins disliked me. There were so many times I pleaded with and begged the Leading Light to make my mother and brothers love me, but I guess he did not hear me. However, on this night, after my tears stopped flowing, I became numb. I had never felt anything like this before, matter of fact, I felt nothing. Maybe this would be a good time to meditate, since I felt so empty inside.

I crossed my legs in padmasana position, lifted my hands towards the sky, and closed my eyes. At first, I saw nothing but darkness, but this was normal because that's all I usually see when I meditate. However, this time a shadow began to appear in the distance. The shadow emerged out of the darkness and was coming closer and closer, until I finally saw a clear image. It was Mother standing there with open arms and a smile. A feeling of happiness came over me as I got up and walked towards her, but it seemed as though the closer I got, the further away Mother was. I tried to run to her, but I could not reach her. And just like that, Meesa was gone.

"Mother, mother!" I cried out.

"Here I am child," Meesa whispered in a gentle voice.

"Where-where are you? I don't see you!" I stuttered.

"Turn around, silly. I'm right behind you," Mother laughed.

I turned around and was face to face with a large two headed demon. This monster stood on two legs, had red eyes, fangs, and hair made of worms. Screaming, I began to run, but it felt like I was running in slow motion. My legs were heavy, as if someone had put weights on them.

"Come here my child. Where are you going? Give your mother a hug," the monster urged, as it flopped on its belly and slithered after me.

"No, get away from me!" I yelled. The creature was getting closer and closer, she reached out to touch me and then I heard tap, tap, tap, tap, tap, tap. The sound awakened me from my meditative state, and I was glad it did!

Two hours had passed as I looked up at the clock. I was always in a meditative state for much longer than I anticipated lately.

"Let me in Aniyas," I heard Father whisper. It was Adrielle tapping at my door.

Getting up slowly, I opened the door. I was dizzy and the room was spinning, but I managed to stay on my feet.

"Pack some garbs and the toiletries you need," Adrielle said.

"Huh, where are we going?" I asked.

"I'm taking you to that sleepover," Father responded. My eyes got bigger than they already were.

"But Meesa said no," I replied.

"I know what she said but you are going. Pack your things, but be quiet so you do not wake her," Adrielle commanded.

I was excited and nervous all at the same time. First, I tiptoed to the washroom to clean the wound on my head. After that, I packed my satchel as quickly and quietly as possible. There was no way I was about to blow this opportunity.

Hurrying down the stairs, I tried not to make a peep. Rushing out the back door and jogging to the car, I entered the vehicle and shut the door lightly. Adrielle was right behind me. A rush of adrenaline jolted through my body, and I could no longer feel the pain coming from my head. Father jumped in the car, and we were off. I rolled down the window and let the soothing breeze tickle my face. As we passed Ms. Saunders' dwelling place, I noticed the empty space where a huge sunflower once stood. I giggled to myself. I was surprised I could find humor in anything, after what just occurred in my home.

Driving to Allura's dwelling place, Father did not utter a word. "Here we go again, never addressing the dysfunction in our home and just sweeping it under the rug," I said to myself. When Mother wakes up in the morning, I'm not sure how she will react to Adrielle disobeying her orders. All I know is, I was glad I wouldn't have to witness it. I would finally be away from my dwelling place, and I was elated. The more I thought about it, these couple of days would not be enough, I wanted to move out of that home and as far away from Meesa as possible.

CHAPTER FOUR

A Mother's Love

We arrived at Allura's dwelling place around midnight. Father walked me to the door, and I rang the buzzard. I hadn't called Allura to let her know I was on my way, so Ms. Haraka was surprised to see us at her door.

"May I help you?" Ms. Haraka asked with a baffled look on her face.

"Hello, I'm Adrielle and this is Aniyas, she's here for the sleepover," Father explained.

"Oh, hi there, Allura talks about Aniyas all the time. It's late so I wasn't expecting you, come on in."

"There was a change in circumstances, so she was able to come. Thank you for opening your home to my daughter."

"No problem at all," smiled Ms. Haraka.

I looked at my father as he said, "Be on your best behavior sweetie and have a great time." Adrielle embraced me, waved, walked to the car, and drove off.

"Allura, Mara, Aniyas is here!" Ms. Haraka called out as she shut the door behind us. Wow, my first sleepover!

Mara and Allura ran down the stairs screaming, "Aniyas!" The pair literally knocked me over with hugs. Despite what had just transpired at my dwelling place, I was overjoyed by the affection being shown to me. We gathered ourselves off the floor and embraced each other once again. Ms. Haraka was watching with a smile.

"Mom is about to make her special hot chocolate for us, so come in the kitchen!" Allura announced excitedly.

"Oh, am I?" Ms. Haraka replied, with the same beautiful smile on her face. I sat my satchel down at the door and followed the others into the kitchen.

"I hope Father makes it home without any trouble," were my thoughts as we sat in Allura's kitchen. We have a twelve-a.m. curfew in Gardash. No matter your age, everyone must be in their dwelling place by midnight, a law ordered by the regime. Not only did my home feel like a prison, so did Gardash. I glanced over at Ms. Haraka while she was making our hot chocolate. Ms. Haraka was stunning, and she looked so young. I wonder why she isn't married. With her looks, it seemed like men would be beating down Ms. Haraka's door. "Did Ms. Haraka have a boyfriend? Where was Allura's father? Why did they move here, in the middle of the academia year? Why did they move so far away?" were the many questions running through my wounded skull. I didn't know much about Allura or Ms. Haraka, but maybe I would get some answers this weekend.

We sat in the kitchen and talked until the entire pot of hot chocolate was empty. I'm not sure what Ms. Haraka put in that hot chocolate, but it was the best hot chocolate I had ever had.

"That was so good, thank you very much," I said to Ms. Haraka.

"You're welcome," she responded warmly.

I had only been around Allura's mother for about an hour or so, but I liked her. She had a welcoming and warm spirit.

"Yes, thank you Ms. Haraka, that was delicious, now let's go back upstairs," said Mara. We all walked out the kitchen, and I grabbed my satchel from the front door.

Unlike my dwelling place, Allura's home was nice and quaint, very earthy. My home was decorated like something out of a magazine, very grand and over the top. Meesa might be crazy, but she has great style and taste. As we walked upstairs into Allura's sleeping chamber Ms. Haraka said, "Good night girls, don't stay up too late because we are going to have a nice breakfast in the a.m."

"Okay," we all responded in unison. Allura's mother went into her sleeping chamber and shut her door.

"Rebecca Hawthorne is pathetic," said Mara. We were all in our pajamas lying on Allura's bed.

"Yeah, she is, she's always trying to start a fight with me, and she's just a mean person period," I chimed in.

"She's probably always trying to pick a fight with you because of the way her boyfriend stares at you," Allura added.

"Who Chase, staring at me?" I replied, with a disgusted look on my face.

"Yes, you Aniyas, he stares at you all the time!" said Allura. I didn't pay Chase much attention, so I hadn't even noticed the stares.

Mara looked at Allura and then looked at me with a weird expression on her face. Allura had no idea that Mara liked Chase.

"Are you sure? I don't think Aniyas is his type," Mara stated.

"His type?" asked Allura.

"Yeah, you know, like Rebecca looks a certain way and then there's me," Mara said. I didn't respond to Mara's comment, and I wasn't exactly sure what Mara meant, but I could only assume she was referring to the fact that she and Rebecca had white to light skin.

"And then there's you?" Allura repeated.

"Yes, me, Chase kissed me about a month ago at academia, and we've been chatting ever since," Mara bragged. This was news to me; I was supposed to be Mara's best friend, and this was the first time I had heard of this kiss.

"Hmm, interesting," I thought to myself because I literally told Mara everything.

"Oh, so you think he likes you. I'm quite sure I see him staring at Aniyas all the time, but I could be wrong," said Allura as she shrugged her shoulders. The room went silent.

Even though we continued to stay up and talk, there was an awkward energy in the room. Mara was sitting beside me, but I could see here glancing over at me strangely, out the corner of my eye. I believe Allura could feel the odd energy too because Allura was looking at me, looking like, can you see how Mara is looking at you. The tension was thick, and I don't think a machete could have cut it. To lighten the mood Allura played some music, but to my surprise it was not spiritual music. I was shocked.

"You're allowed to listen to carnal music?" I asked.

Allura laughed, "They are singing about love Aniyas, how is that carnal?" Allura began to dance, and my eyes bulged out of my head. We were not allowed to listen to carnal music or dance in Gardash.

"What if your mother comes in and sees you?" I questioned.

Allura laughed even harder and louder than before. "I'm allowed," she said.

"What? Meesa would never!" I thought to myself. Mara and I looked at each other with astonishment in our eyes. I then realized, there would be much to learn about Allura and her mother.

I began to dance with Allura, while Mara remained seated and watched. This was the first time I had ever danced outside of my sleeping chamber. We swayed, twirled, and whirled all around Allura's chamber. Allura showed me so many cool dance moves, I wondered where she learned them from. I felt so amazing in this moment, and I felt so free. Allura hopped on her bed, and I followed. Our bodies moved all around as we tried to keep our balance on the bed. The music was so captivating, and my body started to move in ways that I didn't know was possible.

"Okay Aniyas, I see you!" Allura hollered. I blushed while continuing to roll my hips. Allura's door began to open, and her mother came in and joined us.

"Get up Mara! Dance with us!" Ms. Haraka insisted. Mara complied. Ms. Haraka had the moves! She danced so well, and I was impressed. We danced until we were exhausted.

"Good night girls," said Ms. Haraka as she danced back to her sleeping chamber. This was the most fun I had ever had. I never wanted to leave!

We all flopped down on the bed, breathing heavily. Dancing was a workout. Allura went over to turn down the music.

"Wow, that was so fun! I'm not allowed to dance or listen to this kind of music at my dwelling place," I confessed. I heard carnal music before because I caught Landis and Landon listening to it one day. They would sneak and listen to music when mother was not home, but the twins would not allow me join in. I should have told Meesa. I loved the way music made me feel, the drums, the horns, the bass did something to my spirit. I could listen to music all day, if only I were allowed.

"Where did you get this music from?" I asked Allura.

"Mathonia," Allura said.

"Mathonia!" we replied. Mathonia was a place we were told we should never go. It was an evil place filled with scarlets, barbarians, and beast!

"Why would you go to such an evil place, and how did you even get there?" I questioned.

"My mother takes me," Allura responded.

"Your mother?" I replied with judgment in my tone.

"Yes, my mother Aniyas, and if you should know, Mathonia is a wonderful place."

"But-but I've heard so many terrible things about that place," I stuttered.

"Yeah, you've heard, but I've actually been there, so do not judge a place you've never visited," Allura advised.

Mara looked at me, but she didn't say a word.

"But anyway, I'm tired so let's call it a night," Allura said. I fell asleep with so many questions on my mind. Mathonia, maybe it wasn't so bad, and maybe I would get to go there too, someday.

I woke up to a delightful aroma in the air. It was eleven-a.m. and that was the best sleep I'd had in a while. Mara and Allura were still sleeping. Picking up my pillow, I hit them both over the head. Mara jumped up, and Allura groaned and rolled over.

"Really Aniyas?" Mara mumbled. She picked up her pillow and struck me back. I threw my pillow at Mara, but she caught it.

"Ha!" she said while looking down at my pillow. "Aniyas, what is this red stuff all over your pillow?" Mara asked with a concerned look on her face. Reaching back, I felt my head and knew exactly what it was.

While bringing my hand down from my head, Mara saw the blood on my fingertips.

"Aniyas, you're bleeding!" Mara yelled. Mara was so loud she startled Allura.

Allura hopped up, gave Mara a deathly glance and asked, "Why are you yelling like that Mara?"

"Aniyas head is bleeding!"

"Bleeding, what happened to your head Aniyas?" Allura asked.

"I'm not sure," I lied.

"Mom come here; Aniyas' head is bleeding!" Allura called out.

"No, no I'm fine, don't bother your mom!" I stressed, but it was too late. I heard Ms. Haraka rushing up the stairs.

"Are you okay Aniyas? Come, let me examine your head."

"I'm okay ma'am," I replied.

Ms. Haraka looked at my head and said, "That looks deep, come into the washroom with me so I can take care of your wound." I followed.

"Sit there," Ms. Haraka directed. I sat on the toilet bowl. Allura's mom retrieved a towel, antiseptic spray, and a bandage from the cabinet above the sink. She sprayed the antiseptic spray on the towel and applied it to my head.

"Whoa that burns," I laughed. Ms. Haraka looked at me like I was insane.

"It burns, but you're laughing?" she questioned.

Come to think about it, I laugh often when I'm in pain. Last year when I sprained my ankle I laughed. Two weeks ago, when I fell down the stairs and hurt my arm I laughed. Now my head felt like it was on fire, and I was laughing. "That is pretty strange," I thought to myself, but hey it's just the way I am.

"What happened to your head?" Ms. Haraka questioned.

"I'm not sure," I lied again.

"This is a deep gash you have here. Are you dizzy at all?" she asked.

"No ma'am."

"Are you sure you don't know how you received this wound?" Allura's mom inquired again.

"I'm sure," I lied for the third time.

Ms. Haraka looked at me as if she wasn't convinced that I was telling the truth, but she said, "Okay."

Allura's mom applied the bandage to my head.

"All done, now go get the girls, wash your hands, and you all come down for brunch."

"Yes, ma'am and thank you," I replied.

"You're so polite Aniyas and you're welcome. Your mother raised you right," she said with a smile.

"If she only knew," I thought to myself.

The table was set beautifully. There were fresh flowers in the center of the table in an exquisite vase. Pancakes, bacon, waffles, sausage, grits, hash browns, toast, and a bowl of fruit, greeted us. "Cherpinals, yes!" I said to myself.

"Wow, this looks amazing!" I stated.

Mara shook her head in agreement. We prepared our plates and sat down to eat.

"No bacon and sausage Aniyas?" Ms. Haraka asked.

"No ma'am, I don't eat meat," I replied.

"We don't either," Allura responded.

"So, what is this?" Mara inquired as she picked the sausage up from her plate.

"It's plant-based meat," answered Ms. Haraka.

"Eww, I mean oh," Mara blurted out.

"Don't knock it until you try it," Allura said, as she looked at Mara.

"I'm good," Mara muttered with a fake grin on her face, as she placed the sausage back down on her plate. Allura's mom looked at Mara and giggled.

Raised a vegetarian, I was used to eating plant-based meat, but this meat appeared to be authentic.

"The bacon looks so real," I said. "How did you make it?"

"Well, I took some carrots and sliced them thin with a mandoline slicer. Then I put grapeseed oil, liquid smoke, smoked paprika, garlic powder, onion powder, salt, black pepper, and a dash of maple syrup in a bowl and mixed it all together. I added the carrots to the mixture, stirred it all around, and let it marinate for about twenty minutes. After that I pop the carrots into the air fryer, and out comes bacon," she explained.

I picked up a piece of bacon and tried it.

"This is scrumptious," I said.

"Glad you like it. I will give you the recipe to take home to your mother," Ms. Haraka replied. The thought of home made my heart sink, but I just nodded my head and smiled.

"Enough Aniyas," I thought to myself. I ate so much; I was about to explode.

"I'm stuffed! Thank you for the wonderful meal Ms. Haraka," I said.

"You're welcome sweetie." "Did you enjoy your meal, Mara?" asked Ms. Haraka.

"Yes, it was very good," and then Mara mumbled, "I just wish I had some real meat."

"Well, I hope you girls saved room for some lava juice," said Ms. Haraka.

"I've never had lava juice before," I confessed.

"What!" Mara and Allura yelled simultaneously.

"Yeah, my mother doesn't buy it, she says it has a ridiculous amount of sugar in it," I responded.

"Your mother is right but it's one of my guilty pleasures," said Ms. Haraka. "Would you like to try some, Aniyas?" Allura's mother asked.

"Yes please." Meesa would have a fit if she knew I was about to consume so much sugar, but guess what, she will never know.

Ms. Haraka poured a tall glass of lava juice. I placed the glass against my lips, opened my mouth, and swallowed slowly to savor the moment. Lava juice was like a party on my taste buds. Closing my eyes, I took another sip.

"O.M.G. this is so good!" I smiled.

"I am happy you are enjoying it," Ms. Haraka laughed. "Okay young ladies, go get dressed, because after your food digests we are going for a walk," said Allura's mom. I'm not sure if I could move after all that great food, but I would try.

We were off, on our walk. As we walked, Allura and her mom were holding hands. "Aren't we a little too old for that," I was thinking to myself. Mara grabbed my hand, and I snatched it away.

"Don't you want to hold hands too?" Mara asked while laughing.

"Not at all," I replied with a giggle. While we were walking, Ms. Haraka did a little two-step. My eyes moved around swiftly, to see if anyone had seen her. I could not believe Allura's mom just danced publicly. Allura must have seen my reaction.

"Relax Aniyas, nobody saw her," Allura snickered. Carnal music, dancing, and now dancing in public, Ms. Haraka broke all the rules, and I liked it.

Another mile and we would be back at Allura's dwelling place. Allura's mom said we needed to work off all the food we ate. As we were walking, I started to sing.

"You have a really nice voice, Aniyas," said Ms. Haraka.

"Really? Thank you," I replied. I loved to sing and used to dream of being a famous singer, but at home Meesa would always tell me to be quiet. One day I was singing, and my mother said, "Aniyas, why are you always singing, you know you don't sound that good right?" After that day, I stopped singing. So, I surprised myself, abruptly singing in that manner. Ms. Haraka made me feel comfortable, I guess that's why my guard was coming down. I was free to be myself around Allura and her mother, and I loved it!

Finally, I saw Allura's dwelling place up ahead.

"So, Allura told us you took her to Mathonia," blabbed Mara. I was in utter shock. "We aren't supposed to go there," Mara added.

Ms. Haraka glanced at Allura. We all knew we weren't supposed to go to Mathonia, because it was forbidden by the regime. So, I am sure Ms. Haraka did not want Allura divulging that information.

"No, we are not," Ms. Haraka replied.

"Why did you go then?" asked Mara.

"Because I like it there."

"How did you get in and out of your old province?" questioned Mara.

"I have my ways," Ms. Haraka said with a smirk. Allura shot Mara the evil eye, and Mara knew it was time to stop asking questions.

Mara's line of questioning was inappropriate, but I also wanted to know the answers. I wondered to myself, had the mother and daughter duo been to Mathonia since residing in Gardash. If so, how did they get in and out, because Gardash is a lockdown province just like Ratlin. The regime keeps our great wall guarded, and we must get approval to travel from province to province. I had so many questions, but the way Allura glared at Mara, I would save them for another time.

We arrived back at Allura's dwelling place.

"Go freshen up girls, and meet me back in the lounge space," Ms. Haraka commanded. We raced upstairs to shower and change garbs.

"You talk too much," Allura said to Mara, as we entered Allura's sleeping chamber.

"You didn't tell me I couldn't ask about Mathonia," Mara responded.

"Common sense should have told you," Allura countered. Mara rolled her eyes. "For the record, if I tell you something, do not go back and tell my mom, got it!" Allura fumed.

"Yeah, whatever," Mara replied. Allura walked away.

After freshening up, we all met back in the lounge space. There were large comfortable chairs in this space, big enough to seat two people. I sat in my own chair and so did Mara. Allura snuggled right up to her mother as they sat in the same chair. Ms. Haraka kissed Allura on the forehead. At first, the holding hands and cuddles between Allura and her mom made me feel a tad bit uncomfortable, but then I realized, this was a mother's love. I wished Meesa and I could have a bond like this, but I knew deep down it would probably never happen. If only I had a mother as loving as Ms. Haraka, life would be much better.

Ms. Haraka began to read us a story. We were a little old for story time, but I went along with it. To my surprise the book was intriguing. It was a book about fierce warrior women, and it was a true story. I was really engaged, but Mara kept dozing off. Looking at the wall, I noticed there were a lot of ancient looking artifacts.

Interrupting the story, I pointed at the wall and asked, "Are those from Ratlin?"

"No, they are from Mathonia," Ms. Haraka answered.

"What made you all move here from Ratlin?" I inquired.

Allura looked at her mother and then at the floor.

"We just needed a change of scenery," Ms. Haraka replied. Ms. Haraka changed the subject quickly, going right back into story time. I was now aware that Ms. Haraka did not want to talk about Ratlin and by the looks of it, neither did Allura.

The day went by quickly. Before we knew it, it was time for bed. We were all tired from the walk earlier, or should I say hike. Allura's mother wanted to examine my head again before bed.

"How is your head feeling honey?" asked Ms. Haraka.

"It feels fine," I said.

"There isn't much blood on the bandage, so that's a good sign. I will remove the bandage, but you need to clean this wound every day."

"Yes ma'am, also can we keep this between us. I don't want my mother to think I injured myself at your dwelling place, or she will never let me out again."

"Okay," answered Ms. Haraka, while looking at me suspiciously. "I'm all done here. Good night Aniyas," said Ms. Haraka.

"Good night and thank you." As I walked to Allura's sleeping chamber I realized I had to go home tomorrow, and it made me sick to my stomach. I didn't know what was in store for me back at my dwelling place, but I was not looking forward to it.

Adrielle arrived at Allura's dwelling place bright and early. All the ladies walked me to the door to say goodbye. Father approached us.

"Thank you so much for having her. I hope she didn't give you too much trouble," said Adrielle.

"Not at all, you have a wonderful child," Ms. Haraka replied. Allura's mom hugged me and said, "Bye beautiful, hope to see you again."

She called me beautiful; I had never heard those words from Meesa. Matter of fact, my mother never complimented me, she only pointed out my flaws. I embraced Allura and Mara, and I did not want to let go. I was on my way back to misery, and I wanted to cry.

CHAPTER FIVE

Unlikely Pairing

I walked into our dwelling place anxiously, with Father right beside me. Meesa and the twins were sitting in the great space on the couch.

"Hello," I said. Adrielle said hello as well, and no one responded. Landon and Landis got up, walked past us without looking in our direction, and marched out the door. "How rude!" I thought to myself. At that moment, I no longer cared how the twins or Mother felt about me. Their dislike for me was not my problem, and I certainly was not going to sit in my sleeping chamber crying about it anymore. You don't want to speak to me fine, but to disrespect my father and not greet him, that was a problem. Adrielle was too good to all of us to be treated this way. I stormed into my sleeping chamber and slammed the door.

As I fumed in my room, I hoped Meesa didn't come reprimand me for slamming the door. There was so much built-up anger inside of me, I was ready to explode on anyone, including her. A few minutes went by and to my surprise, Mother didn't say anything about the door being slammed shut. Realizing I needed to work on my temperament, this would be the perfect time to meditate. Locking the door, I sat on the floor. It was time to free my mind.

With my eyes closed, I tried to calm my spirit and focus on peaceful thoughts. It was not working, because all I saw was red. Instead of calming down, I became more upset. My breathing became uncontrollable, and it felt as if the room started to shake. Hearing a loud crash, my eyes opened. The lamp had fallen off my chiffonier. My lamp was always placed towards the back of my chiffonier. Had I moved the lamp to the edge of the chiffonier before I left? No, I did not touch the lamp.

"Aniyas, what in the world was that?" Mother yelled.

"I accidentally bumped into my chiffonier and made my lamp fall," I lied. Hmm, the last few times I meditated something unusual happened. "What is going on?" I thought to myself.

It was now Monday, so from one torture chamber to the next I went. Chastis was almost unbearable yesterday, and now I was on my way back to Edgerton. My mind replayed the lamp incident the past two nights. Did I make that lamp fall?

"Aniyas!" I heard Father call.

"Yes Father," I replied.

"Did you hear me talking to you?" he asked.

"Oh, no, I'm sorry." I was lost in my thoughts. Should I tell him about the lamp? No, Adrielle might think I am going insane. We stopped in front of my academia. Father kissed me on my cheek and told me to have a good day.

"I will try to, seeing that I have to learn amongst a bunch of snobs." Sighing, I dragged myself out of the car and walked to the front entrance. Just like home and chastis, I hated it here.

My head was in the clouds during science lecture hall, until I heard my academia master say, we must complete a project with a partner that is due this Friday. We were instructed to create a biome. I rolled my eyes because that was only four days away, and I did not like collaborating with other people. The academia master began to partner us up.

"Aniyas Nguvu and Chase Edgerton, you two will be creating a Savanna," said Mr. Perkins. Not only was I flabbergasted, but I was also disgusted and horrified. I did not want to work with Chase Edgerton.

Looking across the lecture hall, Mara met my gaze, and she did not look happy about the pairing. I hope she knew; I was not happy about working with Chase either. Chase was the last human on earth I wanted to partner with. Usually when we are assigned group projects, the elites are paired together, and so are the conventionals.

I raised my hand and before being called on, I blurted out, "The elites are usually partnered together Sir."

"Well today Aniyas, we are going to try something different. Is that okay with you?" he responded.

"Hell No!" I thought to myself, but I just shook my head yes. I have never uttered a word to Chase Edgerton, and now I have to complete an academia project with him. This should be interesting.

Our academia master informed us the written portion of our projects would be completed in lecture hall, and the construction of our biomes would be completed at home. So, not only did I have to work with Chase, but I would also have to see him outside of academia. Good thing Meesa didn't allow me to visit anyone's dwelling place she didn't know. We would just have to meet at the information center. It was time to partner up.

Chase pulled his desk over to mine with a smile on his face and said, "Hello."

"Hi," I replied dryly and frowned. I was certain Chase knew I disliked him.

Getting straight to the point, I began to talk about our project and our project only. To my surprise, Chase was being polite, and he was smart, not as smart as me though. Chase was also funny, but I made sure not to laugh at any of his jokes. We were supposed to be working, not trying to make each other laugh. Mara looked at me and Chase at least a hundred times. All I could think was, girl I do not want him. Chase is all yours and Rebecca's.

The chime rang and lecture hall was over. I jumped right up and walked out into the corridor. Chase followed.

"Hey, wait a minute Aniyas, we have to schedule a meeting time and place," said Chase.

"Oh yeah, you're right," I replied. Chase handed me a piece of paper with his phone number and address on it.

"Call me after academia, so we can meet up later. Look forward to hearing from you soon, Aniyas."

Snatching the paper from his hand, I swiftly turned to walk

away. "Ouch!" I yelled, as I butted heads with Mara. Stepping back, I wondered if she was standing there the entire time.

"What's on that piece of paper he gave you?" questioned Mara.

"It's just his number, so we can schedule the times and days we will be working on our project," I explained. I omitted the address component, for whatever reason.

"Oh, you have his phone number now huh," sneered Mara. Looking at Mara's face, I could now see this was going to be a problem.

Academia was dismissed for the day. I walked outside of my last lecture hall and there stood Chase. How does he know my schedule?

"I thought you said call after academia, why are you waiting here for me?" I questioned.

"I thought it might be easier to set up our plans in person," he replied. "How about you come to my dwelling place at six, we can start working on our project, and you can have dinner there," he suggested.

I barely wanted to talk to Chase, let alone go to his dwelling place.

"We can just meet at the information center," I responded.

"Okay cool, call me around five thirty and I will be on my way." Chase smiled and walked away.

"He annoys my soul!" I thought to myself. I could not wait until Friday, so I would no longer have to be in the presence of Chase Edgerton.

Allura walked up behind me and gave me a little shove on the shoulder.

"I see you were just talking to your future husband," she giggled. I was appalled.

"Do not play with me like that Allura," I said without cracking a smile.

"Sheesh, lighten up a little," she giggled again.

"I was only talking to him because our idiot academia master paired us together for a project. Now I will be annoyed by him for a full week," I sighed.

"It might not be as bad as you think," Allura shrugged.

"He is a narcissistic, mean, arrogant, bully, how can it not be bad? Anyway, enough about Chase, I'm excited about your party this weekend."

"Me too, are you going to be able to attend?" asked Allura.

"Yes, I will be there for sure!" Allura informed me at lunch, she was throwing a birthday party this weekend, and I was not going to miss it for the world. I don't care what Mother said, I was going to that party, somehow, someway.

Walking into my dwelling place, Meesa was in the kitchen cooking. I said hello and she said hello back. Words were few between us. We had come to an agreement that we love each other but we do not like each other. I still did not think Mother loved me, she just had to say that because she birthed me.

"Chase invited me to his dwelling place because we were partnered on an academia group project. I told him I would not be able to come to his home, but I would meet him at the information center at six."

"Why wouldn't you be able to go to his home?" questioned Meesa, with a puzzled look on her face. My face was even more puzzled. Mother must be playing a trick on me.

"You never let me go to anyone's dwelling place. I've known Mara since I was three and you still won't let me go inside her home."

"Well, this is different, Chase Edgerton is a fine young man. His family is extraordinary. It would be an honor to be in their home."

"Are you serious?" I asked.

"Yes, just leave his number before you go," Mother added.

Wow, I've been a prisoner my entire life, and now I am being set free because an elite invited me to his dwelling place, how shallow! There were so many things I wanted to say to Mother, but I knew it would be pointless.

"Go upstairs and dress in your finest garbs. When you arrive at their dwelling place, be on your best behavior and use your manners," Mother commanded. Turning around, I rolled my eyes to the back of my brain and followed her orders.

Since she is in such a giving mood, let me try my luck. I quickly ran back down the stairs into the kitchen.

"May I go to Allura's home this weekend?"

"No!" Mother yelled. Was I hearing her correctly?

"Did you say no?" I asked.

"You heard me," Meesa replied.

I could feel my blood start to boil. I raised my voice, "So, I can go to Chase's dwelling place but not Allura's?"

Meesa popped me in my mouth.

"Watch your tone when you are talking to me, and don't ever question me again. Now go upstairs and get ready like I said," Mother screamed!

I was so angry my body started to shake, and I was glaring at Meesa in a way I never had.

"If you don't stop staring at me like that and go do what I said, I will knock your head off your shoulders," Mother yelled!

Tears started forming in my eyes.

"You better not start crying, now go get ready and do not come back down until it is time for you to leave!" Mother shouted. Listening, I went back upstairs into my sleeping chamber to pout.

I was infuriated. My breathing was heavy, my teeth were clenched, and my fists were balled tightly. I turned around to close the door. What felt like a force of wind, took over my body as I turned towards the door. The door slammed shut with tremendous force. The mirror on my door crashed to the floor and broke into a million tiny pieces. I was shocked and a little frightened, because I realized I literally slammed the door without touching it.

When that lamp fell off the chiffonier it was no accident, it was me. My head started to spin. What was wrong with me? How was I doing this? Was I crazy? My thoughts were all over the place. I sat on my bed to try and regain my composure. Closing my eyes, I started to breathe slowly and meditate.

"You are in control. You are in control." My anger started to subside, my body began to relax, and my spirit calmed down.

As my eyes opened, Meesa was standing in my doorway yelling because I slammed the door. Mother didn't notice her left foot was bleeding from stepping on the glass. Father warned her about walking around our dwelling place barefoot all the time. After a second or two, I tuned out the yelling. I got up from my bed, walked past my mother, informed her she was bleeding, walked into the washroom, locked the door behind me, and began to get ready. Mother was banging on the door telling me to open it right now, but I ignored her. Looking in the mirror, I began to brush my hair to make sure my bun stayed slick and intact. Pausing, I glared at myself a little deeper. Taking the rubber band out of my hair, I turned on the water in the sink, and placed my head under the stream. I would allow my hair to revert to its true natural state. At that moment I felt liberated. If I had to go to Chase's home, I would be going as my true self.

When I finally pranced out of the washroom, Meesa was standing in my sleeping chamber. I did not want to argue with her anymore, it required too much unnecessary energy.

"Go get a broom and sweep up this glass right now!" she yelled.

"Yes, ma'am," I said, as I tried to follow her orders.

"Wait, stop, what did you do to your hair? There's no time to straighten it again! Now you will be at their dwelling place with your hair all nappy! What a way to set a first impression, Aniyas!" Mother shouted. I went to retrieve the broom without responding.

"Nappy" hair was seen as "bad" hair in our culture and society. I used to harbor the same sentiments when I was younger because I was raised to think that way. My hair was relaxed with chemicals at a very early age. Relaxers kept my hair straight for an extended period of time. It took a while, but I began to let go of the ignorant ideals that had been passed down to us throughout generations of brainwashing. I broke free from those mental chains. My hair is beautiful in its natural state too, and no one would make me think otherwise, not my mother, Father, or society.

Adrielle has hair that society deems as "good" hair because it is wavy. Father never said anything bad about my hair, but I knew he felt the same way about "nappy" hair, because he was raised that way as well. I overheard him asking Meesa to straighten her hair one day when it was in its natural state. No man would ever control how I wore my hair. That same day, I begged Meesa to stop relaxing my hair and she agreed, but I still had to have it straightened with the heating wand. Now, I would start wearing my hair however I pleased, and I didn't care who didn't like it.

I was finally ready for the dwelling place of doom. Mother was still highly upset with my hair, but again I did not care. Walking downstairs, I saw Father in the kitchen drinking a glass of water. This was not the time to talk about what was happening to me, but I would talk to him about it soon.

Meesa walked into the kitchen and shouted, "Do you see her hair?"

Adrielle looked at me and said, "I see you are trying something new with your hair." That was code for he didn't like it.

I responded, "This is nothing new, it is just the way my hair naturally grows out of my scalp." Mother looked at Father and rolled her eyes.

"You are all dressed up, where are you going?" questioned Adrielle.

"Mother is making me go to Chase Edgerton's home, to work on an academia project," I frowned.

"Oh really?" Father replied. "Well let me eat a few bites of food and we will be on our way," said Father.

Meesa didn't drive, so Adrielle took us everywhere we needed to go. I vowed to learn how to drive as soon as I could, there was no way I was going to depend on anyone to take me where I needed to go.

Without finishing his dinner, Father said, "Let's roll kiddo." Off to Chase Edgerton's home I went.

CHAPTER SIX

Deceptive Appearances

We arrived at Chase's dwelling place and there was an armed guard standing at the gate. "They would be this extra," I thought to myself. The guard asked for our names, picked up a communication device, whispered a few words into it, and informed us we were free to come through. The high steel white gate opened slowly, and my mouth dropped. I even drooled a little bit. Chase's home was the most beautiful home I had ever seen. The Edgerton's front courtyard was enormous and manicured immaculately. The lawn was a deep dark radiant green and mowed to perfection. Every light in their dwelling place seemed to be on, which made Chase's home illuminate against the sunset. I was in complete awe.

The Edgerton's dwelling place was composed of three levels, and each level boasted large floor to ceiling windows, with no drapery. There were two massive pillars connected to both sides of the front door, this feature gave Chase's home the appearance of a palace. As we continued up the extended driveway, it circled off, and that's when I noticed three extravagant vehicles. All the vehicles were white, shiny, and gleaming, it was like looking through glass. While soaking in the magnificent sight before my eyes, I wondered how it felt to possess a dwelling place as grand as this. Chase is one lucky kid.

"Wow, do you see this home?" I asked, with a twinkle in my eye.

Father replied, "Yes, it's pretty amazing." Adrielle pulled up to the front door and stopped the car. "Would you like me to walk you to the door?" he asked.

"No, I'm okay. Thank you for the ride. I will call you when I'm ready." As I exited the car, a ball of nerves rushed through my body, and I wasn't sure why. My finger was shaking as I raised it to ring the buzzard.

"Pull yourself together Aniyas! What is wrong with you?" I said to myself. A small man dressed in an all-white uniform opened the door.

"Welcome Aniyas, may I take your overcoat?" he asked.

"Sure," I smiled and nodded.

"Master Chase, your guest has arrived." My left eyebrow raised. Did he just call a minor, master? I rolled my eyes. I did not like how this evening was starting.

Stepping into their home, I marveled at the sight of their living space. The Edgerton's furniture was stylish and modern, you could tell it was expensive. There was a grand chandelier in the center of Chase's entryway, and the staircase was so long it might have reached the stars. Chase came walking down the stairway in all white, grinning from ear to ear.

"Hi Aniyas, I'm glad you could make it. You look beautiful and I love your hair." That caught me off guard, I just knew Chase would hate my hair. As Mara previously insinuated, Chase has a certain type, and I did not fit that mold. His words felt genuine, so maybe Chase is not as shallow as I assumed.

"Would you like to take a tour of my dwelling place?" asked Chase.

"Yes, I would like that, thank you."

Walking around Chase's extravagant home made me feel like I was in a movie, at every turn there was modern elegance. The Edgerton's spared no expense when it came to decorating this dwelling place. As soon as I thought it couldn't get any better, the doors swung open to the back terrace. It felt like I was on another planet, I had never seen anything like it.

Chase's home had to be built on a million acres of land, and there was a leisure pool with a lighting system that flashed several different colors. Looking up, I observed the balconies of the home stacked on every level. By the look in Chase's eyes, he could tell I was impressed. Gathering myself, I tried to play it cool.

"Nice dwelling place," I said dryly.

"Thanks," he laughed.

My acting wasn't as good as I thought. Chase could clearly tell I was more excited than I tried to let on.

"I could sit out here and watch the stars all night." Oh no, did those words just literally come out of my mouth.

"You're welcome to do just that, you can come here anytime you want Aniyas," Chase said as he stared into my eyes.

Quickly, I darted my eyes in another direction. It was getting weird, so I had to redirect my focus.

"Can we go back in?" I asked.

"Let's go, dinner should be ready. Follow me." I followed Chase back into his dwelling place.

To my surprise, Chase pulled my chair out for me. "These place settings are stunning," I said. Two workers in all-white placed our plates on the table. Snap, I forgot to tell him I do not eat meat, but to my surprise I didn't see any meat sitting before me.

"Do you not eat meat?" I asked Chase.

"Yeah, I do, but I know you don't, that's why we are having a meatless dinner this evening."

How does he know I don't eat meat? Is he a stalker? Chase must have noticed the look on my face. My facial expressions always gave away my true feelings.

"I overheard you telling one of the lunch guardians that you don't eat me." So, he's spying on me, that is a little stalkerish. "Let's eat!" Chase shouted. He didn't have to tell me twice, I dived into my plate!

"Where are your parents, are they coming down?"

"My parents are not here. Most of the time I'm home alone and have dinner by myself," Chase replied.

"Aww, he must get lonely," I thought to myself. Meesa would

have a heart attack if she knew I was home alone with a boy. Mother didn't even check to see if Chase's parents were going to be here, but I guess she didn't think she had to because he's an Edgerton.

"Where are your parents?" I pried.

"My father works long hours, I barely see him, and my mother is probably out somewhere getting drunk, she's always drunk," Chase said nonchalantly.

Alcohol was forbidden in Gardash, but then again, the Edgerton's are elites, they never follow the same rules we do. Chase's dwelling place was a dream, but I was starting to realize his home-life might be a nightmare.

Dinner was amazing, the food was delicious, and there was constant laughter and chatting throughout. I'm not a big talker when I don't really know someone, but with Chase my words flowed effortlessly. Even though I wanted to keep my guard up, it was coming down.

"Now it's time for dessert," announced Chase. One of the workers sat a platter of cherpinals topped with whip cream on the table. Did Chase know cherpinals are my favorite fruit? "Okay, he might really be stalking me," I said to myself.

"How did you know cherpinals were my favorite fruit?" I questioned Chase.

"I didn't know, cherpinals are my favorite fruit, that's why I selected them for dessert."

"Oh, okay," I replied. Whew, so Chase isn't a stalker!

"That's two things we have in common now, we both love star gazing and cherpinals," Chase smiled. This evening was not what I expected, Chase Edgerton was actually a decent human being.

Dinner was over and it was getting late. Chase and I had a plan laid out for our project, and we would start to execute those plans tomorrow. To my astonishment, Mother had not called to check on me one time, not even at this hour and it was an academia night. Calling Adrielle, I let him know I was ready.

"Do you want to watch something on television until your father arrives?" Chased asked.

"Television!" I screeched.

Televisions had been banned many years ago in Gardash, and the conventionals and indigents would surely be fined or punished if we were caught with one. Elite privilege was most definitely real!

Chase looked at me and said, "I know I am allowed to do several things you are not allowed to do, and it's not fair, but it's the world we live in."

I did not respond. Chase was aware of his privilege, interesting. I wish Chase would use that privilege to help the conventionals and indigents, instead of watching television.

"Follow me," said Chase. We walked into the lounge space, sat on a huge comfortable chair, and began to watch television. I had no idea what I was watching but it was hilarious. Chase moved closer to me, touched my hair, and told me I was beautiful. A lump formed in my throat, and simultaneously I slapped Chase's hand down from my hair.

"Don't touch my hair!" Chase jumped back, looked at me like I was insane, and apologized. I hopped up from the lounge chair and said, "I will wait for my father by the door."

With a puzzled look on his face, Chase replied, "Okay." Was he trying to put the moves on me? Chase has a girlfriend he is cheating on with Mara, and I just overheard him telling a guy in academia how pretty Allura was. Chase Edgerton clearly does not have a type. He loves us all.

Waiting by the door, I heard a car pull up. The front door flung open, and Chase's mom came stumbling inside. She stopped, looked me up and down, and asked, "Who do we have here?"

"I'm Aniyas ma'am. Nice to meet you."

"Well, aren't you just so well-mannered you-you wild headed child," she stuttered. You could clearly see Mrs. Edgerton was extremely intoxicated. She was slurring her words and she could barely keep her balance. Chase looked embarrassed.

"You are home early Mother. I was not expecting you back until your usual time of much later," he mumbled. "I will get you to bed." Chase struggled to get Mrs. Edgerton into the elevator. Yes, the Edgerton's have an elevator in their home.

"Do you need some help?" I asked.

"No, I got it." Before the elevator door closed, Chase looked at me with sadness in his eyes. I never thought I would feel sorry for Chase Edgerton, but now I do.

Watching Chase struggle to care for his mother in her intoxicated state, was a sad sight to behold. Earlier at dinner Chase stated his mother was always drunk, what a burden for a child to carry. It was unfair that Chase was responsible for looking after his mother, while still being a minor. As I waited by the door, I wondered if Mr. Edgerton would be home soon, too. I was now curious to see how Chase's father behaved. Looking out the door, I saw Adrielle pull into the driveway. Without saying goodbye, I left.

CHAPTER SEVEN

The Radiant Ones

Entering the car, Father gave me a kiss on the cheek.

"Did you enjoy your evening honey?" asked Adrielle.

"It was interesting, to say the least," I replied.

I did not mention the incident with Chase's mom. Father was unusually silent the rest of the ride home. Adrielle talks nonstop most of the time. Father will speak to anyone at any time about anything. Adrielle will talk to himself, a chair, a bear, a tree, a cat, a dog, a frog, that's just how much he talks. My father was the definition of an extrovert.

As we pulled into the driveway, I wondered should I inform Father about what I had been experiencing. This would be a great time because we were alone, but would Adrielle think I was a weirdo or a freak? Taking a deep breath, I told Adrielle about the vision I had while meditating, and how I think I've been moving objects without touching them when I get upset. He's going to think I'm crazy!

Father turned to me and said, "I knew it, you are a radiant one!"

"I'm what?" I questioned, confused.

"My child, this is going to be a long conversation, and we have a lot of work to do, so sit back, listen, and pay attention," commanded Adrielle. At this moment, I knew my life was about to change forever.

Adrielle began to tell me a story.

"Our last name Nguvu means powerful in Swahili. We originate from a bloodline of warriors, and some of those warriors possessed abilities and strengths others did not have. Meditation is the key to unlocking and keeping those abilities and strengths, that's the reason I encourage you to meditate as often as possible. The regime knows there are still individuals that may possess these gifts, so they put toxins in the air, our water, and our food to suppress those abilities. My child, your gifts were strong enough to push through those barriers. Aniyas Nguvu, you are truly special.

"I am not sure if you are the only one with abilities, but I have not heard of anyone possessing these gifts in many years. Honey, I used to be just like you, you inherited your abilities from me. Unfortunately, I was stripped of my abilities like many others, years ago. Like you, I had visions, and I could also move objects without touching them from harnessing my energy within. The real motive behind meditation being deemed evil and outlawed is because the regime did not want to risk us regaining or using our gifts. The regime is fearful that we will reclaim what is rightfully ours.

"Most of the indigents descend from the same bloodline of powerful warriors that possessed these gifts as well. We are separated from the indigents by ranking, but we are all connected by our origin. We are indigents, Aniyas. The indigents are not oppressed because they are helpless, they are oppressed because the regime knows their true power. If the indigents were to tap into their inner self, and realize who they truly are, the world would shift in our favor."

I sat there speechless, but this was just the tip of the iceberg. Father had much more to say.

"You were always much faster and stronger than girls your age, Aniyas. As you grew older you grew exceptionally faster and stronger than your brothers, that is when I had the inkling you might be a radiant one. This is where the real work begins Aniyas, you must train harder now, you must meditate even longer, and you must practice controlling your abilities. So far, we know you can move objects without touching them when you are upset, but now you must learn to harness that energy when you are calm and in any situation. You've also had a vision, so we must figure out the depth of your visions and unlock any other abilities you may have.

"You cannot tell a soul about this Aniyas, not Mara, not your mother, not your brothers, not Allura, no one! If anyone were to find out about your gifts, I'm not sure what they would try to do to you, but we both know it would not be good. So, we must be very careful and lowkey with your advanced training, and never let anyone see you using your abilities. Do you understand?" Father asked firmly.

"Yes, I understand." I didn't know how to feel or what to think. I always knew I was different from others, but I didn't know I was this different. When others were following the crowd, I never did. I always marched to the beat of my own drum. While most people craved popularity, I didn't care to be popular or conform to the new ways of the world. Shock instantly hit my body, Aniyas the radiant one, that was a whole other level of different.

Father carried on with more information. "Some of the indigents and conventionals have been completely brainwashed. They have accepted the ways of this power structure and long to be accepted by the elites. I can only hope they wake up. Then there are the indigents and conventionals that want to break free. The individuals that are tired of the unfair treatment and senseless killings by the guardian patrol, are ready to take action. We must be ready Aniyas!

"The indigents have been meditating, secretly training, and developing their combat skills. There has been no mention of abilities being unlocked, but that does not mean it has not happened. Some indigents may be keeping their gift's a secret just as we must for the time being. We don't know who we can trust, but I believe we can trust the Abrafo's. Keir and his father train on a regular basis."

"So, that's why Adrielle was so fond of Keir," I thought to myself. Not only was Keir handsome and kind, but he was also a warrior. I think I'm in love! "Come on now, focus Aniyas, this is not the time for that, pay attention," I said to myself. Looking at

Father, I continued to listen.

"If we should ever go to war with the regime and elites, there are three major factors in our victory and survival. We must know how to defend ourselves; we must know how to feed ourselves, and we must own land. When all those factors are in order, the indigents will come together and take a stand. Now as for you, we will increase your training time. You will train for a few hours after you come home from academia tomorrow."

"Okay, I will tell Chase I can't come over to work on our project," I responded.

"No, you must follow your regular schedule. If you deviate from your schedule people might get suspicious. We will complete two hours of training and then you will go to Chase's home. Remember, do not tell him or a soul about anything we've discussed tonight!"

"I won't!" I said with certainty. "Why didn't you tell me any of this information before?" I questioned Father.

"I didn't want to risk you revealing this information to someone."

"Understandable," I replied. Unlike Father, I could hold water, so these secrets were safe with me.

A tap on the car window startled me, it was Meesa. "We will finish this conversation later," Adrielle said.

"You've been sitting in this car forever. What are y'all doing out here?" questioned Mother.

"We are coming in now," Father said, as he gave me a look. My lips were sealed.

Walking into our dwelling place, I knew I was about to get the third degree from Meesa. I still hadn't processed all the crucial information I just received from Adrielle, so I really did not want to talk or answer any questions right now. "Let the interrogation begin," I said to myself.

"How was their home? I just know it's beautiful. Was Chase a gentleman? I'm sure he was because he's such a sweet boy."

What kind of cars do they have? How many workers do they have? Is their dwelling place extremely large? Do they have a lot of land? Is there a leisure pool? Did he invite you back over? Are his parents nice? The questions from Meesa went on and on, but my answers were short and sweet. I just wanted this conversation to be over. "His mother is so beautiful," stated Mother.

Chase's mother was a thin, tall, plain looking woman. She had small sharp features, which was our societal standard of beauty, but Mrs. Edgerton was average looking if you asked me. I know beauty is subjective, but Chase's mother wasn't beautiful. Meesa was just a colorist and didn't realize it.

Mother would always say fair skin women were beautiful, no matter what they looked like, and women with darker skin were unattractive no matter how pretty they were. It was so odd to me because Mother had dark skin, but she had been brainwashed like so many others. Meesa equated beauty to skin color and hair texture, when logically it should be measured by your facial feature set up. I started to wonder, does Meesa even like her own dark skin. Mother went on to ask a thousand more questions but thankfully she finally ran out of them. Up to my sleeping chamber I went, but not to sleep. It was time to meditate. It was time to focus on what I could truly become.

CHAPTER EIGHT

Friends to Foes

I felt a tremendous amount of weight on my shoulders. Learning I was a radiant one was mind blowing. I have the power to change Gardash, and I was taking it seriously. Last night during meditation, I had the clearest vision yet. Standing in a large empty field, surrounded by darkness, a small orb of light appeared in the distance. The light became brighter and floated in my direction. As the light moved closer, I tried to move back but I could not. I was frozen. The light drew nearer, and my temperature began to rise. What was once a small orb of light, was now massive and radiating heat. Panic started to set in because I still couldn't move. Sweat was dripping from all my pores, and in an instant, I was engulfed by the massive orb of light. The orb then burst into flames, and I just knew I had been burnt alive.

To my amazement, the flames were not harming me, I was one with the flames. My body was illuminated, and I felt extraordinarily powerful. Focusing all my energy on moving my body, I tried to walk, but I still could not move. I became frustrated and the flames began to fizzle out. Again, I was standing in darkness. Taking three extremely deep breaths I opened my eyes, and I was no longer in a meditative state.

"That's it Aniyas, that's how you release yourself from a meditative state, three deep breaths!" I thought to myself. This was the first time I was in control of my abilities. I had a long way to go with cultivating my gifts, but this was a step in the right direction, and I was excited.

On the ride to academia, I didn't tell Father about my vision. I was excited about releasing myself out of a meditative state, but I was not pleased that I couldn't control my body during the vision. Adrielle did not need to know about my failure.

"Aniyas!" Father yelled. I was engrossed in my thoughts. "Wake up kiddo, it's time to use that awesome brain of yours and remember to keep our little secret to yourself. Love you and have a good day," said Adrielle.

Smiling, I nodded my head and exited the car. Waving goodbye to Father, I said, "I love you too."

When I turned around, Allura was heading my way. We walked into academia together and to our first lecture hall. As we walked, I began to tell Allura about my visit to Chase's dwelling place. It wasn't enough time to tell Allura everything, so I would tell her the full story during lunch.

It was time for science lecture hall, and for some reason I felt butterflies in the pit of my stomach. I wasn't sure what to say to Chase after seeing that episode with his mother, not mentioning it at all would probably be the best thing to do. Chase walked through the door and sat right next to me.

"I'm sorry about my mom."

"It's okay, you have nothing to be sorry about," I replied.

"If I'm not mistaken, I think Aniyas Nguvu is starting to warm up to me. I know you didn't like me very much."

"I still don't," I whispered.

 Chase chuckled.

"No seriously, I thought you were the biggest jerk known to man, but last night I saw a totally different side of you. I liked that side."

Wait a minute, his cheeks were flushed. Chase Edgerton blushing, I never thought I would see the day.

"Despite what you may think of me, I am a good person Aniyas," Chase said.

"So why are you such a bully and so mean in academia?" I asked.

"Well, there is a lot going on in my home, and sometimes I let that anger out the wrong way. I also have this image to uphold, people expect me to be the bad boy. For some reason people respect and admire the bad boy persona."

"I understand you are going through a lot at home, but that does not give you the right to take your troubles out on other novices, seek help. You also shouldn't care about keeping up a persona, just be yourself," I stressed.

"You're right," Chase responded.

That's it, he agreed with me. I was expecting an argument. Chase Edgerton is the complete opposite of what I thought he would be. He was growing on me.

Mara walked into lecture hall glaring at me. I smiled and she didn't smile back. Chase observed our awkward exchange but didn't say anything. Why would he? Chase did just have his tongue down Mara's throat a month ago, who knows it could be happening daily. Mara only informed me about the kiss because Allura thinks Chase likes me. Chase didn't tell me about the kiss either. I'm sure Chase wouldn't tell anyone about that kiss because he's dating Rebecca. There is no way Chase should be dating Rebecca, kissing Mara, and trying to put the moves on me last night. He knows Mara is my best friend. My mood instantly changed, and I gave Chase the side eye. We began working on our project and I was noticeably short with him. There would be no more laughing, and no more unnecessary conversations with Chase Edgerton. It's straight back to business between the two of us!

Lecture hall was over, and it was time for lunch. Mara exited lecture hall quickly without looking my way. When I arrived at the dining hall, Mara and Allura were already seated.

"Hey Mara, Hey Allura," I said.

"Hey Aniyas!" Allura responded.

"Hi," Mara replied dryly.

Allura looked at me with a what is her problem face. I shrugged and got up to get my lunch. There were much bigger things I needed to worry about besides Mara and her attitude. While walking to the lunch line, Chase hopped out of his seat and practically skipped over to me. I looked around to see if anyone noticed, and sure enough Rebecca and her pawns, Allura, and Mara were gawking at us.

Chase approached me, flashing those perfect pearly white teeth.

"What do you want?" I snapped.

"Whoa, I just wanted to know what time you were coming over later, so we can work on our project. We forgot to set a time in lecture hall."

"Oh, I'll be there around six," I replied.

"I'll see you then," Chase said with a smile.

He returned to his seat next to Rebecca. I can tell she was upset by the expression on her face. I looked at Rebecca, smiled, and turned my back. I knew that would piss Rebecca off even more and that was the point.

Returning to the lunch table, before I could even sit down, Allura asked, "What was that about?"

"He just wanted to know what time I was stopping by to work on our project," I mumbled.

"Excuse me, stopping by, you've been to his dwelling place Aniyas?" questioned Mara.

It's so funny that Mara was barely speaking to me, never told me what was really going on in her life, but had the nerve to question me.

"Yes, I have," was my response and that's all she was going to get. I told Mara about the good, bad, and ugly going on in my life and I finally realized, she told me nothing. No longer did I feel obligated to inform Mara about anything that was going on in my life. My new motto is you get what you give.

"Aniyas, finish telling me about your visit to Chase's home. You left off at how beautiful his dwelling place was and how Chase was such a gentleman," Allura recalled.

"We will talk about it later," I replied. Even though we aren't seeing eye to eye right now, I know Mara likes Chase. I don't want to throw my experience with Chase in her face. I love Mara, so I would never do anything to intentionally hurt her feelings.

"So, you can tell the new girl you went over to my guy's house but not me?" Mara screeched.

"Last time I checked he was never your guy but Rebecca's guy," I responded.

"You know what I mean Aniyas, you know Chase kissed me last month. So, whatever happened between you and Chase doesn't matter anyway."

"Okay," I said as I ate my lunch.

"I called Chase last week and asked him to meet me at Dover's Creek. We hung out, made out, and had a great time," Mara bragged.

Wow, something else Mara hadn't told me. Also, the timing of her telling me this information and how she said it, made me wonder if Mara was intentionally trying to make me feel a way. It was also interesting that shortly after she found out Chase may like me, she made sure to call him and make out with him again. Mara had been acting really weird lately, and I was starting to wonder if she was really my friend.

Mara was going on and on about the wonderful time she had with Chase, while I listened in silence. She then goes on to say, Keir had flirted with her on several occasions. This was the first I had ever heard of Keir flirting with her, and now I was not sure if I believed her. Mara knows I like Keir. I now knew she was intentionally trying to hurt my feelings. I could not believe she was acting like this, and I had done nothing to her. I've always been a good friend to Mara. All this just because she thinks a boy that she likes, who has a girlfriend, likes me. Mara was being ridiculous.

Allura had had enough. "Just shut up Mara! You are really making yourself look like an idiot right now," Allura fumed.

"No one is talking to you newbie!" Mara screamed, as she stood up.

"I'll be a newbie!" Allura yelled, as she stood up. I was in the middle of the two, so I stood up to make sure this argument did not escalate into anything further.

"Whatever, I don't have time for this. I'll leave you with your new best friend Aniyas. You two were made for each other!" Mara yelled, as she stormed out of the dining hall.

Everyone was staring at us, and Rebecca had a look of satisfaction on her face. Mara had been my friend for many years, this issue wasn't that big. We would get over this, hopefully.

As soon as I walked in the door from academia, my name was being called.

"Aniyas, come here!" I went into Mother's sleeping chamber to see what she wanted. "Remember a while ago when I told you your garbs and shoes were disappearing, well I figured out where they went. I got a call from Mara's grandmother asking if I had given Mara some garbs and shoes. She went on to say there was a bag of garments and a few pairs of shoes she found in Mara's closet that she didn't purchase. Mrs. Smith brought the bag over, and sure enough all the items belonged to you." This was news to me; I was in disbelief.

"Did you let Mara borrow these items?" Meesa asked.

"No, I didn't, I didn't even know she had them," I replied.

My mind was blown. Mara had been stealing from me, when all she had to do was ask to wear the garbs. Mother was also shocked that Mara would do this. Meesa called Mara's grandmother to inform her Mara had taken those garbs and shoes without permission. "That girl can no longer come over here. I will not allow a thief in my home. Do you understand?" Mother said. "Yes ma'am," I replied. Meesa stormed out of her sleeping chamber.

This situation made me recall when I snuck to meet Mara at the shopping square a few days ago, to find garbs for Allura's party. They had an underground boutique, where you could find beautiful garbs of all different colors. I had no idea about this place, but Mara said Allura told her about it. Mara arrived first and pulled dresses. Mara didn't like any of the dresses she tried on, so I asked if I could try them out. I was larger than Mara, but most of the dresses were made from a stretchy fabric.

As I tried on the dresses and looked in the mirror, Mara said, "Ugh I'm never coming shopping with you again, everything looks good on you. I didn't know you had all that body."

"Cut it out Mara, everything looks good on you as well," I reassured her.

I loved one of the dresses Mara didn't want. The dress was black with long sleeves and sequin all over.

"This is the one," I said to Mara while admiring myself in the mirror.

"You can't wear that one Aniyas, you are going to outshine me at the party," Mara laughed.

"I'll find something else," I responded.

"No, no I was just joking, get the dress," she urged.

"Are you sure?" I asked.

"Yes, Aniyas, I'm sure!" As I paid for my dress, I noticed Mara stuffing garbs into her satchel. I was shocked but I didn't say anything, and frankly it was none of my business. But now, not only was Mara stealing from boutiques, she was also stealing from me, and that was a problem. Snapping out of my flashback, I stood there dumbfounded. I was starting to realize; I didn't really know Mara at all.

It was almost time to train with Adrielle. "Today has been one hot mess," I thought to myself. I now knew how to release my mind from a meditative state, so I would meditate for a few minutes to clear my mind. Closing my eyes, I tapped into my inner self, chanting, my soul is at ease. My spirit began to smile. Opening my eyes, I stood up and was ready for training. No bad days, only bad moments, always keep pushing Aniyas, always keep pushing.

Training was intense today. Father showed no mercy. He pushed me to my limit. We worked on harnessing my energy to move objects. I became angry because I could not move the plate that was before me. It wasn't until I became angry that I made the plate crash to the ground. Knowing that anger should not be the driving force behind my abilities, I screamed out of frustration. After that episode, Adrielle said we were done for the day.

"You are greatness Aniyas, always remember that!" Father said as we wrapped up. He was right, I am greatness, and I'm going to master my gifts one day.

My body was drained, but I knew I had to go to Chase's dwelling place to work on our project. When I arrived, I was short and straight to the point. I even skipped dinner because I just wanted to hurry up and get in my bed. Chase didn't eat because I didn't eat, but he grabbed a bag of stechuls to snack on, another luxury he was afforded with his privilege. Indigents and conventionals didn't have stechuls in our markets, they were removed. Matter of fact, I hadn't seen stechuls in years.

"Would you like some?" Chase asked.

I really really wanted the stechuls, but I declined.

"Is everything okay?" he questioned. "You are acting a little strange this evening."

"I'm fine. I'm just tired," I replied.

"Okay, we will finish this section and resume tomorrow, so you can get home." About twenty minutes later we were done, and I was on my way home to get some much-needed rest.

At academia the next day, to my astonishment Mara had pulled another stunt. About a week ago I shared with Mara and Allura that I wanted to sell politically motivated garbs, with slogans about social reform. During research hall, which was basically a free period in academia, Mara was holding up a colorful poster that stated, "Social reform garbs coming soon." Not only had she stolen my garbs and didn't reach out to apologize, now she was stealing my idea. Mara had done a few questionable things throughout our friendship that I ignored, but she was starting to go too far.

Walking directly up to Mara's face, I asked, "What are you doing?"

"What are you talking about, Aniyas?" she replied.

"You know exactly what I'm talking about Mara. I told you I was going to be selling garbs like this just a week ago!" I raised my voice and stepped closer.

"Well, I had the same idea and was working on it too," Mara said.

"If you were working on the shirts when I shared my ideas, you should have informed me. We could've worked on the shirts together!" I shouted. "Not only do you steal garbs, but you also steal ideas, you thief!"

"I have no idea what you're talking about Aniyas," Mara lied. My feelings were extremely hurt, and I couldn't believe this was happening.

By this time Allura walked up and grabbed me.

"Get off of me!" I screamed.

"Calm down Aniyas, it's not worth it," Allura reasoned.

Snatching away from Allura, I walked into the washroom to gather myself. Allura followed me.

"I can't believe Mara stole your idea."

"She was also stealing my garbs and shoes too."

"What!" Allura yelled.

"Unfortunately, yes," I responded.

"What is wrong with her? I hate to say this, and I know I haven't been around that long, but from what I've seen, Mara is not your friend."

At this point I had no more words, but I was starting to agree with Allura. Mara had been my friend for a long time, but it was time for me to distance myself. With friends like that, who needs enemies.

CHAPTER NINE

Build, Destroy, Rebuild

"This week has flown by," I thought to myself. It was the day before our science project was due. We were almost done, I just had to add a few finishing touches to the scenery. After training, I would go to Chase's for about an hour. Between training, academia, and the Mara drama, I was exhausted, but I had to keep pressing forward. I was determined to get faster, stronger, and learn how to control and unlock any other abilities I may possess. Allura's party was also coming up this Saturday, and I still had not asked my parents for permission to go. Even if they said no, I was going to that party by any means necessary.

While in my sleeping chamber, I began to practice the dance moves Allura taught us. Looking in the mirror, I dipped, swayed, and rolled my body, imagining I was dancing with Keir. I really hope he's able to make it. I wondered who would attend Allura's party. Allura said she only invited a few people, people who she thought she could trust. Parties are forbidden in Gardash, and we can only have spiritual gatherings. Ms. Haraka was taking a huge risk by allowing Allura to host this party. If anyone alerted the guardian patrol, we would surely be punished. Hopefully everything would go smoothly, and everyone would keep their lips sealed.

"Ouch!" I yelled as I laughed. I had hit my baby toe on my bedpost. I injured a part of my body at least every other day. I'm shocked that clumsy ole me was blessed with my abilities. I guess I wasn't clumsy when it mattered the most. Walking into the kitchen, Landon and Landis were sitting at the table eating breakfast. Mother had made a huge spread on a Thursday morning, which was unusual. The twins moved into their own place a few weeks ago, so I assumed this was an I miss you breakfast.

"Grand rising," I said to my family.

"What in the world is grand rising?" Landon questioned.

"I'm sure she meant good morning," Landis added.

"Nope, I meant exactly what I said, grand rising."

"What does that even mean, Aniyas?" Mother asked.

"Well, some people believe it's just a better way of saying good morning. In African spirituality words hold power, what you speak may come to pass, like a spell. Morning is a homophone for mourning, even though they have two different meanings, they sound the same. Mourning is typically an unpleasant word, meaning a time of grief, and the universe can't differentiate which way we mean the word, so, we say grand rising instead, because both of those words have positive meanings."

"Girl, really?" said Landis.

"Don't interrupt me, I have not finished my thought." I continued my explanation.

"Grand means magnificent and rising means awakening, new, going up, increasing, and so on and so forth, so, we should think, speak, and use words with positive meanings. If you put positivity into the universe, that's what you will receive back. Others believe your spirit travels while you sleep, so upon awakening people say grand rising because they are giving thanks for their spirit being returned to their bodies, and they are happy to be rising again," I explained. Mother and the twins were looking at me like I was insane. It was fine though; I had grown used to being the black sheep.

"African spirituality, spells, the universe, spirits traveling, Aniyas stop bringing all that voodoo mess in my dwelling place. Where did you even get this evil nonsense?" Mother questioned.

"There is nothing evil about anything I just mentioned, everything I said was about positivity. Did you know voodoo wasn't made to be bad, there are just some people who use it in negative ways. You know just like back when people were in bondage and the bondsman masters used the Pathway to justify their evil ways. It's so typical for people to denounce things they know nothing about," I responded.

"Girl, I don't care about anything you are saying right now. The only divine power you may speak of in my dwelling place is the Leading Light, understood?" Mother said. I didn't respond.

"Here you go Aniyas, you're always coming up with this weird mess. Where do you get this stuff from?" Landon asked.

"After everything I just said, all he could come up with was weird mess," I thought to myself. "Actually, there is nothing weird about anything I just said and I'm learning a lot from Allura and her mother."

"That's exactly why I don't like you hanging around people I don't know, they are filling your head with stupidity," Meesa scolded. I wasn't going to win this battle, so I decided to just keep my mouth closed.

There was no way Mother would allow me to go to Allura's home this weekend, after that exchange. Meesa was always so judgmental of anything that differed from her way of thinking. I almost fell into that way of thinking, but the more I meditate, the more I become open to new information. There was way more knowledge out there other than what had been forced upon us, and I was eager to learn. Grabbing a cherpinal, I headed out the door.

It was going to be awkward seeing Mara today after our blow up. Most of our lecture halls were together, so it wasn't like I could avoid her. I walked into my first lecture hall and Mara was already seated. We didn't speak to each other, we acted as if we didn't even see one another. I'm not sure if we would ever be friends again, but for the time being I really didn't care. I was over Mara at this point.

Allura walked in and spoke to both of us, but she headed straight towards me.

"Hey girl, are you going to be able to make it to my party Saturday night?" she asked.

"I'm going to try my best to make it, but I know Mother isn't going to let me come," I whined.

"Just sneak out your window," Allura said nonchalantly. I never ever snuck out of my home before. If Meesa caught me, I'm sure she would place me in a grave.

"Mother would kill me, if she caught me," I whispered.

"Well don't get caught," Allura whispered back. I did say I was going to that party by any means necessary. It was time for my first sneaking out of my dwelling place adventure, this should be interesting.

The day was going by fast, just how I liked it. It was time for lunch, and I was starving. "Well, what do we have here?" I said to myself. Mara was sitting at Conny and Samantha's table. If they knew how much crap Mara talked about them, they wouldn't want her anywhere near them. "That child is something else," I mumbled.

Before I could even sit down, Allura said, "Do you see who Mara is sitting with now?"

"Yes, I do, but I don't even care to talk about it."

"Okey, dokey," Allura responded. Mara no longer existed in my world.

Chase came and flopped down right beside me.

"Why are you sitting at my table?" I questioned.

"Because I want to eat lunch with you," he said.

"There is no way Rebecca is allowing that."

"I am a free man. We broke up last night. So, Rebecca has no authority to tell me who I can and can't sit with," Chase smiled.

I'll be damned! The king and queen of Edgerton were no longer an item.

"Breaking up with someone shouldn't be a joyous occasion Sir, why are you smiling about it?" I asked.

"To be completely honest, I never really liked Rebecca that much. I only dated her because we were both popular and everyone expected the most popular boy and girl to be together at academia."

Wow, that was not what I was expecting Chase to say.

"I've had my eye on someone else for a while though," he smiled again.

"I bet, your eyes are always on someone else," I thought to myself. Mara is going to be elated when she discovers Chase and Rebecca are no longer together. Wait, why was I thinking about her? As Chase and I ate lunch together, I was getting dirty looks from Mara and Rebecca. Little did they know, I did not want Chase Edgerton, Keir Abrafo was the only man for me.

Academia was over for the day and now it was time for training. Adrielle had been focusing on combat skills for the past couple of days, but today we would work on harnessing my energy again.

"Everything comes from your spirit, focus on the energy coming from your spirit," Father said.

I closed my eyes and tried to connect my mind with my spirit.

"I am one with my spirit, I am one with my spirit," I repeated to myself. A sense of calm came over my body. Opening my eyes, I felt the same calming but powerful feeling. I raised my hands and there was a small orb of light mixed with darkness in my left hand. This had never happened before, I was thrilled!

While continuing to concentrate on the orb, images began to form. It was the guardian patrol, and they were headed to Allura's dwelling place. Inside Allura's home I could see people dancing. This must be her party. How did the guardian patrol find out about the party? The patrollers were getting closer and closer to Allura's dwelling place. Ms. Haraka moved swiftly to the upstairs hallway and when I say swiftly, I mean I had never seen anyone move that fast in my life. Ms. Haraka opened a hidden window and saw the guardian patrol coming. Allura somehow appeared right behind her mother.

"Go turn off the music now and direct the kids to the safe space in the cellar," commanded Ms. Haraka. Allura jetted down the stairs with lighting speed, she was even faster than her mom.

"The guardian patrol will be here any minute, everyone please be quiet and follow me," Allura yelled. The orb in my hand faded out and disappeared. I was shocked. I had finally unlocked one of my abilities with control. I was truly a radiant one.

"Did you see that, Father?" I shouted with excitement.

"Yes Aniyas, I saw the orb. I'm so proud of you!" he gleamed.

"Did you see images in the orb?" I asked Adrielle.

"No, I didn't see images, just the orb. Did you see images?" Father questioned.

"No, I didn't," I lied.

I now knew that the orb could be seen by others, but only I could see what was materializing inside of the orb. I lied to Adrielle about not seeing any images because he would know about the party that wasn't supposed to be happening.

Should I warn Allura? What if the images were just a part of my imagination? There was no guarantee my vision would come to pass. I wouldn't be able to say anything to Allura about my vision anyway because she would have too many questions. Allura would want to know how I obtained the information. I most definitely had to be at this party for sure now, to see what really goes down.

It was time to head to Chase's dwelling place to finish our project. Overall, I was having a really good time working with him and I still couldn't believe it. Upon arrival, I was greeted by Chase at the door with a bouquet of flowers and his beautiful smile. I blushed and said thank you. No one had given me flowers before, and this was my first gift from a boy.

"Why did you give me flowers?" I asked.

"I enjoyed working with you. You are a really cool girl Aniyas, and I like you." Chase leaned in to kiss me on the lips, but I turned my head. Looking into his eyes, I saw the disappointment. Chase just ended things with Rebecca, and he was just kissing Mara. Besides, I like Keir. There was no way I was getting involved with Chase Edgerton.

"Listen Chase, you have proven to be a nice guy, but you just got out of a relationship. Mara also told me you hooked up with her a few times. Even though Mara is no longer my friend, I don't think she would be too fond of us hooking up. I also like someone else," I explained.

"I already told you the Rebecca thing was just for show, and yes, I kissed Mara a couple of times but that's in the past. I really like you; I want to be with you." This was shocking news to me;

Chase was really putting it all out there.

Was this just him running a game on me or had Chase Edgerton always liked me? He sounded sincere. Before I even realized what was happening, Chase grabbed my face and kissed me, and I kissed him back. Coming to my senses, I pushed him away. Oh no! How was Chase Edgerton my first kiss? I've liked Keir for years and we haven't even kissed yet. Not to mention, Mara would lose her mind if she found out.

"We can't do this Chase!" I pushed past him and walked to the table to complete our project. Chase dropped his head and followed me.

There was a lot of awkward tension in the air. Every time Chase looked at me, I turned away. We were finally finished with our project though, and it looked amazing.

"Will you stay for dinner?" Chase asked. I stayed. Dinner was so delicious, but we didn't speak much. I was still feeling weird about the kiss. I couldn't believe Chase liked me.

"I don't want to hear your excuses!" I heard a man's voice yell as the side door flung open. It was Chase's dad, and Chase's mother was stumbling in behind him. Oh boy, she was drunk again. "There is no reason I should be getting calls from the high society club, saying my wife is there drunk and acting like a fool!" Mr. Edgerton yelled again.

"Well, maybe if you were home more often, I wouldn't have to entertain myself so much!" Mrs. Edgerton screamed. I wish I had some popcorn, because this fight was intense and entertaining.

Chase jumped up from the table and said,"Mom, dad,we have company."

"Oh, I didn't know we had a guest," Mr. Edgerton responded with a slight hint of embarrassment on his face.

"I don't care who is here! I am sick of this crap!" Mrs. Edgerton said as she continued with her rant.

"Calm down dear, not in front of the kids please," Mr. Edgerton pleaded.

"Don't tell me to calm down, you jerk of a husband!" Mrs. Edgerton lunged at her husband, but he stepped out of the way. Mrs. Edgerton stumbled, tripped, and came crashing down on our project! I stood up and gasped. All our hard work was gone in a split second. Everything we had just built, Mrs. Edgerton destroyed. Mad was an understatement, I was furious!

Mr. Edgerton went to help his wife up and started to escort her upstairs. He looked back at us and mouthed, "I am so sorry." Mrs. Edgerton could barely walk, and she was crying hysterically.

"What was going on with this woman?" I thought to myself.

"There is no way we can complete another project of this magnitude by tomorrow," I said to Chase.

"I'll just tell the academia master we need more time," he replied nonchalantly. Here we go, Chase could ask for more time and not be penalized, I would for sure receive a failing grade. I did not have the same privileges as Chase Edgerton, and I wish he could understand that.

"Life doesn't work the same for me Chase. You have privileges that I don't!" I yelled.

"You're blowing this way out of proportion," Chase responded.

This project was half of our grade, Meesa would kill me if I failed!

"You know what I'm leaving! I will figure something out Mr. Privileged!" I shouted, as I walked out the door. Chase followed behind me. "Please don't follow me. I'll wait for my father outside alone!" I slammed the door behind me. I was waiting for Chase to come after me, but he didn't.

I was still fuming on the ride home, all that hard work, gone! Father knew something was wrong, but I didn't want to talk about it. I had another thing in common with Chase, our mothers were crazy! Arriving home, I ran straight upstairs to my sleeping chamber and slammed the door. Meesa walked into my sleeping chamber shortly after.

"Why are you slamming doors, what happened?" she questioned. I usually don't tell Mother anything that's going on in my life because we don't have that type of relationship, but for some reason I told her everything that transpired this evening at the Edgerton's home.

I went on and on about how I'm going to fail because it's too late to complete a whole new project by tomorrow. Meesa listened.

"Maybe I can come up with something," I said aloud. I ran downstairs and tried to piece something together with whatever I could find around our dwelling place. Nothing was working, everything looked horrible! My frustration started to take over me, but I calmed myself down quickly and accepted the fact I was going to receive a failing grade. I went back upstairs and went to sleep.

Waking up in the a.m., I sat on the edge of the bed and became infuriated again. Maybe I should fake an illness so I won't have to go to academia today, yeah that's what I would do. Jumping up, I put on my robe and my best sick face. Walking into the kitchen, my mouth dropped. Meesa was standing by the table next to a newly created project. This savannah was absolutely amazing, it was one hundred times better than the one Chase and I had created.

"I was up all night working on this project for you," Mother said. I couldn't believe my eyes or ears; this was the most thoughtful thing Meesa had ever done for me. I wanted to cry.

"Wow, thank you, thank you, thank you so much!" I shouted, as I hugged Mother.

"You're welcome," she smiled. Meesa and I never hug at home, only at chastis for show. The hug felt a little awkward, but I meant it. I was extremely grateful Mother did this for me, and this would certainly be the best project turned in. In a matter of a week our project was built, destroyed, and rebuilt. Maybe this could be the start of building a relationship with Mother, I was optimistic.

CHAPTER TEN

Secrets Revealed

I woke up Saturday still reveling over receiving the highest score on our science project. When I informed Mother that everyone was in awe of her work, she was elated. Getting out of bed, I locked my door and tried on my dress for the party tonight. "I look good!" I said aloud. Once again, I began to practice my dance moves. Tap, tap, tap, I turned towards my window, and it was Keir. I dropped down to the floor.

"Turn around now, I don't want you to see my dress!"

"What, why?" questioned Keir.

"Just do it!" Hopping up, I ran to put on my robe.

"Okay you can turn back around now. Did you see my dress?" I asked.

"Barely."

"Good, but what are you doing here so early?" I questioned.

"I wanted to see my favorite girl." I blushed. Leaning in, I kissed Keir. He kissed me back. After the kiss we both looked surprised. I couldn't believe I made the first move, and by the look on Keir's face, he couldn't believe it either.

There was nothing but dead silence for a few seconds, but then Keir leaned in to kiss me again. We stopped, and locked eyes. Suddenly, the kiss I shared with Chase crossed my mind. I quickly shook the thought away. I could never tell Keir about that kiss.

"You have to go before Meesa catches us," I said, grinning

from ear to ear.

"I will see you tonight," smiled Keir, and he was off.

"I can't wait to see him this evening!" I said to myself. My first party with Keir will be a night to remember!

In the kitchen, I hummed and smiled as I prepared my breakfast. I could not stop thinking about Keir. It felt like I was floating on clouds.

"What has you in such a good mood?" Mother asked as she walked in the kitchen.

"Just thinking about how our science project crushed the competition."

Meesa smiled. "After you eat, go prepare for chastis," Mother commanded. Meesa was usually tired from preparing all day Saturday, for chastis Sunday, so she went to bed early on Saturday nights. Father also went to bed early the night before chastis. This was perfect, because my parents would be fast asleep by the time I left for Allura's party. Tonight, could not get here fast enough!

I was watching the clock like a hawk. Why was time passing so slowly? The thought of sneaking out of my home had my anxiety at an all-time high. What could I do to pass the time? Picking up a book, I began to read. A few hours passed and my parents were finally off to bed. Grabbing my satchel, I stuffed my dress and shoes in it and dropped it out the window. "Okay, I'll just climb down the side of the gutter like Keir does," I said to myself. One foot out and secure, the next foot out and secure, I had a tight grip on the gutter, so far so good.

I'm not sure what happened, but in the blink of an eye I was falling. I wanted to scream but I couldn't. I was about to fall to my death or break a million bones. Either way I was dead, because Meesa would kill me once she caught me sneaking out. As I watched myself plummet towards the ground, my life flashed before my eyes. Closing my eyes, I prepared for the worse, but to my surprise I landed feet first in a side squatting position. "Hmm, must be my abilities," I thought to myself. Standing up, I looked around to make sure no one saw me. I grabbed my satchel off the ground and ran all the way to Allura's dwelling place.

Allura didn't live far from our home, it was a ten-minute drive.

Looking down at my watch, I ran to Allura's dwelling place in five minutes. "Whoa, that's fast!" I thought to myself. I pressed Allura's buzzard.

"Aniyas, you made it!" Allura yelled, as she hugged me.

"Eww, you are sweaty."

"Sorry, I ran all the way here. Can I hop in your shower please?"

"Sure, but hurry up because everyone will be here soon." In the shower, I decided to take my hair out of my bun and wet it. The only person that had seen my hair in its true natural state besides my parents and brothers was Chase. Chase informed me he wasn't coming tonight, and I was relieved. I did not want to be anywhere with Chase and Keir at the same time.

The steaming hot water pouring down on my hair felt incredible. Getting lost in my zone, I closed my eyes and started to sway.

"Hurry up Aniyas!" yelled Allura.

Well, that was short lived, I rushed to finish showering. I applied leave-in conditioner and some oil Allura had on the sink to my hair. I donned my dress and shoes and admired myself in the mirror. Allura walked into the washroom.

"Wow Aniyas, you look amazing, and I love your hair like that!"

"Thank you, you look amazing too," I replied. The door buzzard chimed.

"Okay, here we go, people are starting to arrive," Allura said and gave a little shimmy. I shimmied right behind her. I couldn't believe I was at my first party, and I couldn't wait to see how the night would unfold.

"How many people did you invite?" I asked Allura, as we walked down the stairs.

"Twenty," she replied.

"Twenty! That was a lot of people for a party that was not supposed to be happening," I thought to myself. Allura was a social butterfly, I on the other hand, was not. Look up the word introvert in the dictionary and you would find a picture of Aniyas. Keir, Mara, and Allura were my only friends. I mean it's not like people didn't try to befriend me, but humans are weird, and I didn't trust them. Example, look how things unfolded with Mara, and she was my best friend. Keeping people at a distance was my thing, but for some reason I allowed Allura into my circle. Anyway, back to the matter at hand, I was ready to have some fun!

Allura must have said dress to impress with her invites, because after those hooded robes came off, everyone looked spectacular. Doing a three sixty, I further scoped out the space.

"What the hell is she doing here?" I mumbled. There was Mara, standing in the center of the living space. I was convinced Mara wouldn't come to the party after everything that transpired between us. Then again, she probably thought Chase was coming, so Mara wouldn't miss this party for the world. Little did she know, ha-ha, Chase Edgerton would not be at this gathering. Even though I saw Mara, I acted as if I didn't. I looked straight past Mara and walked over to the food. One thing for certain, two things for sure, I'm going to eat.

As I was chomping away on carrot sticks and ranch dip, I started to do a little two-step. A body pressed up against me, turning around to see who it was, it was no one other than the handsome Keir Abrafo.

"You look beautiful," said Keir.

"You don't look too bad yourself," I replied. We embraced, and I almost melted in Keir's arms.

"Did you see Mara? I am surprised that you two aren't together, you are usually inseparable."

"We are no longer friends, but I really don't want to talk about that situation right now. I just want to have fun and enjoy the night," I replied.

"My lips are sealed on the subject," Keir responded. We embraced once more.

Keir grabbed my hand and led me to the dance floor. "Wait, I'm still eating!" I screeched. Oh well, I'll just get more food later. I shoved one last carrot in my mouth and swallowed it quickly. Oh no, I have ranch breath! What if Keir tries to kiss me? What if he thinks I can't dance? What if I step on his feet? I've never danced with a boy before. "You are over thinking again Aniyas, just relax and have fun," I said to myself. As Keir continued to pull me over to the dance floor, I saw Mara watching, and I was about to give her a show.

Every dance Allura taught us, I executed. Looking out the corner of my eye, I saw Mara roll her eyes at me a time or two, and it made me giggle inside. "Mission accomplished," I thought to myself, now let me focus on this good-looking boy in front of me. To my amazement, Keir could dance very well, we looked good together. The music slowed down, and Keir pulled me close. My heart fluttered like a butterfly's wings in the springtime. While resting my head on Keir's shoulder, I closed my eyes and it felt like no one else was in the living space.

After a while, this strange feeling came over me. Opening my eyes, Chase was standing close by watching us intensely. "What is he doing here? He said he wasn't coming. How long has he been here?" I thought to myself. Panic rushed through my veins. I looked at Chase and gave him a half smile. Chase started walking towards us. Now why did I go and do that?

"Keep cool Aniyas, keep cool," I said to myself. As Chase was walking over, Mara stepped right in front of him. I guess I was happy Mara came after all, she just saved the day! Oh no, Chase mouthed a few words to Mara, politely pushed her aside, and continued to walk in our direction. When Mara saw Chase walking towards me, she rolled her eyes, folded her arms, and stormed out of the living space.

Chase snatched my hand and said, "I need to talk to you!"

"Whoa buddy, can't you see we are dancing?"

"I'm not talking to you indigent!" Chase yelled at Keir.

"Chase!" I scolded.

"Well, I'm talking to you!" Keir responded. Keir dropped my other hand and stepped closer to Chase.

"Guys please!" I pleaded.

"Get out of my face before I punch you in yours!" Chase threatened.

"Try it!" Keir responded, as he moved even closer to Chase.

Before I could interject again, Chase swung at Keir's head. Keir ducked, grabbed Chases' legs, and tackled him to the ground.

"Stop, stop!" I screamed, as I tried to pull Keir off Chase. Despite my attempts, I could not stop the fight.

Ms. Haraka and Allura entered the living space and helped me break up the fight. Once Chase and Keir were off the floor and separated, Ms. Haraka asked, "What is going on here?" Standing by Keir's side, none of us said a word. "There will be no fighting amongst peers in my dwelling place. If you cannot behave, leave!" Ms. Haraka shouted. I'd never seen Ms. Haraka upset before, I didn't even think she could get angry.

Chase looked at me and said, "I'm out of here!" Chase pushed through the crowd and walked out the front door. I wanted to go after Chase, but I was frozen. Mara had made her way back into the living space to witness the action. She had this look on her face like, I can't believe they were fighting over her. Well, I couldn't believe it either.

Everyone at the party was staring at me and Keir.

"Okay kids, go back to having fun, dance, eat, and party," Ms. Haraka commanded.

"What was that about?" questioned Keir.

"I-I-I don't know," I stuttered.

Allura must have sensed I was in a predicament. "Girl washroom break," she announced, as she pranced over and grabbed my hand.

Looking back at Keir, I yelled, "I'll be right back!" We entered the washroom, and Allura shut and locked the door behind us.

"Aniyas, what is going on?" she asked.

I shared with Allura that I kissed Chase, and I also informed her I kissed Keir the very next day.

"Well, I'll be damned, Aniyas the player. I must admit, I didn't think you had it in you," Allura joked.

"It's not like that, the kiss with Chase was an unexpected mistake," I explained.

"Whatever you say Aniyas," Allura smirked. "You have two fine boys tearing up my dwelling place over you. Teach me your ways sis, teach me your ways," she laughed.

Rolling my eyes, I said, "Let's just get back to the party."

"Alright player," Allura giggled. I put my hand on my head and shook it, unlocked the door, and walked back into the party. Now, what was I going to tell Keir? I had to get my story straight and get it straight right now.

Walking back up to Keir, I grabbed his hand.

"Is everything okay?" he asked.

"Yes, everything is fine," I replied. I was waiting for Keir to question me about Chase again, but he didn't. If he's not saying anything else about it, I'm not saying anything about it, my lips are sealed on the subject. Glancing around, I didn't see Mara anymore. Knowing how much Mara liked Chase and thinking about it, I started to feel bad. It was never my intention to hurt Mara, whether we were still friends or not.

"Are you sure you're okay? You are staring off in space." Keir questioned.

I snapped out of my thoughts and said, "Yes, I'm great, now let's dance!"

We danced to a couple of songs, and then Keir looked around and led me upstairs. Once we were in the hallway, Keir pulled out a locket and placed it around my neck. Wow it was beautiful, but we aren't supposed to wear jewelry in Gardash. Where did he get this? "Oops, here I go again. Aniyas, just be quiet and enjoy the gift," I said to myself.

"Thank you, it's beautiful, I love it!"

Keir pulled me close and kissed me. Closing my eyes, I was enjoying every second of our kiss. Suddenly, a sensation came over me that I had never felt before. With my eyes still closed, I could see the guardian patrol heading our way.

Backing away from Keir, I shouted, "The guardian patrol is coming!"

Keir looked at me like I was insane. I'm not sure how Ms. Haraka heard me over the music, but she was upstairs in the blink of an eye. She opened a hidden window and saw the guardian patrol. Allura somehow appeared right behind her mother.

"Go turn off the music now and direct the kids to the safe space in the cellar," commanded Ms. Haraka.

Allura jetted down the stairs with lighting speed, she was even faster than her mom. "The guardian patrol will be here any minute, everyone please be quiet, grab your robes, and follow me," Allura ordered.

My orb vision was coming to pass, except I did not see Keir in my orb vision back at home. I wasn't sure how things were about to unfold but I was about to find out. We followed Allura to the cellar.

All the party attendees rushed into the safe space. My mind began to wonder. Not only were Allura and her mom mega humanly fast, why would they need a safe space? "Omg, they are radiant ones!" I thought to myself. I had so many questions but now wasn't the time, we were all in danger.

"Everyone put your robes on and then remove your garbs from under your robes," ordered Allura.

Boom, boom, boom, the guardian patrol was pounding on the door excessively hard. There was a vent in the safe space that was connected to the living space, so we could hear everything that was going on upstairs. While surveying the safe space, Alexis was crying. I went over to comfort Alexis and to keep her quiet.

"May I help you?" asked Ms. Haraka.

"We have intel that an unlawful event is taking place in your home, and we would like to check the premises," I heard a voice say.

Now who went and snitched to the guardian patrol? I bet it was Chase or Mara.

"Do you have a guardian entry pass?" questioned Ms. Haraka.

"Ma'am we don't need one, we make the rules around here," I heard the same voice say. The guardian patrol was always abusing their power, it was ridiculous!

"Stop, do not take another step! You are not welcome in my dwelling place without a guardian entry pass!" Ms. Haraka raised her voice.

"Move, now!" I heard the same voice shout.

"No, I will not, this is an unlawful entry! Do not come into my dwelling place!" Ms. Haraka shouted back.

The next thing I heard was a bunch of commotion, and Allura took off up the stairs. I followed.

Looking back, Keir was right behind me, but the other kids

were huddled in the corner of the safe space. All the children were frightened half to death. However, I didn't feel an ounce of fear in my heart, and I was ready for whatever. Running into the living space, my eyes opened wide. Ms. Haraka was fighting off six guardian patrollers, and not just any ole fighting, she was very skilled. Allura and Keir jumped right in. This was impressive!

After my short state of shock, I joined in on the action. I wasn't surprised that Keir was ready to battle and was such a skilled fighter because Father had already informed me, but to see Allura and Ms. Haraka in action, I was amazed. Allura and her mom were so fast and kicking butt. Keir was fighting two guardian patrollers. He punched one guardian patroller so hard, the patroller flew across the room, and was knocked unconscious. Keir then picked up the other patroller by his legs and tossed him like a doll. Wow, he has mega strength! Keir is a radiant one, too!

While I was amazed watching everyone else, I was also fighting two patrollers with ease. It felt like the guardians were moving in slow motion, and all their moves were so basic. The years of combat training with Adrielle had really paid off for me. Dodging a blow to my head and kick to my face, I punched one patroller in his eye. The other patroller I kicked in the temple, and they were both knocked out. I looked across the room and Allura and her mom had also knocked out the patrollers they were fighting. We all stopped and stared at one another in awe. We all had some explaining to do!

"Allura go get some rope and duct tape out of the safe space," Ms. Haraka commanded.

"Yes Ma'am!" Allura responded. Allura was back in a flash. No one had asked any questions yet; we were just working together at this point. We all helped tie the guardian patrollers up and duct tape their mouths closed. Keir picked the patrollers up like they were babies and placed them in the pantry.

"Mom, what are we going to do about the kids in the safe space? They know the guardian patrol has been here, they heard everything! I don't want to move again!" Allura pleaded. So that's why they moved to Gardash, someone must have found out about Ms. Haraka and Allura's abilities.

"Don't worry Allura, bring all the kids back into the living space," Keir said.

"But why?" she questioned.

"Just trust me," he replied. Allura followed Keir's instructions.

She rounded the kids up and brought them into the living space. The children looked scared and confused. Alexis started asking questions about the guardian patrol.

"Go turn the music back on Aniyas," Keir ordered. I followed Keir's directions without question.

"Nothing remains, everything changed, there is nothing that happened here ten minutes ago that you shall retain. Nothing remains, everything changed, there is nothing that happened here ten minutes ago that you shall retain," Keir chanted.

"Ms. Haraka, Allura, Aniyas, start dancing," Keir commanded. We all gave Keir the side-eye, but we started to dance and so did he.

Within two seconds all the other kids were dancing as well, they did not look scared or confused anymore. Oh, my, goodness, nothing remains, everything changed, there is nothing that happened here ten minutes ago that you shall retain, Keir had erased their memories with an incantation. To my amazement, Keir had more than one ability too. So far, Keir had shown mega strength, and he could erase moments from people's memories. Never in my wildest dreams could I have imagined this would be my world, this was crazy!

Allura and Ms. Haraka realized what Keir had just done as well. Ms. Haraka walked over to the speaker and stopped the music.

"Okay kids, I'm glad you all could make it, and I hope you had fun, but the party's over now. It's time to go home before it gets too late," she announced.

"Nothing remains, everything changed, our Pathway study was great, and we must do it again. Nothing remains, everything changed, our Pathway study was great, and we must do it again," Keir chanted.

"Great Pathway study Allura," some of the kids said as they walked out of the front door.

"We will see you at academia Monday," others said. Not only could Keir erase moments from people's memory, but he could also add memories. We couldn't risk any of the kids reporting this party, so it was smart of Keir to add those Pathway memories. Keir was even more than I could imagine, and I couldn't wait to learn more about him.

Allura went outside and checked around their dwelling place to make sure none of the kids were lingering around. Opening the pantry, the six guardian patrollers had awakened. The patrollers were trying to yell, but all you could hear were muffled sounds.

"Allura and Aniyas go collect the children's garbs from the safe space and put them into bags. Keir load the patrollers into their guardian patrol van," Ms. Haraka ordered.

At first, the patrollers resisted, but when Ms. Haraka drew her gun, they all hopped right into the van. I didn't see that one coming from Ms. Haraka!

"So, what's the plan?" I asked.

"We are going to drive them into the woods, let Keir do his thing, and leave them there," Ms. Haraka answered.

I didn't even know we had woods in Gardash, but I replied, "Sounds like a plan."

The four of us were silent the entire ride to the woods, while the guardian patrollers kicked the sides of the van and tried to scream through their duct tape. "Idiots!" I thought to myself. This ride seemed like it was taking forever. I sure hope we made it home by curfew, because I had had enough excitement for the evening. We finally arrived, and never in my life had I seen this part of Gardash. All the leaves on the trees were green and had brown trunks, unlike the colorful trees where we lived. I wondered why this location in Gardash had been kept a secret. How did Ms. Haraka know this area existed?

As we dragged the guardian patrollers out of the van one by one, I saw fear and panic in their eyes. I wondered if the patrollers saw that same fear and panic in the eyes of all the innocent victims they had slaughtered.

"Let's just kill them and bury them!" I yelled. The patrollers really started to panic.

"No Aniyas, we are sticking to the original plan!" Ms. Haraka responded.

"Fine," I mumbled.

"You are on Keir," said Ms. Haraka. It was time to watch Keir work his charm.

"Nothing remains, everything changed, you will not remember anything that happened today. In ten minutes, do not roam but find your way home. Nothing remains, everything changed, you will not remember anything that happened today. In ten minutes, do not roam but find your way home," he chanted.

All the guardian patrollers were suddenly asleep. We untied the patrollers, removed the duct tape from their mouths, and got back in the van. The conversation on the ride back home was about to be extremely interesting.

"Where do I even start," said Ms. Haraka. "How did you know the guardian patrol was coming, Aniyas? There is only one hidden window in that hallway that no one can see," she questioned.

"I saw them coming, I have visions. Well, I saw the patrollers coming yesterday in my orb vision, but I wasn't sure if it would come to pass. Today, a few minutes before the guardian patrol arrived at your dwelling place, I saw another vision of them heading to your home," I explained.

"Wow, so you are a radiant one. I observed that you were a skilled fighter, but you also have an ability," stated Ms. Haraka. Allura looked at me in amazement, and I smiled.

"I actually have two abilities that I know of. Besides my visions, I can also move objects by harnessing my energy from within. My father had the same two abilities, but they were stripped from him. Father has been training me in combat since I was small, but I discovered I have abilities and that I am a radiant one just a little while ago," I confessed.

"Those are some amazing abilities Aniyas," Ms. Haraka said.

"Thank you!" I replied. At that moment, I felt extremely proud.

"Ms. Haraka, how did you hear me yell from downstairs over that loud music?" I questioned.

"Allura and I have two abilities as well, mega hearing and mega speed. Many radiant ones that are my age had their abilities stripped away many years ago, but no one discovered my abilities. I noticed Allura was a radiant one early on, at the age of three. Allura repeated something to me I whispered to a friend. The catch was, Allura was in the kitchen, and we were standing outside in the courtyard. I was horrified that she heard what I said, but I was excited to learn she inherited an ability," Ms. Haraka confessed.

"I have always been nosey," Allura giggled. We all chuckled.

"My mom discovered I had mega speed when I was six, because a dog was chasing me," Allura laughed. We all laughed again.

"Long story short, it was difficult hiding a child with abilities, so we had to move often. If I suspected the least bit of suspicion, it was time to go. That's why we are here in Gardash now, my last boyfriend started asking too many questions, and I wasn't sure if he knew about our abilities or not. In the middle of the night, we ran away again, from Ratlin to Gardash. Our lives have been full of adventure to say the least," Ms. Haraka stated.

"You think you know, but you never really know a person," I thought to myself. Now let's see what Keir's story was all about.

"So, Keir the muscle man, picking up grown men like toys, when did you find out you were a radiant one?" I joked. Keir laughed.

"Around the age of ten my mega strength started to develop, and just last year I cultivated my ability to erase moments of people's memories and add memories. My dad always knew I would develop his abilities, he just didn't know when. Like your dad Aniyas, my father has also been training me in combat since I was a small child. He also trains others."

"Others?" questioned Ms. Haraka. We all waited for Keir's answer in suspense.

"There are hundreds of indigents that have been training in combat for many years as well," Keir explained.

"Does your mom have abilities?" I asked Keir.

"No, she does not, but she oversees a lot of the combat training and is also a skilled fighter."

"How cool," I replied.

"Aniyas, does your mother have abilities?" questioned Allura.

"No, and she doesn't even know I have these gifts. My father told me not to tell a soul, including my mother. Mother is so wrapped up in chastis and Emperor Kadar, we aren't sure if she would turn me in to the guardian patrol or not."

"Your mother would never!" Allura said.

"I'm not so sure," I thought to myself, but I just smiled.

"It seems as if you all have two abilities that you inherited from one parent," Ms. Haraka acknowledged. "Well, our secrets are out," she added.

We conversed more on the drive home. I would have no choice but to tell Adrielle what transpired tonight, and Keir would tell his parents as well. We decided to gather at Allura's dwelling place after chastis tomorrow. Ms. Haraka parked the patroller van a few rows from her home. We walked back to Ms. Haraka's dwelling place and entered her vehicle. Ms. Haraka dropped me off at my home first. I climbed back up the gutter, through my window, and straight in my bed. Usually, I didn't get into my bed with my outside clothes on and without showering, but after everything that had taken place this evening, I was exhausted. Tomorrow would be another long day of chastis, but I was looking forward to meeting up with the radiant ones.

CHAPTER ELEVEN

Chastis of Doom

Even though I was exhausted when I returned home last night, I didn't get much sleep. I tossed and turned all night, replaying everything that happened at Allura's party. Learning that Keir, Allura, and Ms. Haraka were radiant ones, was astonishing. Jumping out the bed, I put on my robe and ran downstairs to the cellar where Father was. Adrielle was in the washroom shaving.

"I have so much to tell you Father!" I said eagerly.

"Good morning to you too," he replied. In order to tell Adrielle what happened, I would have to tell the truth about attending the party. Hopefully Father wouldn't punish me.

Closing the washroom door, I whispered everything that transpired last night, in Father's ear. Adrielle was shocked, but he also seemed excited. Father had many, many questions that I had to take the time to thoroughly answer. I informed Adrielle we would all be meeting after chastis at Allura's dwelling place.

"Aniyas, are you down there?" I heard Mother call.

"Yes ma'am," I responded.

"What are you doing? Come get ready so we won't be late for chastis!" Meesa urged.

"Coming!" I yelled.

"We will finish this conversation later," said Adrielle.

While getting ready for chastis, I wondered how many more radiant ones were out there. I had a feeling I would find out soon enough.

Upon arriving to chastis, something was wrong. No one was being allowed in, and everyone was being directed to the side of the building. When we turned the corner, everyone was lined up in front of a wooden gate grouped by their rankings. To my surprise the indigents were standing in the front. I saw Keir and his family right in the center, and I began to worry.

"What is going on?" I questioned my parents.

"I have no idea," Father replied. Meesa just shrugged her shoulders.

Glancing around I saw Mara, and we made eye contact. Mara quickly looked away. I was still pondering over if she or Chase outed us to the guardian patrol. Things weren't that great between any of us right now, but I would never put Chase or Mara in danger with the guardian patrol. Well, Chase would never be in danger when it came to the guardian patrol because his privilege would always protect him. Snapping out of my thoughts, my eyes searched for Allura and her mom, but I didn't see them. So many thoughts were running through my head, and none of them were good.

Finally, the gate opened, and there stood Emperor Kadar on a wooden platform. I had never been on this side of the building, seen the wooden gate, or this platform before. Everyone was chatting, and most looked confused. Emperor Kadar raised his right hand, and there was instant silence.

"I regret to inform you all that an unlawful act has been committed against the guardian patrol," Kadar announced. The six guardian patrollers from last night walked onto the platform. Some of the patrollers had black eyes, others had bruises, and one even had a sling tied around his arm. A lump instantly formed in my throat, that I had to swallow. Adrielle looked at me out the corner of his eye with concern. What was about to take place?

"These patrollers were found walking along a dark row after curfew, by an indigent last night. The patrollers had no idea how they arrived at that row, or any remembrance of anything that happened that day," Kadar explained. "Obviously we can all see they have been violated, but again, the patrollers cannot remember what happened to them. We will find out what happened and find everyone that was involved. There will be grave consequences for the perpetrators," threatened Kadar. Kadar directed the patrollers off the platform and out into the crowd. I wasn't sure what was about to happen, but I did not have a good feeling about it.

A few seconds later I heard a man screaming, "No, no, no, please don't!" Looking back up at the platform, two large men with red mask on were dragging out the man that was screaming. The screaming man had a black cloth over his head. The men stopped in the middle of the platform, and the man with the black cloth over his head was brought to his knees. The large masked men removed the cloth from the man's head. Terror was written all over his face. I didn't know his name, but I recognized him. The man looked sorrowfully into my eyes.

"This is the indigent that found the guardian patrollers and brought them back to the patrol base," Emperor Kadar stated. "Allegedly he was helping them, but my question is, why was an indigent out after curfew driving down a dark row? Why was this indigent so far from the quarters? Being outside after curfew is already a punishable offense, but to have six beat and broken guardian patrollers in your vehicle on top of that, is very suspicious."

"I promise, I promise all I was doing was helping them. I had nothing to do with anything bad happening to the patrollers," the indigent pleaded. Emperor Kadar struck the man in his mouth, and some people in the crowd gasped. I could not believe this vile treatment was happening again, right before our eyes.

"Silence!" Kadar yelled. "Who helped you do this?"

"No one Sir, because again I tell you, I had nothing to do with anything bad happening to them! I promise!" cried the indigent, as blood streamed from his mouth.

"You had something to do with this, but of course you are going to deny it. Gardash does not and will never tolerate any violence brought upon our great guardian patrol, therefore, you are sentenced to death by hanging!" Kadar shouted. My heart dropped and I'm sure many others did as well.

The indigent was on the platform pleading, crying, and begging for his life. His wife was in the crowd crying as well, trying to reach him. The guardian patrol was holding her back. I could not believe what I was hearing and seeing. There was about to be a public lynching in Gardash. The indigent didn't get a trial, he was assumed guilty with no tangible evidence, and sentenced to death like an animal. I felt sick to my stomach. "I knew we should have killed and buried those patrollers," I thought to myself.

A rope began to drop from a high beam above the platform. The indigent's wife screams became more frantic. "Charles, Charles, please, no Charles," she cried. So, Charles was his name. Charles began to struggle, but he couldn't get away. The masked men were just too large and strong. A tall slender man, who donned a red mask, walked onto the platform and placed the rope around Charles' neck.

Most of the elites began to yell, "Hang him, hang him, hang him!" To my surprise, some of the conventionals, and a few indigents were yelling hang him as well. I was absolutely baffled and disgusted!

Turning towards Meesa, her eyes closed, and her head dropped. Landis and Landon were standing next to Mother with their eyes glued on the platform. I still could not believe this was happening. The execution of Charles was not about to go down, not on my watch. I began to move towards the platform, but Adrielle grabbed my arm and pulled me back. Looking back at Father, I snatched my arm away and then I heard a loud thump. The floor beneath Charles had dropped, his head was now the only thing visible on the platform. Charles' eyes began to roll in the back of his head as he gasped for air. His life was being choked away.

There were cheers and cries heard throughout the crowd. As Charles tried to hold on to whatever life he had left, his wife fainted. Charles' eyes began to bulge. A few seconds later, he was dead. I couldn't hold it in any longer, vomit poured from my mouth, and tears poured from my eyes. Even though there had been many murders of innocent men, women, and children by the guardian patrol for many years, this was the first unjust murder I had witnessed right in front of me. At that moment, I vowed it would also be the last.

After having a man hung in front of every man, woman, and

child in Gardash, Emperor Kadar still went on with chastis. That man had no soul at all. Kadar even spent extra time collecting the chastis tax today. "What an evil sicko!" I thought to myself. I was infuriated! Why were we all sitting here like nothing had happened? We are so weak! How could we keep allowing things like this to happen to other human beings? Tears began to well up in my eyes, but I held them back. The more I looked at Kadar, the more I hated him.

Anger and rage filled my heart. Did I personally know Charles? Not at all, but that didn't stop me from feeling deep empathy for Charles and his wife. Charles was someone's child, someone's husband, someone's friend, and his life was taken away, like he was nothing. Looking over at Meesa, she looked disturbed. Landis and Landon had their normal goofy looks on their face. I couldn't read Adrielle though; I wonder how he was feeling about all of this. Suddenly, I became infuriated with Father. Why did he stop me? Why did he let Charles die like that? Then my mind wandered to Keir and his family, they were right in the front. Why didn't they stop the execution? Where was Allura? Where was her mom? "We all could have saved him; we all could have saved him!" I screamed to myself. A tear trickled from my eye, and I quickly wiped it away. Soon enough I'll be making Emperor Kadar's wife and children shed tears, soon enough.

Chastis always seemed long, but today it felt like an eternity. Kadar ended chastis with these words from the Pathway, "Heed your masters laws, bow with fear and respect, obey them just as you would the Leading Light."

I almost vomited again after hearing those words. Kadar was a monster! As we were walking out of chastis, many of the elites, some conventionals, and a few indigents were smiling, talking, and laughing as if they hadn't just seen Charles' innocent life taken away. I was mortified!

How could people be so heartless? How could you see Charles' wife break down like that and still be okay? If I could smack all of them right now, I would! Most of the indigents were walking out of chastis somberly. They had just lost another one of their own, and they were feeling it. We had just lost another one of our own,

I should say. We were the indigents, and the indigents were us, it was time to realize that and come together!

Landis and Landon decided to visit our dwelling place after chastis, so they walked back with us. The twins were laughing and joking around just like the other heartless elites, conventionals, and indigents. I was about to unleash everything I was holding inside on Landis and Landon if they did not shut up! Father must have read my face.

"Are you okay Aniyas?" Adrielle asked.

"Am I okay? Am I okay? No, I'm not okay! I just saw Charles get executed on a public platform, like he was trash!" I screamed. This was my first time ever yelling at Father, and he was shocked.

"Don't yell at your father young lady!" Meesa chimed in.

"Instead of acknowledging my hurt and pain, hence the reason I am yelling, you just yell right back at me, to tell me to stop yelling, typical!" I screamed at Mother.

Meesa was about to respond to me, but Father interjected. "You are upset, I understand, but we must control our emotions at times like this."

"Control our emotions?" I questioned. "Why do we always have to control our emotions, while our supposedly trained authority figures can just lose all control and beat and murder innocent men, women, and children, whenever they feel like it!" I did not want to have this conversation anymore. I had to walk off, or I would explode.

"Well technically he wasn't innocent. He was outside after curfew, which is an offense!" Landon yelled. I turned around and stormed back to where Landon was standing.

"So, being out after curfew warrants death? You are so ignorant!" I screamed in Landon's face.

"All people have to do is obey the rules. If he'd obeyed the rules, he would still be alive," Landis added. My ears or brain could not fathom what I was hearing right now. Meesa and Adrielle had raised two straight Uncle Rukos! I was ashamed to be a part of this family!

"Say his name, his name was Charles! Charles was a living breathing soul that did not deserve to die, even if he was out after curfew! A curfew is more important than a human life? Why do adults have a curfew anyway? You two are ridiculous, shut up talking to me!" I yelled. I turned and ran ahead of my family before my yelling turned into swinging fists.

"Aniyas, watch your mouth and stop yelling before a guardian patroller hears you!" Mother ordered. Meesa was ridiculous! We weren't allowed to say shut up in front of our parents, but we were allowed to watch Charles be murdered, how preposterous.

Turning back around, I shouted, "Screw the guardian patrol!" Meesa's mouth dropped. Landis and Landon stopped in their tracks, and Adrielle just kept walking in silence.

While running the rest of the way home, the waterworks started flowing like a river. When I reached our dwelling place, I ran upstairs into my sleeping chamber. I crashed down on my bed and the tears just kept coming. No matter how hard I tried, I couldn't stop crying.

"Aniyas, get down here right now!" Mother ordered.

"Let me go talk to her," I heard Father say. "Honey, can I talk to you for a minute?" Adrielle asked. Even though I heard him, I remained silent, but I was listening.

"I know you are hurting right now, and I know there are things you just don't understand, but there is a time and a place for everything. This is a very sorrowful time, but you cannot allow your grief to completely take over you, or you will be stuck in that emotion. Let's go take a walk," Father suggested.

My body felt limp, I wasn't even sure I could move. All my energy was drained, from how heavy my heart felt. Adrielle came over and picked my head up off the bed. Sitting up, I wiped away my tears.

"Get yourself together, wash your face, and meet me downstairs at the front door in ten minutes," Father commanded. Ten minutes, I'll meditate for five, the universe knows I need some peace right now.

Even after meditating, I still felt horrible. Charles' face, I couldn't stop seeing Charles' face, and thoughts of Charles' frantic wife also kept entering my head. "Is she okay? Did anyone see where the guardian patrol dragged her off to? Did they kill her?

Were the thoughts running through my head. Again, tears began to well up in my big almond eyes. "What is crying going to do, Aniyas? Nothing, so be strong," Meesa's life lessons played in the back of my skull. Finally, I mustered up the strength to pull myself together and walk into the washroom.

After washing my face, I walked to the front door. Mother, Landis, and Landon were eating dinner at the kitchen table. Eating was not on my agenda for the day, my appetite was completely gone. I knew I was drowning in sorrow because I rarely passed up a meal.

"Come eat, Aniyas," Meesa said.

"I'm not hungry," I replied.

"You, not hungry?" Landon questioned.

Just as Mother was about to insist that I eat again, Father walked into the kitchen and said, "Let's go Aniyas."

"Saved by the dad," I thought to myself.

"Where are you two going?" Meesa asked.

"We are going for a walk, Aniyas needs to let off some steam," Adrielle explained. Mother didn't respond, and just continued eating.

"Aniyas, hurry up, we are going to be late," Adrielle said.

"Late for what?" I asked.

"Late for the meeting with the other radiant ones. Come on Aniyas, get your head together." I forgot about our meeting, chastis had my head all over the place. Hearing those words put a little pep in my step. First thing on the agenda, we would plan our revenge for Charles.

I looked around at all the other hooded gray robes walking down the row, wondering if they were as upset and heartbroken as I was. I was still in disbelief at how out of touch the twins were, how could they not see Charles' death was unjustifiable. Meesa on the other hand, even though she hadn't said much about it, I could tell she was bothered by the whole ordeal, but she would never speak out against Emperor Kadar. We were almost at Allura's dwelling place, and a surge of adrenaline rushed through my body, it was time to put a stop to all this madness.

We entered Allura's home. Keir and his parents were sitting at the kitchen table with Ms. Haraka. Usually, I would be happy to see Keir, but right now I felt numb. Father and I said our greetings.

"Where is Allura?" I asked.

"She's upstairs in her sleeping chamber, she's not doing so well with what she witnessed at chastis today," Ms. Haraka replied.

"Oh, so they were there," I thought to myself. Poor Allura, her heart must be broken, just like mine.

"Can you please go upstairs and bring her down, Aniyas?" Ms. Haraka asked.

"Yes ma'am." I ran upstairs to console my friend.

"Allura, it's Aniyas. Can I come in?" I asked, while simultaneously knocking on her door and opening it.

As I opened the door, Allura hopped up and wiped her eyes. I walked over and embraced her. This was the first hug I received all day, and it was much needed. Adrielle would have hugged me in the past, but we really don't hug anymore.

"How could they do Charles like that, Aniyas, how?" Allura questioned.

"It's their world and their rules and if we keep abiding by these unjust rules, they will keep killing us off. If we don't take a stand, nothing will ever change," I explained.

"Well, I'm ready for change!" Allura shouted.

"So, let's go downstairs and start plotting our revenge," I urged. We were ready for war!

Back downstairs, we all sat around the dining space table. "While you two were upstairs, we briefly talked about our abilities," said Mr. Abrafo.

"Can you two please explain your abilities to us?" Mrs. Abrafo asked.

"I don't want to talk about abilities, let's talk about how we plan to avenge Charles' murder," I snapped.

"No Aniyas, vengeance belongs to the Leading Light," Mrs. Abrafo responded. Looking over at Father, he was shaking his head in agreement. They were all brainwashed, stupid, and brainwashed!

"Did you all forget a soul for a soul? Now let's go get Emperor Kadar," I replied.

"Listen Aniyas, I know you are angry and so are we, but we are not prepared to go up against Emperor Kadar and the regime right now, we aren't organized enough yet. You yourself just found out about your abilities a little while ago, you don't even know how to fully control your gifts yet. So, before we go on the attack, we must truly be ready," Adrielle explained.

I was tired of hearing all the excuses, if we weren't talking about avenging Charles' murder, I didn't want to talk at all.

"I don't believe in all that Pathway and Leading Light stuff, but I do agree with your father on this one Aniyas. We can't go in blindly," Ms. Haraka added. The looks Father and the Abrafo's gave Ms. Haraka when she said she didn't believe in the Pathway or the Leading Light, were unlike any looks I have seen. You would have thought they saw a spirit. I looked over at Keir, he had been extremely quiet.

"This is what we are going to do this evening, we will discuss our abilities, and give each other advice on how to control and enhance those abilities. We will then set up a daily time you all can come down and train in combat with the other indigents. We will start training together tomorrow," Mr. Abrafo explained. He continued to talk but I just tuned him out. I was going to find a way to get to Emperor Kadar, even if I had to do it all by myself.

CHAPTER TWELVE

The Source Bearer

I really didn't want to go to academia. Charles continued to linger on my mind, and I was in a horrible mood. My training with the combat indigent warriors started this afternoon, so a change of mindset was needed. It was time to for me to get focused, no matter the circumstances. Suddenly, Mother popped into my head. Where would Father tell Meesa we were going every day after academia, Mother would for sure want to know. Keeping this secret from her was becoming more difficult by the day. Meesa was an intelligent woman, and I had a feeling eventually, somehow, someway, she would find out what was really going on.

Looking out the living space window, I saw Meesa and Adrielle talking in our courtyard. Was Father telling Mother my secret? The conversation looked intense. At that moment, I wished I had Allura's mega hearing. Mother threw her hands in the air and started walking towards the front door as Father followed. Hurrying away from the window, I rushed to the ice chest, grabbed a cherpinal, and sat at the kitchen table.

My parents walked into the kitchen and said good morning. I replied with grand rising and pretended like I didn't see their exchange. Meesa didn't mention anything about our abilities, so Father couldn't have told her. They were fighting about something else, and I wondered what about.

"Let's hit the road kiddo," Adrielle ordered. "Bye."

"Bye Aniyas, have a good day. I will see you after academia," Meesa responded.

"We are going to be helping at the colony garden after academia for a few weeks. Yesterday was rough on Aniyas, I think it will help her let off steam and relax her mind," Father announced.

"Oh okay, that sounds like a good idea," Mother agreed. For someone who told me I shouldn't lie, Adrielle was extremely good at it, things that make you go hmmm.

Adrielle dropped me off in a hurry today, which was odd. Father never rushed. Entering academia, I went straight into the washroom, pulled out a towel, bottle of leave-in conditioner, and homemade flaxseed gel from my satchel. Turning on the water, I took the bun out my hair and stuck my head under the running stream. After letting the water run on my hair for a couple of minutes, the shrinkage began. I then put the towel around my neck, so the water dripping from my hair wouldn't run down my uniform. I applied the leave-in conditioner to my hair and then raked the gel through my coils with my fingers. This would be the first time I've worn my natural hair out at academia. Looking in the mirror, I wasn't sure how the other novices would react to my hair, but I didn't care, it was the hair that naturally grew from my head, and I was going to wear it.

As I walked down the corridor, the stares and whispers began. Rebecca and the doublemint twins were a few steps ahead of me, this should be interesting.

"Eww, look at her hair!" Rebecca yelled, as I walked past her. A few years ago, Rebecca's comment would have upset me, because back then I hadn't accepted my hair. I have now learned to love and embrace the way the Leading Light, the universe, or whoever created me, made all of me. My hair is beautiful!

I could also say a lot about Rebecca's damaged, thin, limp, non-versatile, lifeless hair, but I wouldn't. Good hair is healthy hair, no matter the texture, and Rebecca's hair was not healthy at all. Sticking my head up even higher in the sky, I kept walking without looking back or responding. Rebecca was not worth my energy anymore. Someone grabbed my hand, I turned, and it was Chase.

"Your hair is beautiful and so are you," Chase said loudly. Rebecca looked furious. Chase's words made my heart smile.

Staring into his eyes, I smiled and said, "Thank you." We walked to my lecture hall hand and hand.

The stares lingered on as I navigated the academia corridors. When lunch time rolled around I walked into the dining hall confidently and all eyes were on me. Allura was already seated at our table.

"Okay Aniyas, I see you're rocking your natural hair out again, and I love it!"

"Thank you Allura," I blushed.

"Here comes boyfriend number two," Allura joked. Chase came and sat down right beside me. Surprisingly, Chase didn't seem upset about what happened at Allura's party, he hadn't even mentioned it. Keir didn't mention their confrontation either. Come to think of it, Father never talks about any of the problems we face at home. I was starting to assume; men just don't like talking about their issues.

Speaking of Allura's party, it slipped my mind that Chase could possibly be the culprit that called the guardian patrol on us. Should I ask him about it? "No Aniyas, you shouldn't. If Chase is the informant, he will know you had something to do with those guardian patrollers being beaten and having memory loss. Chase would surely tell," I thought to myself. This situation was complicated, was Chase a friend or a foe? I guess only time would tell, but until then I would keep a close eye on Chase.

Lunch was over and it was time for our next lecture hall. While walking out of the dining hall, I saw Mara. I looked at her, but she quickly looked down and kept walking. Was that an omission of guilt? Mara couldn't even look at me. Was she the informant? As I continued to walk down the corridor, I heard my name on the overhead speaker.

"Aniyas Nguvu, please report to Dean Master Powell's chambers," the academia secretary announced.

"What could he possibly want with me?" I asked myself.

Entering Dean Powell's chambers and seeing the look on his face let me know this wasn't about to be a pleasant meeting.

"Young lady, have you read the academia handbook before?" he questioned.

"Not in its entirety," I replied.

"Have you read the section on dress code?" he asked.

"I can't say I have."

"Please pick up the handbook right beside you and turn to page 56, section 21.3 and read it out loud," Dean Powell instructed.

I did as he asked. "All novices shall come to academia properly groomed, with a professional look," I read. Looking up at him, I now knew where this conversation was headed, and I was infuriated.

Dean Powell had an issue with my hair. How did he even know how I styled my hair today; this was my first time seeing him.

"Your hair is to be well groomed; your hair usually looks nice, whatever this new look is, it's unprofessional. It's almost the end of the day, so I won't send you home, but tomorrow wear your hair like you normally wear it," Dean Powell commanded. My blood was boiling because this entire discussion was absolutely ridiculous.

Just because my hair didn't look like his, Dean Powell viewed my hair as being ungroomed.

"What about my hair is unprofessional or ungroomed? This is my hair in its natural state, the way it naturally grows from my scalp."

"I will not go back and forth with you; you heard what I said. You are dismissed!" Dean Powell scolded.

Standing up, I took a step towards Dean Powell and replied, "You cannot tell me I can't wear my natural hair. I do not see that rule in the handbook, so I will continue to wear my hair as I please."

"Aniyas, if you come to academia with your hair like that tomorrow, you will be suspended," he cautioned. Turning my back and exiting his chambers, I didn't say another word, because tomorrow I would walk right back into this academia with my hair exactly how it is now, natural and beautiful!

The academia day was finally over, and it was time to go meet with the indigents.

"Hey dad," I said, as I hopped into the car. I was still upset about what transpired with Dean Powell, but it was time to focus on being ready for today's training.

"Your hair is different from this morning," Adrielle acknowledged.

"Yeah," I replied. Father didn't need to know about the hair controversy because I was going to handle it myself. Also, Adrielle would probably just tell me to put my hair back in a bun. Father always tries to avoid confrontation, and he's too nice at times.

We were getting closer to the quarters, and a jolt of excitement hit me.

"Almost there," Adrielle announced. Looking around, the scenery started to change. I couldn't help but feel a little sad about the conditions the indigents had to live in, everything always looked so dingy and gloomy. Come to think of it, the entire province of Gardash was kind of gloomy. I couldn't remember the last time we had a bright and sunny day. There also wasn't one tree in sight in the quarters, at least the conventionals and elites had the vibrant color of trees where we reside.

"How did the quarters get like this?" I thought to myself. Why was every other place in Gardash beautiful, except where the indigents lived? Thinking about it, I'm sure the regime had something to do with the conditions the quarters were in. Now that I'm waking up to what's really going on around me, I'm going to start getting answers to these questions, and I'm going to find solutions to fix them.

We were almost at Keir's dwelling place, the thought of him lifted my spirits and made me smile.

"What are you over there smiling so hard about?" Father asked.

"Oh nothing," I replied. Adrielle looked at me and raised his eyebrow with suspicion. I giggled. We arrived at Keir's home. Before the vehicle completely stopped, I opened my door and jumped out.

"Aniyas wait until the vehicle is fully parked before you get out!" Father cautioned. Ignoring him, I ran straight to Keir's door and started knocking.

Mrs. Abrafo answered the door.

"Welcome, I'm so glad you both could make it." Walking into the living space, I saw Keir and my face immediately lit up.

"Hello Keir."

"Hello," he replied dryly and without a smile. That was strange, Keir was always happy to see me, but I just shrugged it off.

"Follow me please," Mrs. Abrafo ordered. As we walked behind her into their small hallway, she opened a closet door. There was nothing but cleaning products and towels in the closet. I know we did not come here just to clean. "This better be a joke," I said to myself.

Mrs. Abrafo kneeled and moved the towels to the side on the bottom shelf. There was a small latch that she flicked back. After she flicked the latch, she stood up and took a step back, and so did I. To my surprise, the side of the closet began to open. Mrs. Abrafo walked into the tight dark opening, grabbed a lantern, and we all followed. If this were any other family besides the Abrafo's, I would be very leery about this, but I trusted them. I was thrilled to see what we were about to walk into.

This walk was taking longer than I imagined, we had been walking for at least fifteen minutes. Mrs. Abrafo made a right turn after walking in one straight direction the entire time. She then reached up, and my eyes followed her hand. There were at least fifty small latches on a ceiling above, that seemed to appear from nowhere. Mrs. Abrafo then clicked several different latches, almost like it was a code. Another passageway opened, but this time it was to a flight of stairs. Walking down the stairs, the space became extremely tight. Once at the bottom of the stairs, Mrs. Abrafo clicked three latches on the wall and placed her right palm beside the last latch she clicked. The wall then slid open from both sides, and we were welcomed by two armed men. We walked past the guards, to two large doors. Mrs. Abrafo put her right and left palm on the doors, and they opened. My mouth dropped in amazement; the walk was more than worth it.

"Welcome to our training facility," Mrs. Abrafo said. This place was humongous! There had to be a few hundred people in this space, filled with men, women, and children. The people were split into different groups, and they were all training in some form of combat. I looked to the left and there were two large spaces with clear windows. One space was filled with every kind of weapon you could imagine: machine guns, rifles, pistols, swords, shields, war staffs, knives, daggers, bow and arrows, grenades, battle axes, darts, javelins, machetes, and so much more. In the space next to it, there was a shooting range, where people were practicing. The space had to be soundproof, because I didn't hear one shot being fired, but I could see them shooting. I couldn't believe my eyes, but I was ready to see more.

Looking to my right, there were also two large spaces with clear windows. There was a large leisure pool in one of the spaces, and I could see small children swimming laps back and forth under the supervision of five adults. Next to that space, there was a space, and the lights were dim, people were meditating. Straight in front of me, there were large screens placed on the wall. On one screen you could see everything that was taking place in the training facility, on a second screen you could see the passageways we walked to get to the training facility. I was now looking at a third screen and you could see the Abrafo's living space, and the hallway with the closet that led us here. Focusing on the fourth screen, you could see the outside of the Abrafo's dwelling place and an overview of the quarters. On my way here I wasn't sure what to expect, but I for sure wasn't expecting all of this.

How long has this facility been here? How long had they been training here? How did they get the money to build this? There were a million questions running through my head. Did Adrielle know about this place? I remember him saying he knew the Abrafo's and some indigents trained, but did he know they were training like this? Instantly, I felt out of place. Yes, I've been training since I was small, but not to this capacity. I had never even touched a gun before, or half of these weapons. I don't even know how to swim. There was so much to take in, so much I needed to learn, and I began to feel overwhelmed.

Keir must have felt my energy shift, and my face probably gave away how I was feeling. My face always showed my true emotions.

Keir placed his hand on my shoulder and said, "Don't worry, you are a fast learner. You will catch on to everything you don't know in no time."

That was much better than the dry greeting Keir had just given me.

"Thank you, Keir," I smiled.

Turning towards Father, I asked, "Did you know about this place?"

"No, I didn't. I'm just as surprised as you look."

"I know this might be a lot for the both of you to digest right now, but I promise we will explain everything to you shortly," Mrs. Abrafo assured us. At that moment, I became speechless. All I could do was nod my head, but I was ready to hear everything Mrs. Abrafo had to say.

A few minutes later Mr. Abrafo, Allura, and her mom entered the training facility. Looking at Allura, she looked just as astonished as I felt.

"Allura!" I called out to her. She found my voice very quickly in this room full of people and jogged over to me. Ms. Haraka and Mr. Abrafo followed Allura.

"Aniyas, can you believe this place?" Allura asked, as she stood next to me.

"I'm in awe," I responded.

After exchanging pleasantries, Mr. Abrafo walked to the front of the space and up on the platform. He grabbed a sound transmitter and said, "Man, woman, and child illuminated by the sun. We are familia. We are one." Every single person in the facility stopped what they were doing and repeated after Mr. Abrafo. The people in the side spaces joined the rest of us in the large main space. "Familia, we have four new radiant ones, please give them a warm welcome," Mr. Abrafo announced.

"Wait, so all these people here already knew about the radiant ones. Are they all radiant?" I asked myself. I had so many questions and I hoped they would all get answered today.

"Can the Harakas and Nguvus please come up to the platform," Mr. Abrafo instructed. A ball of nerves instantly shot through my body; I hate being the center of attention. As we walked onto the platform the crowd began to clap.

"Man, woman, and child illuminated by the sun. We are familia. We are one," Mr. Abrafo said again. The crowd repeated after him and so did I this time, and then there was complete silence. Outside of the training facility to the conventionals and the elites Mr. Abrafo was just an indigent, but inside of these training facility walls he was like an emperor.

Mr. Abrafo introduced us and proceeded to tell the crowd everything he knew about all of us, including what abilities we possessed. I hope our secrets are safe here. "The Nguvus and Harakas will be training with us on a regular basis. Please make them feel at home," Mr. Abrafo said, as he ended his welcome speech. "You all may commence with your training," Mr. Abrafo ordered. Still in awe, I scanned the space again. Mrs. Abrafo tapped me on my shoulder and told me to follow her. Father, Allura, Ms. Haraka, Keir, and Mr. Abrafo were close by. We followed Mrs. Abrafo into a small space behind the wall the large monitors were on. There was a long wooden table and we all took a seat.

Mrs. Abrafo spoke, "I know you all must have many questions, but before we get to your questions I would like to say a few things. So please listen attentively." I tend to have problems listening but now I was all ears.

Mr. Abrafo continued, "You are the first conventionals we have ever allowed into our training facility. You are also the first conventionals we have learned are radiant ones. All the indigents here are not radiant ones, only a few are. The way you all differ from the radiant ones here, is that you all have two abilities. Besides Keir and his father, all the other radiant ones only have one gift, so that makes each of you special, and possibly one of our children could be the source bearer."

"The source bearer, what is that?" I interrupted.

"The source bearer is the child that will lead our people out of true bondage," Ms. Haraka chimed in.

"This child will have more than one ability and be a skilled and fierce fighter, according to The Book of the Radiant," added Allura. Allura knew about all of this? I felt so lost, and I didn't like it.

Why was I the only one who seemed to be in the dark? "How

do you know all of this? What is The Book of the Radiant?" I questioned.

"My grandfather taught my mother before he passed away, and my mother passed along the knowledge to me," Allura responded.

"Everyone, please let us finish explaining everything first, and then you all can say whatever you like and ask as many questions as you like," Mrs. Abrafo interjected. My mind was now racing with excitement, frustration, and so many questions. I would do my best to sit back and listen, but honestly, I wasn't sure if I could.

"Let me start from the beginning," Mr. Abrafo picked up where Mrs. Abrafo left off. "Everything the regime and Emperor Kadar has told you is a lie. We pretend to believe in the Pathway, only to survive and to blend in, you never truly know who you can trust. Our people were stripped of all their true beliefs when they were brought here in bondage from Mathonia. We all originate from Mathonia. Mathonia isn't evil, they only tell us those lies to keep us away from our homeland so we won't reconnect to our roots. Reconnecting with our true roots would be extremely powerful for us as a people. That's also why the regime has a travel ban to Mathonia. Mathonia wasn't its original name though, its true name is Kemtopia. The Book of the Radiant has all this information in it, but they took all the books, burned them, and replaced them with the Pathway, well at least they thought they burned them all." This was getting deep and the Abrafo's had my undivided attention.

Mr. Abrafo continued, "A few of our antecedents worked hard to keep The Book of the Radiant alive and passed it down throughout the generations. We aren't sure how many more of these books are out there, but our family is the keeper of this one, and we shall continue to guard it with our lives. Many of the indigents, conventionals, and elites have never heard of this book. There have been whispers about radiant ones before but not about this book. I'm sure all the elites in power know about The Book of the Radiant, though." I turned my head to look at my father. Adrielle had never mentioned this book to me. He couldn't have possibly known about any of this, or did he?

Keir took over, "In The Book of the Radiant, they speak of the source bearer and how evil beings will seek to destroy this child and the child's tribe. They don't give specifics on who the child will be, but it does tell us that this child will possess many gifts and abilities. As my mom said, one of us could be the source bearer because we possess more abilities than the other radiant ones. Being the source bearer holds great responsibility, but I'm sure any one of us can manage it. There could still be others like us out there, so we will send out a coded message that only radiant ones will be able to understand. They will have seven days to respond. After that week, we will train for a month before we attempt The Extraordinary Assessment of Valor. During this assessment, our skills, abilities, and bravery will be tested. Only one radiant one will shine bright, and that will be the source bearer." There was so much information to grasp, but I made up my mind at that moment, I would be ready for The Extraordinary Assessment of Valor.

I asked a million questions after Keir was done speaking. The Abrafo's were patient with answering them all. The Abrafo's then took us on a complete tour of the facility and personally introduced us to a few of the radiant ones. Everyone was so nice; it was good to know that there were others out there just like me.

"Today was just a day to welcome you all to the familia, and if you didn't know, familia means family in Swahili," Mr. Abrafo explained. "We will see you all tomorrow at the same time. Keir will escort you out," Mr. Abrafo added. We said our goodbyes and Keir showed us back to their dwelling place. Outside, Allura and I chatted for a few seconds, while Father spoke with Ms. Haraka. The guardian patrol was always in the quarters harassing people, so we made our conversations quick and left.

On the ride home I asked Adrielle why he didn't tell me about The Book of the Radiant or the source bearer. Father went on to explain that he himself didn't know about a lot of that information. Adrielle was raised by parents that were heavy into the Pathway and the Leading Light, and he was taught any other affiliations were evil. Father never told his parents about his abilities because he didn't know how they would react. Adrielle had to figure out plenty of things on his own. The rest of the ride home was in silence, many thoughts were racing through my head. I couldn't believe that the training facility had been there for five years, five whole years! Keir could really keep a secret! I also wondered who the elite was that paid for the facility to be built. The Abrafo's wouldn't reveal his name, but I sure hope this elite was truly trustworthy. I hoped it wasn't a trap.

"We are home," Adrielle said, awakening me from my thoughts. My life had turned into a complete whirlwind, and I had a feeling it was only going to get crazier.

CHAPTER THIRTEEN

The Rebellion

It was the next day, and I was ready for academia. I was feeling rejuvenated! My hair was in full fro mode, and I was ready to go. Looking in the mirror, I said aloud, "I am beautiful! I am smart! I am strong! I am confident! I am brave! I am enough!" I then strutted down the stairs into the living space where Meesa was.

"Aniyas, you cannot go to academia with your hair like that." Ignoring Mother, I walked straight out the door.

"Get back in here, right now!" she shouted. Disobeying Meesa, I continued walking.

"Where are you going?" Adrielle yelled after me.

"I'll be walking to academia today, Father!" I yelled back. My parents didn't say another word, they just let me be. As I walked to academia, I prepared myself for whatever was about to go down.

Prancing into the academia doors, I saw Dean Powell at the end of the corridor. Pretending I didn't see him, I walked straight to my first lecture hall. I'm sure he saw me because my hair was kind of hard to miss.

"Ms. Nguvu! Ms. Nguvu!" I heard Dean Powell call. Overlooking him, I continued my prance into lecture hall and took my seat.

Shortly after I was seated, Dean Powell was standing in the doorway.

"Ms. Nguvu, report to my chambers now!" he commanded. I

ignored him.

"Ms. Nguvu, did you hear me? Report to my chambers now!" Dean Powell repeated.

"Why?" I questioned.

All the novices and the academia master turned and looked at me in shock, because no one ever questioned Master Dean Powell.

"Ms. Nguvu, I am going to ask you one last time to report to my chambers!" Dean Powell yelled angrily. Looking straight forward, I ignored him again. Out of the corner of my eye, I saw Dean Powell charging towards me, but I didn't flinch. My heart was racing because I knew this was about to be a trainwreck.

Dean Powell grabbed me by the collar, pulled me from my desk, and down to the floor while simultaneously shouting, "You indigent!"

That was odd, because technically I was a conventional. Dean Powell was literally dragging me out of the lecture hall. My blood began to heat up with anger. I grabbed Dean Powell's hand to release his tight grip from my collar.

"Stop fighting me!" he yelled. Fighting him? I was just trying to release myself from this choke grip he had on me. It was taking all the self-control I had within not to fight Dean Powell.

"You are in control. You are in control," I repeated to myself, because if I lost control, I would hurt Dean Powell and my secret would be revealed.

Dean Powell dragged me into his chamber and released me violently. I hit the floor hard.

"Who do you think you are to question me?" he yelled.

"Oh wow, he has really lost his mind!" I thought to myself. Jumping up from the floor, I yelled, "Don't you ever put your hands on me again!"

This situation reminded me of the time a conventional assistant dean master kicked me in my behind because I was not walking to my lecture hall fast enough at my old academia. Meesa went to the academia and had her fired. That was one other time Mother had my back, and that meant everything to me.

Mrs. Forte must have heard the commotion because she came rushing into Dean Powell's chambers.

"Is everything okay in here?" she questioned.

"No, it's not! He dragged me and threw me on the floor all because he doesn't like my hair!" I shouted.

"Is this true?" Mrs. Forte asked Dean Powell.

"Her hair violates our dress code!" screamed Dean Powell.

"How so?" questioned Mrs. Forte.

Dean Powell went on to explain to Mrs. Forte, everything he had said to me the first time he confronted me about my hair. He even pulled out the handbook.

Mrs. Forte said, "Can you please excuse us for a minute, Aniyas."

I stepped outside of Dean Powell's chambers and shut the door. Here is another time I wish I had Allura's mega hearing ability.

Ten minutes later, Mrs. Forte walked out of Dean Powell's chambers smiling at me.

"Go back to lecture hall, Aniyas," said Mrs. Forte. Confusion was written all over my face. Moments ago, Dean Powell was livid about my hair and now I could just go back to lecture hall.

"But," I started to speak but Mrs. Forte cut me off.

"Don't question anything Aniyas. It's been handled, so just let it go," warned Mrs. Forte.

"Okay," I replied.

"I love your hair by the way," said Mrs. Forte, as she walked into her chambers.

Walking back to lecture hall, I couldn't help but think how weird that entire situation just was. I couldn't believe Dean Powell just dropped the issue at hand like that, he never lets anything go. It was Dean Powell's way or the highway! I wondered what Mrs. Forte said to him, but that I will never know.

I continued the rest of the academia day with this strange feeling in the pit of my stomach. Even though Dean Powell had miraculously dropped everything, and Mrs. Forte advised me to let it go, I still felt uneasy about the way I was man-handled. I was treated like an animal all because of my natural hair, and it was not acceptable at all! During lunch I told Allura everything that transpired.

"Oh, hell no Aniyas, you do not let that go! Tell your parents so they can come and handle Dean Powell!" Allura stressed. That's exactly what I was going to do. As soon as I returned home, I would inform my parents, and Dean Powell was going down!

Academia was over and I rushed outside to tell Adrielle how Dean Powell violated me. To my surprise, Father wasn't here yet. Adrielle had never been late picking me up. Twenty minutes went by, and I started to worry. Not only had Father never been late coming to get me, but he had also never forgot to get me from academia. While pacing back and forth, it hit me. I stormed out of our dwelling place this a.m., and said I was walking to academia. Therefore, Adrielle probably assumed I would be walking back home. "Welp, I guess I better get going," I thought to myself.

Arriving home, I barged through our dwelling place door. Mother and Father were sitting at the kitchen table talking. Rudely, I interrupted and went on a rant about what happened with Dean Powell today.

"Well, Aniyas you shouldn't have worn your hair like that to academia in the first place," scolded Meesa. Hold up, wait a minute, I know that was just not Mother's response! This can't be the same woman who got the conventional dean fired for kicking me in my behind! What was going on here?

"Are you serious?" I yelled. "Dad!" I shouted, as I threw my hands in the air.

"Aniyas, you know the rules honey," replied Adrielle.

"What? You two must be kidding me! There is no rule saying I can't wear my natural hair!" I shouted.

"Stop screaming at us right now!" Mother screamed.

I continued yelling, "This large male, man-handled me and called me an indigent as an insult, just because I was wearing my hair the way it naturally grows out of my head, and y'all are okay with this? Unbelievable!" Parents are supposed to protect their children, but my parents didn't even care about what I had just experienced. After rolling my eyes at Meesa and Adrielle, I marched upstairs into my sleeping chamber and slammed the door.

There was a knock on my door and then Adrielle walked in.

"Aniyas, you have to get ready to leave for training shortly," said Father.

"I'm not going," I responded.

"You must go; The Extraordinary Assessment of Valor will be here before you know it. You must be prepared!"

Without looking Adrielle's way, I repeated, "I'm not going."

"You will!" Father shouted! I was shocked because Adrielle had never raised his voice at me before.

"I won't!" I shouted back.

"Fine," said Adrielle as he exited my sleeping chamber. Tears started to form in my eyes, but I held them back.

"It's fine! I don't need them! I don't need anybody! I will handle this myself!" I shouted.

"Breathe Aniyas, regain control," said a voice in my head. Wait, did I just hear a voice talking in my head or was I just talking to myself? I was utterly confused. I began to breath and regained control of my emotions and thoughts, this would be a great time to meditate.

As I cleared my mind, I saw myself standing at the top of a hill. There were people standing below me, but I couldn't make out their faces. I was giving a speech, but I couldn't hear the words. As I raised my hands towards the sky, a force of wind struck me from behind, the clouds parted, and the sun became visible. The rays from the sun beamed down on our bodies and then everything went black. I waited to see if any other images would appear, but everything remained black, so I released my mind from its meditative state.

Looking around my sleeping chamber, I wondered what the vision meant. The vision had nothing to do with the situation at hand, nor did it offer any solutions. It was fine though; I was more than capable of producing a solution to this Dean Powell problem. Light bulb! I went downstairs to call Allura. After speaking with Allura, she was down for my plan of action. I knew I would be able to count on her. Tomorrow would be the most interesting day Edgerton had ever seen.

I arose early in the a.m. to get ready for academia. Careful not to wake my parents, I gathered everything I would need for the day. I stretched my hair last night to make sure my fro was as big as it had ever been. Tiptoeing through our dwelling place, I walked out the front door backwards and shut it quietly.

"Ah!" I yelled. "Allura! What in the world? You scared me!" I said, as I began to laugh. Allura was standing right behind me as I turned around from shutting the door.

"I'm sorry," giggled Allura.

"Please, please, please don't let my mother and father wake up," I beseeched. Allura's mom was waiting in the car. We hoped in, and Ms. Haraka drove off.

"I am so sorry about what happened to you," stressed Ms. Haraka.

"Thank you," I replied. At least someone cared.

We arrived at Allura's dwelling place and went straight to work.

"Those signs look good girls!" said Ms. Haraka.

"I hope we have enough," Allura replied.

"We have to hurry, so we can arrive at Edgerton before anyone else does," I said eagerly.

"All the girls confirmed they are coming, right?" I questioned Allura.

"Yes, they said they will be there at the scheduled time."

"Are you girls hungry?" asked Ms. Haraka.

"I'm too anxious to eat."

"I don't want anything either," added Allura.

"This is the last poster, and I am done," I stated.

"Okay, I will be right back," replied Allura. Allura walked back into the kitchen about five minutes later, with her hair combed into a large afro.

"You look beautiful!" I said.

"Thank you, if I'm going to represent, I have to represent the right way!" blushed Allura.

"Are you girls ready to go?" asked Ms. Haraka.

"Ready!" we said in unison. It was time to take a stand!

When we arrived at Edgerton, no one was there yet. Allura confirmed at least fifty novices said they would be here, but I didn't see one soul. Everyone was just probably running behind.

"Be patient Aniyas," I said to myself. Fifteen minutes passed by, and a car pulled up. Christine, Amanda, and Alexis exited the car.

I rolled down the window and shouted, "Hey guys, we are over here!"

They walked over and entered the vehicle. Handing them their signs, I asked, "Are y'all ready?"

"We are ready!" they shouted.

"Thank y'all so much for coming! You just don't know how much this means to me!" I expressed.

"No problem at all. It was ridiculous the way Master Dean Powell handled you. He can't get away with this!" said Amanda.

"You're right. He can't get away with this!" I repeated.

It was almost time to take our places, and we were still the only ones here. Out of fifty people who promised to stand with us, only three showed. I felt frustrated and a little defeated. How can we make real change if we don't show up for each other when one of us is wronged. We must stick together! No matter how I truly felt inside, I still had to fight for what was right!

"Well girls, it looks like it's just us," I sighed.

"That's a shame," muttered Alexis. Ms. Haraka must have sensed our morale was down.

"It only takes one, to take a stand. It's five of you here and that is enough to have your voices heard, and I will also join you. So, hold your head's up girls and let's go!" Ms. Haraka commanded. It absolutely meant the world to me that Ms. Haraka was going to be out there with us, she most definitely lifted my spirits back up.

Dean Powell and the academia masters would be arriving any minute now. We stood in front of Edgerton's front door, blocking the entrance, and holding our signs high! My sign read, "MY NATURAL HAIR IS NOT A CRIME!" Ms. Haraka was standing to the left of me, and her sign read, "MEN SHOULD NEVER PUT THEIR HANDS ON GIRLS or WOMEN!" Allura was right by my right side and her sign said, "MY HAIR IS BEAUTIFUL!" Mrs. Forte was the first one to arrive.

"Wow Aniyas, this is incredible! I was handling things from my end, but I see nothing wrong with protesting for your rights," said Mrs. Forte.

"Thank you for the support!" I responded.

"Now excuse me," Mrs. Forte said. "

I'm sorry but I can't let you pass," I replied.

Mrs. Forte looked at me for a second, she then turned around and walked away saying, "I'll just use the side entrance." There were two side doors and a back door at Edgerton. If everyone had showed up, we would have more than enough people to block all the entrances. There were only six of us and we had to stand together as one unit. We could not split up. The other doors of Edgerton would remain unguarded.

A few minutes later, Dean Powell entered Edgerton's driveway. My heart began to race! As he approached us, we all stood a little taller.

"Ms. Nguvu, what is all of this?" he questioned.

"We are standing up for our rights!" I yelled.

"This was already handled, young lady," Dean Powell replied, while looking at Ms. Haraka.

"It was not handled! Your actions were unwarranted and extremely inappropriate!" I stressed.

"You had no reason to put your hands on her and that will be the first and last time you will ever touch Aniyas or any other girl! If I ever hear of any such thing happening again, there is going to be major consequences!" Ms. Haraka added.

Stepping in front of Ms. Haraka's face, Dean Powell asked, "Are you threatening me?"

Ms. Haraka took a step closer to Dean Powell, looked him straight in the eyes and said, "It's not a threat, it's a guarantee!" Things were getting heated, and I was ready for the fire.

Allura went and stood between Dean Powell and her mom. "Back up!" she cautioned.

"I got this, Allura," Ms. Haraka said, as she moved Allura out of the way.

"You all better listen and listen well! Disperse from this area right now or there will be consequences!" warned Dean Powell. We didn't flinch!

"Christine you will be graduating this year. You have scholarships to think about. Do you really want this on your record?" he questioned.

Christine looked at all of us with regret in her eyes and said, "You guys, I can't lose my scholarships. My family can't afford the institute fees on their own." Christine dropped her sign and ran towards the side entrance of the academia. One down, who else would fold.

"I will give you all twenty minutes to leave," warned Dean Powel, as he turned and walked away.

"Hell no we won't go!" Amanda shouted. I looked at Amanda and giggled a little bit, not because the situation was funny, she just caught me off guard with that one. In forty minutes, the academia day would start. Dean Powell wanted us gone before the other novices arrived.

"Our voices will be heard!" I yelled.

"I'm so proud of all of you!" announced Ms. Haraka. Dean Powell wanted us to leave, but we weren't going anywhere!

Twenty minutes later, Mrs. Forte and Dean Powell were at the front entrance together.

"Can you ladies please come in so we can all talk?" urged Mrs. Forte.

"First and foremost, I am the only lady out here, these girls are still children, need I remind you. Secondly, unless Dean Powell is ready to apologize to Aniyas and some form of disciplinary action is going to be taken against him, there is nothing to talk about," said Ms. Haraka.

Dean Powell laughed and went back inside.

"Aniyas, please, please come in and talk to me," Mrs. Forte urged again.

"No!" I stated firmly. Mrs. Forte sighed, as she also went back into the building. No one was going to stop me from standing my ground!

Novices were starting to arrive. We tried to get them to join us, but they wouldn't listen. Mara walked straight passed us with her head down. Even the novices that originally agreed to protest wouldn't join us. I was extremely disappointed, but I would continue to stand strong. Looking over to my left, I saw Chase approaching me.

"What's going on Aniyas?" he asked. I explained to Chase what we were doing and why. Without a second thought, Chase picked up the sign Christine dropped and stood with us. Tears started to form in my eyes, but I held them back. It touched my heart to see Chase supporting us.

As the time went on, a few more novices joined us. Dean Powell appeared at the front entrance again.

"You have five minutes to leave the premises," he warned and walked away.

We all looked at each other but none of us budged. We continued to chant, "My hair my right, we will stand up and fight! My hair my right, we will stand up and fight!" I looked over at Chase as he repeated the words with so much passion. There is no way Chase could be the informant, there's just no way.

Five minutes later we heard sirens. Dean Powell had called the guardian patrol. Mrs. Forte rushed out the front entrance.

"Please, all of you come in now!" begged Mrs. Forte. We all looked at each other again and stood firm. We were not leaving.

"Ms. Haraka, if you have any sense, you will make these children get in here right now!" urged Mrs. Forte. Ms. Haraka ignored her. As the sirens grew louder and louder a rush of adrenaline surged through my body.

"Okay the guardian patrol will be here any minute now. We can't bend or break!" I shouted.

"Yeah, I can't do this, I don't play with the guardian patrol!" one of the novices said, as he ran into academia. "And then there were nine," said Allura.

The guardian patrol hopped out of their vehicles and approached us. "I am Guardian Patroller Rogers. You all have been asked to leave numerous times. Leave now or you will be detained!" shouted Rogers. I recognized his voice; he was the rude patroller I heard talking when the guardian patrol showed up at Allura's party. It was odd though because Patroller Rogers was not there during the fight, I would have to get to the bottom of that later. Dean Powell walked out of the building and stood next to Guardian Patroller Rogers.

"You can't make us leave! We have the right to protest!" yelled Amanda.

"You do not have the right to protest on private property if the owner does not want you to, and Master Dean Powell wants y'all to leave now," stated Rogers. Okay, Patroller Rogers was taking it there, well I was ready to go there!

"Last time I checked, Dean Powell was not the owner of Edgerton, he's a worker," I rebutted.

"My name is Master Dean Powell to you, indigent!" Dean Powell shouted, as he turned red. Everyone turned to look at him. This was the second time Dean Powell had called me an indigent, when I was a conventional

"There are no indigents here," Mrs. Forte responded. Dean Powell did not reply.

Chase chimed in, "Technically I am the owner of Edgerton because my family owns it. So, I say we can stay."

"It doesn't work like that young man, and you know it," replied Guardian Patroller Rogers.

"We aren't going anywhere!" I reiterated.

"This is your last warning, disperse now!" yelled Rogers.

"No!" I yelled back. Guardian Patroller Rogers then grabbed my arm. This was about to go from bad to worse.

"Get off of me!" I shouted, while simultaneously snatching my arm away.

"There is no need to touch her!" shouted Mrs. Forte. Rogers grabbed me again, and I pulled away.

"Stop resisting!" warned Rogers. The next thing I know, I was on the ground with my face smashed against the pavement. Rogers had slammed me to the ground and pinned me down.

"Get off me! Get off me!" I squirmed.

Patroller Rogers was unusually strong. Looking around me, there was nothing but commotion. Allura and Ms. Haraka were trying to pull Rogers off me, but two other guardian patrollers slammed them down to the ground as well. Mrs. Forte was shouting for everyone to calm down. Dean Powell was standing there with his arms crossed, with a look of satisfaction plastered on his face. Amanda and Alexis had also been slammed on the pavement. The other novices that were there with us ran. Chase was trying to get to me, but two patrollers were holding him back. The patrollers knew not to slam Chase Edgerton to the ground. My blood began to boil. I couldn't take this anymore, it was time to show the guardian patrol and Dean Powell what I was really made of.

"Aniyas, no!" yelled Ms. Haraka. I hadn't even made a move yet, but I guess she could sense I was on the verge of exploding. "You are in control!" she shouted. How did she know those were the words I spoke to myself? "This is not the time; this is not the place, not yet!" shouted Ms. Haraka. She was right, this was not the time or place to handle this situation like I really wanted to. I stopped moving and became very still.

"That's more like it!" snarled Rogers. The patrollers lifted us all off the ground.

"Wait until my father hears about this. You all are finished!" yelled Chase.

"We will see about that," replied Rogers.

"Chase, go to lecture hall!" commanded Dean Powell. "The rest of you are going down to the patrol base," said Rogers.

"They are minors. You just can't take them down there without informing their parents!" challenged Ms. Haraka.

"She's right," added Mrs. Forte.

"I bet I can," smirked Patroller Rogers. They walked us over to the patroller vehicles and placed us all into separate cars.

CHAPTER FOURTEEN

The Lost One

I was in the back of a patroller vehicle, handcuffed like a common criminal on my way to the patrol base. All I wanted was respect. All I wanted was the freedom to be my natural self. All I wanted was to be heard. Is that too much to ask? Why can't they just let us be! Here come the tears again, but I was not going to give these patrollers the satisfaction. They love to see us hurting. They love to see us scared. They love to see us in pain. They love to make us seem like the aggressors, after they have provoked a situation. They love to see us angry, well you know what, I wasn't going to give them any of that, not now, not anymore.

We arrived at the patrol base, and they placed me in a small holding space. Twenty minutes later, Guardian Patroller Rogers walked in. He asked me a question, but I did not answer.

"Call my parents please. I will not answer any questions until my parents arrive," I said.

Rogers asked me another question, and I ignored him.

"Answer me girl!" he ordered.

"I will not answer any questions until my parents arrive," I re-iterated. Rogers slammed his fist down on the table, and a piece of wood flew off from the impact. Either this table is weak, or again, Rogers is unusually strong.

"You think you're so smart huh, just because you go to Edgerton. You are not smarter than me!" Rogers ranted. I was lost and confused by his comments. Who said I was smarter than him? Where was all this coming from? Rogers continued with his rant,

"You indigents need to learn your place!"

"I'm a conventional just like you," I replied.

"Don't interrupt me girl!" scolded Rogers. Even though I had recently found out that technically I am an indigent, it was odd that Dean Powell, and now Patroller Rogers had called me an indigent. Rogers was still talking, but I tuned him out.

Mrs. Forte walked into the room. What was she doing here?

"Let's go Aniyas!" ordered Mrs. Forte.

"Ma'am you can't take her anywhere!" interjected Patroller Rogers. Mrs. Forte handed Rogers a piece of paper. Patroller Rogers looked up at her, glanced at me, and handed Mrs. Forte the paper back.

"Unhandcuff her now!" commanded Mrs. Forte. Rogers followed her orders.

"Let's go Aniyas," said Mrs. Forte, as she walked out the door. I followed while smirking at Rogers. I was so grateful for Mrs. Forte; she had proven that she would always have my back.

"Thank you so much! How did you get me out of there without my parents? What was on that paper?" I questioned.

"We will talk about it later, but not here," said Mrs. Forte. We were still walking out of the patrol base, so she should be leery of speaking behind these walls.

"Where are the others?" I asked with concerned.

"I'm not sure but I'll find out later."

"Later! I need to know if they are okay, now!" I complained.

"Listen Aniyas, I need you to calm down and trust me," advised Mrs. Forte.

"Where are we going?" I asked.

"I am taking you home. I have a lot to discuss with your parents," said Mrs. Forte. I hopped in the passenger seat and did not utter another word.

We arrived at my dwelling place. I entered the code on our keypad to unlock the door.

"Mom, dad!" I shouted. My mother came walking down the stairs.

"You were gone before we woke up this morning, so I just figured you walked to academia early, but what are you doing home in the middle of an academia day?" questioned Meesa. Mother reached the bottom of the stairs, and a puzzled look spread across her face. "Who do we have here?" asked Meesa, as Father also entered the living space.

"Hello, how are you? I am Mrs. Forte, the novice advisor at Edgerton. Nice to meet you both," said Mrs. Forte.

"Nice to meet you too, but why are you here with Aniyas?" questioned Meesa.

"Can we all please be seated?" asked Mrs. Forte. Mother looked at me with worry in her eyes.

"Yes, let's go to the kitchen table," answered Father. Looking at Mrs. Forte's expression, I was starting to get a little concerned myself. What in the world was she about to say!

"As you both may know, there was an incident between Dean Powell and Aniyas the other day," said Mrs. Forte.

"Yes, we are aware," replied Meesa.

"Well, that situation escalated this morning," revealed Mrs. Forte. Mrs. Forte went on to tell my parents everything that had transpired from the protest, to being taken to the patrol base, to the detainment, she told it all. Mother was baffled.

"Aniyas, you went and got yourself arrested!" yelled Meesa. Mrs. Forte had just told them everything that went on, including me being slammed to the ground by Patroller Rogers, and this was Mother's response. Why am I even surprised? I must stop expecting what I would never get from Meesa.

Adrielle just sat there without saying a word, which didn't surprise me.

"You are so lost Aniyas! Why do you love to cause confusion and chaos?" questioned Meesa. I didn't respond. "Oh, so now you want to be silent," said Mother.

"Unfortunately, Aniyas has been suspended for ten days and Dean Powel has recommended expulsion to the academia board," informed Mrs. Forte.

"Expulsion!" Meesa screeched. Mother went on to say, "You go to the best academia in Gardash. Do you know how hard it was to get you into Edgerton? Oh, you know but you just don't care. You are ruining your future young lady. Where did I go wrong with you? You are truly a lost soul!" Again, silence from Father. I was the black sheep of the family, the lost one, and I was going to wear that title with pride.

I was hurting inside, but I would not allow myself to show it. Meesa's words and lack of support cut deep, and Adrielle's silence cut even deeper. I'm not sure if Mrs. Forte could sense my pain, but she looked over at me with concern in her eyes and asked, "Are you okay Aniyas?"

"I'm fine," I lied.

"I'm going to do everything I can to try and stop the expulsion, but it may be difficult. Dean Powell's chief complaint is that Aniyas incited a riot. He is also moving forward with the guardian patrol to press charges," revealed Mrs. Forte.

"That is a lie! A protest is not a riot! Press charges, against me? He put his hands on me and Patroller Rogers put his hands on me!" I shouted. I could not believe this!

Mother responded by saying, "You know better, do not say the word lie or liar in my presence Aniyas, and look what you've done, your future is ruined! Our family name is ruined!"

"Can I please have a word with you two in private?" asked Mrs. Forte, as she looked at my parents.

"Aniyas, go to your sleeping chamber and close the door!" ordered Meesa. As I sat in my sleeping chamber, I tried to hear what they were saying, but I couldn't hear a thing. Allura is never present when I need her. Speaking of Allura and the others, I needed to check on them ASAP!

Fifteen minutes later, Mrs. Forte was gone. She didn't even say goodbye. Mother opened my door with a black leather belt in hand, and yelled, "Lie on the bed!" Mother whipped me on my butt and legs until she was exhausted. She had to strike me at least one hundred times. I used to cry hysterically during my beatings, but now I don't even shed a tear.

"You are on punishment young lady! Do not come out of this sleeping chamber until I tell you to!"

"You beat me and now I'm on punishment! On punishment for

what? I'm on punishment for standing up for myself and all the other girls that look like me!" I yelled.

"Say one more thing to me if you want to," Mother warned. Meesa rolled her eyes at me and began to exit my sleeping chamber.

"Wait, wait, I need to check on my friends," I pleaded.

"Punishment means no communication device!" replied Mother.

"I need to check on them!" I demanded.

"Let her check on her friends dear," said Adrielle, as he entered my sleeping chamber. I rolled my eyes. Where was he when I was getting lashed?

"Here you go, always undermining my authority," whined Meesa. Mother walked out of my sleeping chamber into hers and slammed the door.

"Go check on your friends honey," said Father. He didn't have to tell me twice; I flew down the stairs.

"Come on Allura, pick up," I thought to myself, as Allura's communication device went to the sixth ring. I hung up and called again, still no answer. I was beginning to worry. "Let me try one last time," I said to myself. Ring, ring, ring, ring, ring, ring, no one was answering. Come on, please answer! Frustrated, I slammed down the device.

While I was walking back upstairs, the communication device rang. I almost fell down the stairs trying to answer it.

"Hello!"

"Aniyas, thank goodness you are home," Allura said from the other end.

"Omg Allura, I was so worried about you and everyone else. Where is your mom and the others?" I asked.

"Everyone is home now. Chase came to the patrol base with his father, and Mr. Edgerton got us all released." Look at Chase coming through, there is no way he's the informant. He protested with us, was willing to get detained, and he had his father get everyone released from the patrol base. Chase Edgerton was most definitely solid!

"How did you get out? You were already gone when Mr. Edgerton inquired about you," questioned Allura.

"Mrs. Forte," I answered.

"Oh wow, I wonder how she pulled those strings," said Allura.

"I have no idea, but I am elated to be out of that place. Mrs. Forte has been immensely helpful, and I'm so grateful for her," I responded.

"That's great to hear, Aniyas. We are all meeting up at my dwelling place at nine p.m. Be there!" ordered Allura.

"I'm on punishment," I sighed.

"On punishment for what? You know what, I almost forgot who your mother was for a second, don't even answer that. I'm sure you will find a way to get to us, you always do. See you soon!" said Allura.

"See you soon," I replied, as I hung up the communication device.

As I watched the people pass by from my sleeping chamber window, an orb appeared in my hand. Looking into the orb I saw five guardian patrollers at my front door, and Patroller Rogers was leading them. The orb disappeared. I wondered how soon before this orb vision would occur. This would be a good time to meditate, but all I could do was pace back and forth. It had only been two hours since I had been shut up in my sleeping chamber, but it felt like an eternity. I felt like a caged animal. How long would Meesa keep me locked up here? I Imagine for the rest of my life!

A tap on my window snapped me out of my thoughts. It was Keir! Opening the window I whispered, "Omg I am so happy to see you."

Keir climbed through the window, and I jumped into his arms! I definitely needed this embrace. Keir tried to pull away, but I held on to him even tighter. I finally released him from my hold and went and locked my door.

"I heard what happened and rushed right over," explained Keir.

"What did you hear?" I asked. Keir went on to tell me a story that was full of lies. Someone told him I assaulted Patroller Rogers, which was so not true. I explained to Keir what really happened and asked him to go and spread the truth. "I'm on it!" assured Keir.

"Okay, you have to go now before Meesa tries to pop in here," I warned. We embraced one more time and Keir left.

I must have dozed off! Jumping out of my bed, I looked at the clock, and it was already eight fifty-five. Without a second thought, I jumped out of my window and landed directly on my feet. I ran all the way to Allura's dwelling place. Before I rang her buzzard, I checked my pockets to see if I still had a mint from earlier, because I knew my breath was not fresh. Yes! I had one. Allura opened the door and said, "I see you made it." We squeezed one another tightly.

Chase, Amanda, and Alexis were already there, they all stood up and embraced me.

"Is everyone alright?" I asked. I'm good. I'm okay. We are fine, were the different answers I heard.

"Dean Powell and Patroller Rogers came to all our homes this evening and told us we were suspended, going to be expelled, and would probably be sent to The House of Corrections," explained Alexis.

"Well, everyone except Chase of course," added Amanda.

"I spoke with my dad. He said he is going to get you all the best attorney money can buy," promised Chase. I can't believe my hair had caused this much commotion; it was all just too much.

"I wonder if word about this situation has reached Emperor Kadar?" questioned Amanda.

"I'm so scared y'all! If Emperor Kadar finds out, we are dead!" cried Alexis.

"Stop crying and be strong! This is not the time for tears!" I snapped. Alexis wiped the tears from her face. The others looked at me with shock on their faces.

"No one is going to die! I will not let that happen!" said Ms. Haraka, as she walked into the kitchen. "Calm down Alexis. Everything is going to be fine," assured Ms. Haraka. Ms. Haraka was correct, none of us were going to die, especially on my watch.

We chatted for an hour or so, and then Chase, Alexis, and Amanda went home.

"Okay girls, I spoke with Mrs. Abrafo. We will all be going to train at the facility in the a.m. now, since you both are suspended from academia," said Ms. Haraka.

"What if someone follows us to the quarters?" I asked.

"I don't think anyone will follow us, because I don't think they suspect our abilities, but we must double check our surroundings at all times," stressed Ms. Haraka.

"Did you all hear anything at the patrol base?" I asked.

"No, we didn't, our mega hearing is selective. We can't choose what conversations we want to hear," replied Allura.

"Well, that sucks," I thought to myself. "I need to get back to my dwelling place before my parents realize I'm not at home," I sighed.

"Be careful and we will see you in the a.m.," said Allura. We all embraced and back to my dwelling place I went.

Standing outside, looking up at my window, I decided to try something. Pushing off my heels, I jumped with all my might. "Uhm," I grunted, while grabbing on to my window seal. I had jumped two stories high! Wow! Was that another ability? I wasn't sure. I peeked around my sleeping chamber, before I opened my window. The coast was clear. I climbed in quietly. My door was still standing, so I know Mother or Father had not tried to enter my sleeping chamber. Today was an exceedingly long and extremely stressful day. I prepared for bed by taking a shower, and boy did that shower feel good! This would be a wonderful time to meditate.

Locking my sleeping chamber door behind me, I sat on the floor, closed my eyes, and began to slow my breath. Images began to appear. Patroller Rogers was in Dean Powell's chambers at the academia. Mrs. Forte walked in. They all appeared to be arguing. I could still only see images; I could not hear what they were saying. A few seconds later Mr. Edgerton walked in and handed Dean Powell a piece of paper. Dean Powell smiled. Mrs. Forte shook her head and exited Dean Powell's chamber.

The images began to fade away. I saw a flash of white and the image of the guardian patrollers at my front door appeared again. Another flash of white and the images were gone. This was the second time I saw the same vision twice. So, the guardian patrol would be coming to my dwelling place at any moment now. I don't know why but whatever the reason, I would be ready for them.

CHAPTER FIFTEEN

Training Day

"Aniyas wake up. Aniyas wake up!" I opened my eyes, and Adrielle was standing at my bedside. I thought I locked my door. Anyway, I was exhausted because I was up all night expecting the guardian patrol, but they never showed. "It's time for training. Get up and get ready!" Father ordered.

"I'm up, I'm up!"

"Meet me downstairs in twenty."

"Yes Sir, Father Sir, as you command!"

Adrielle laughed. I've been upset with Adrielle for the past few days. He did not protect me. There had to be a good reason he was allowing these people to treat me in this manner, there just had to be. I was going to get to the bottom of this issue, today!

"Why did you allow those men to put their hands on me?" I blurted out, as we drove to the quarters.

"Honey, I don't want to cause an uproar right now. You were supposed to be keeping a low profile. You have training, and The Extraordinary Assessment of Valor is coming soon. You haven't perfected your gifts, and we aren't even sure if you have more abilities to unlock. We don't know what we might have to face as things unveil. We are not prepared yet. This was not the right time for a protest."

"So, when is the right time?" I questioned. "If I were a parent and a grown male touched my daughter, I would be in The House of Corrections right now!"

"Aniyas, trust and believe their day will come, but right now I am doing what is best for you and the indigents as a whole," said Father. I didn't have any more words for Adrielle at that moment.

There weren't many people at the training facility this a.m. I only saw Allura, Ms. Haraka, The Abrafo's, Father, and two trainers. Allura was training in combat when I arrived. I was directed to the swim room. After a few minutes, my trainer walked out. I introduced myself, "Hi, I'm Aniyas. What's your name?"

"I am trainer 332."

"You don't have a name?" I asked.

"I'm not allowed to reveal my name."

"But you know my name," I replied.

"And you will not know my name," he responded.

"Well okay then," I said, tilting my head back and twisting my lips. I found it very odd that I couldn't know his name, but I'll let it go for now. My trainer informed me there was a bathing suit in the changing space for me. As I changed, I became nervous. I didn't know how to swim, and quite frankly large amounts of water frightened me. I'm not sure I wanted to do this, I stood there frozen in place like an ice cube.

"Get it together, Aniyas!" I mustered up the courage to walk back to the leisure pool. The trainer must have sensed my fear.

"You must be strong! You can do anything you set your mind to!" 332 encouraged.

"This water looks deep. Where is the shallow end of the leisure pool?" I questioned.

"There is no shallow end Aniyas, now come stand next to me." I wanted to tell him, don't say my name, since I can't know yours, but I didn't. I was silent and did as he said.

"Now remember, you can do anything!" he reiterated, as 332 pushed me into the leisure pool. Had he lost his mind! I began to panic!

The trainer shouted, "You are a radiant one! You can do anything!" I can do anything! I can do anything! I began to float, my legs began to flap behind me, and my arms stroked in front of me. I was swimming! After my sixth lap, I jumped out the leisure pool.

"I told you you could do anything!" stressed the trainer.

"Since I can already swim naturally, I guess we are done here."

"We are not done at all. We are just getting started!" 332 said. I did not like the sound of that.

I was ordered to get back into the leisure pool and tread water for ten minutes. There was a large timer on the wall. The timer hit eight minutes and forty-five seconds and I was still treading water with no problem at all. The timer struck nine minutes, and down I went. Sinking, I was sinking! Before I knew it, I was at the bottom of the leisure pool, and I could not move. There was a large boulder attached to my leg by a chain. Where did this thing come from? Frantically, I pulled at the boulder, but I could not get it off. Oh Lawd, he is trying to kill me!

"Think Aniyas, think!" trainer 332 yelled.

If he could hear me through this water I would have yelled, "Shut up and get this thing off me, now!"

I am in control! I am in control! Remain calm! Think Aniyas, think! I closed my eyes and harnessed the energy within me. I felt a surge of electricity throughout my body. When I opened my eyes, I was engulfed in an orb of light. I focused all the energy into my hands and aimed it at the chain around my leg. The latch opened, and I was free! I jumped out of the water but this time a large amount of water came with me. The trainer was standing there drenched in water, looking at me with his mouth wide open.

"I've never seen anything like it in my life!" The trainer was still staring at me in amazement, while he explained to the others what happened. Apparently, when I jumped out of the leisure pool, I was still engulfed by the orb of light. That wasn't the only thing, I also emptied out half of the water inside the leisure pool, when I jumped out. Oops! I was really feeling myself in this moment.

"Listen up everyone, I have something to announce! I am the source bearer!" I blurted out. I have three abilities, I had to be the source bearer.

Ms. Haraka looked at me and asked, "How do you know this Aniyas?"

I explained how I can jump from extremely high places and land on my feet and how I could jump from the ground to exceedingly high places. Ms. Haraka giggled.

Mrs. Abrafo giggled as well and said, "Keir must be the source bearer too, because he can also do that."

"Allura discovered she had a jumping ability two days ago," Ms. Haraka added.

Oh, was my response. Oh, was all I had. Oh, was all I could say because I was embarrassed.

Mrs. Abrafo went on to say, "You must also remember Aniyas, we still have one more day for any other radiant ones to come forward, and you all still have to complete The Extraordinary Assessment of Valor."

"I got a little ahead of myself there guys. Forgive me!" I yelled, as I exited the space. Allura laughed and followed me.

"When were you going to tell me about your jumping ability, Aniyas?"

"When were you going to tell me about yours?" was my response to Allura. She just looked at me.

"Allura report to the meditation room. Aniyas report to combat training," someone said on the overhead speaker. I did not recognize the voice, but I obeyed.

My combat trainer was trainer 135. She looked so sweet and innocent. Ten minutes later, I changed my mind. Sweet and innocent, she was not! 135 was kicking my behind!

"Concentrate, Aniyas!" she shouted. "Hit me! Hit me!" No matter how hard I tried, I could not strike this woman. She dodged every blow I sent her way. Trainer 135 was extremely skilled and fast.

"What am I doing wrong?" I thought to myself. I tried to hit her again. Miss! "What are you doing wrong, Aniyas?" I asked myself again. You are over thinking. I am over thinking! Once I relaxed my mind, trainer 135 was in trouble. She could barely stop me from landing a punch.

"This is remarkable! You and Allura are the only trainees that have ever been able to strike me," 135 revealed. "We are done here for the day, report to weapons training."

"Yes 135, I am on my way."

Before coming to indigent combat training, I had never touched a gun in my life. Now every gun you could think of was right within my reach. I was back with trainer 332. He showed me how to load the guns properly, hold the guns properly, and shoot the guns properly. Once again, I was a natural. Missed the center of the target a few times, but everything else was a direct hit. Again, the trainer was amazed to see how well I was doing.

When we were done with the guns, it was time for bow and arrow training. Learning how to use the bow and arrow was coming to me easily, just like everything else. We moved on to the sword, piece of cake, the staff, the sword staff, the blade staff, too easy. Next it was time to practice throwing the javelin and spear, another simple task.

"You are truly special Aniyas."

"Thank you 332," I said, as I blushed.

"Keir is also extraordinary with weapons. You two are extremely gifted," he added. "It is time for you to report to the meditation room. After that you are done for the day."

"Thank you 332. I will see you tomorrow." I pranced right on over to the meditation room. Today is turning out to be a wonderful day!

There was no one in the meditation room but me, it was time to dig deep. The first image materialized. It was Mrs. Forte, Patroller Rogers, Mr. Edgerton, and Dean Powell all seated at a round table. My body jerked, and there appeared Patroller Rogers and the other patrollers at my front door again. Why do I keep seeing this image? A flash of black and there stood Keir, alone in the meditation room. He dropped to his knees and began to cry. I could feel his pain. My heart began to ache for my friend.

Keir vanished, and then Chase appeared. He was watching television. His father walked into the room with papers in his hand. Mr. Edgerton said a few words and handed the papers to Chase. Chase looked over the documents and shook his head. Mr. Edgerton began to talk. Chase threw the papers in the air and walked out of the lounge space. Mr. Edgerton collected the papers off the floor, and then everything faded to black. No other images materialized, so I released my mind from its meditative state. What did all this mean? I am sure I would find out soon.

Keir was standing alone in the middle of the main floor when I walked out. If Keir was here, that means he was done with academia for the day, which meant it was around three-thirty p.m. There were no clocks in the training facility, only timers. Keir saw me walking his way and frowned. Was I imagining things, or did he just frown at me?

"Hi, Keir. How are you?"

"I'm fine," he said in a tone I had never heard from him before. Keir was angry.

"You don't sound fine. What's wrong?" I questioned.

"Aniyas, leave me alone right now." Keir walked away from me, and I followed him.

"Wait! Tell me what is going on, please!" I begged.

"You kissed Chase!" How did he know that?

"How do you know that? Who told you that?" I asked.

"That is the first thing that came to your mind. Wow Aniyas!" Keir walked away again, this time with haste. I jogged after him.

"I'm sorry! I'm sorry!" I yelled. Keir stopped in his tracks.

"That should have been the first thing you said to me, not how do you know. It doesn't matter who told me, what matters is, you should've been the one to tell me."

I stood there in silence. For the first time in my life, I didn't know the right words to say.

This was our first argument, and I did not like it.

"You were my girl. How could you do this to me?" Wait! I was his girl? Hold on, he said you were my girl, that's past tense, which means I'm not his girl anymore. Technically, I was never his girl because we never made anything official. Keir continued, "That's why Chase was so upset when he saw us together at Allura's party. How could you keep this from me and then kiss me after the fact?"

"Technically, I was not and am not your girl, Keir. You never asked me to be your girlfriend, and you want to talk about secrets, you've known about this facility and your abilities for years and you never said a word to me about any of it!"

"Come on now Aniyas, that is not the same thing, you cannot compare the two. Don't try to switch this up on me. You know what, I'm done with this conversation." Keir walked away from me again, but this time I did not follow.

"Everyone please meet in the conference space," the unfamiliar voice said from the overhead speaker. I was the first one in the conference space. Keir walked in next without looking at me, and he made sure to sit far away from me. Following closely behind were the Abrafo's, Adrielle, Allura, and Ms. Haraka.

Everyone took a seat. Mrs. Abrafo started the conversation, "Allura and Aniyas, I hope you both enjoyed your day. I heard extraordinary things about the both of you." Allura smiled and so did I. "Do you girls have any questions or anything you would like to talk about from today's training?"

"No Mrs. Abrafo," we both replied.

"Okay, let's move on. We have a lot to discuss.

"Two individuals responded to our coded message, and they are indeed, radiant ones. They will both be visiting tomorrow in the a.m." I looked at Allura as she looked at me, we were probably thinking the same thing. Who would these two individuals be? Mrs. Abrafo continued, "It has also come to my attention that Emperor Kadar has been made aware of the incident that happened at Edgerton with Allura and Aniyas. I'm not sure if you all know or knew, but protesting is prohibited in Gardash. The law was passed last month. There has been no word on what Emperor Kadar plans to do about this situation, but we should be on high alert, especially at chastis this week. Emperor Kadar is not going to let this go." Looks like my time had come to avenge Charles, and I was ready!

"We will wait for one another before entering chastis. I will also alert all the indigent warriors and radiant ones, so they will be prepared to fight, if need be, "continued Mrs. Abrafo. "Hopefully, Kadar will spare you both because you are children, but if he tries to proceed with harsh punishments or deadly force, we will all step in. Neither one of you will be harmed or lose your life, I promise you that." I'm happy Mrs. Abrafo made that promise, but I would not stand there and let Kadar take my life or the life of my friends, he would lose his first.

"Now girls, tell me about your day and how your abilities have been evolving," said Mrs. Abrafo.

"Besides the fact I almost drowned, my day was amazing," I blurted out. Allura giggled. Keir sat there with a stone face. He was still upset, and I felt horrible.

"I heard about you being engulfed in a black orb that glows, has that happened before?"

"No, it was the first time."

"We will focus on that ability tomorrow, and we will also do some training in the woods. I would like you all to learn the terrain." I was not too fond of wild animals, so I was not excited about training in the woods, but I smiled a nodded my head.

"Allura, are there any new developments with your abilities?" asked Mrs. Abrafo.

"As you already know I have the jumping ability now, besides that nothing else. I do wish I could hear all conversations, though."

"You can't hear everything?" questioned Keir.

"No, if I could hear everything we would always be one step ahead, don't you think. My mega hearing, just like my mom's is selective. Well, I wouldn't even say that, the conversations choose us," Allura explained. I guess it would make someone insane if they heard several conversations all day long. It made sense that their mega hearing only activated in times of danger, or when necessary.

"Okay girls, go home, eat a good meal, and get some rest. We will see you both in the a.m.," said Mrs. Abrafo. Everyone exited the conference space.

On my way out, I tried to speak with Keir again, but he didn't want to talk. Allura noticed the tension.

"What's going on between you and Keir?"

"I don't mean to be rude, but I honestly don't want to talk about it right now."

"That's fine. I'm here to listen if and when you are ready."

"Thanks Allura, I appreciate that." Swiftly, I walked to the car. I was silent on the ride home. Thoughts of Keir flooded my mind. Adrielle noticed my energy was off.

"Do you want to talk about it moo-moo?"

"Not right now dad, thanks for asking." Staring out the window, I truly hoped Keir would forgive me. He was one of my best friends, and I didn't want to lose him.

CHAPTER SIXTEEN

No Going Back

Meesa was waiting for us at the door. "Dean Powell called. Your expulsion hearing is tomorrow morning. I still can't believe you put yourself in this predicament, Aniyas!" Mother ranted. Ignoring Meesa, I went straight to my sleeping chamber. I was not in the mood to be yelled at. Today was a day of highs and lows, and I wanted to focus on the highs. Unlocking a different ability with my orb was the highlight of my day. My gifts were starting to evolve quickly and it was thrilling.

"Can I come in?" Adrielle was at my door.

"Yes, come in."

"I know you probably don't want to discuss this right now, but we need to." I sighed.

"Tomorrow at your expulsion hearing, please maintain your composure."

"We can't draw unnecessary attention," I finished Father's sentence as I rolled my eyes.

"I'm serious Aniyas."

"I know you are. I will be the humble, meek, docile conventional that you want me to be," I said sarcastically. Adrielle, not pleased with my response, left my sleeping chamber without uttering another word.

After waking up from a nap, I was starving. The aroma of delicious food filled my nostrils. As I walked into the kitchen, Landis and Landon were sitting at the table eating. This was a surprise because the twins rarely visited since they moved out.

"So Aniyas, I hear you are still causing trouble," pried Landon.

"

She's always the problem," Landis added. Both twins would be ignored, their comments did not deserve a response.

I grabbed some food and went down to Adrielle's man cave. Father was gone as usual, so I had the cellar to myself. I liked being by myself, it was peaceful. When I finished my food, I returned to the kitchen to wash my plate. Landon and Landis were gone. Good, they were so annoying! Meesa walked into the kitchen.

"Next time, do not eat my food since you think it's okay to ignore me."

"Okay," I said, as I made my way back to my sleeping chamber. Mother wanted a fight, and she was not about to get one from me. I surrender.

As I prepared for bed, thoughts of Keir flooded my head again, and I dismissed them quickly. Keir was important to me, but I had more imperative issues to worry about. My expulsion hearing, combat training, cultivating my abilities, these are the things I need to focus on. I was my main priority. Meditation would be good right now, I entered my mind into a meditative state, and braced myself for what I was about to see.

Nothing, I saw nothing! Fifteen minutes later, and not one image had materialized. What was wrong with me? Why couldn't I see anything? I will try again in a few minutes. I went to grab a glass of water and cherpinal. Okay, I was feeling better after I put some sustenance in my system. "All I needed was some energy, now let me try this again," I said to myself. No matter how hard I tried, all I saw was the color white. Panic began to sat in. Again, I spoke to myself, "Calm down Aniyas. You had an intense day of training. You just need some rest, and you will be good as new tomorrow." I was sure everything would be okay in the a.m.

My alarm sounded. I could not believe it was time to get up already. My mind and body felt like I had only been asleep for ten minutes, but the clock let me know I had been asleep for eight hours. Why did I feel so drained? Okay, time to meditate! Again, nothing, I could only see the color white. This could not be happening to me; my visions were gone! "Do not freak out Aniyas, there must be a reason. They will come back," I reassured myself. In the meantime, I would get ready for my expulsion hearing. Today I would fluff and stretch my afro to the limit. All of this was because of my hair, so today they would see hair!

My parents were in the kitchen waiting for me.

"Oh no Aniyas, we are not doing this today. Go put your hair in a bun now!" yelled Meesa.

I calmy responded, "No."

"Remember what we talked about yesterday, Aniyas. You need to cooperate today," insisted Father.

"No," I repeated. Mother charged at me, but Adrielle grabbed her.

"I'm so sick of this girl, I don't know what to do!" she yelled.

Father looked at me and said, "We do not have time for this today, we are going to be late, and we can't afford to be late."

"Okay, let's go then," I said, as I walked outside to the car. My parents followed. The first battle of the day had been won. I was ready to go to Edgerton and fight the next one.

When we arrived at Edgerton we were escorted to the conference space. Five minutes later, Dean Powell, Mrs. Forte, and Emperor Kadar walked in. My mouth dropped. What was Emperor Kadar doing here? My parents looked nervous and quite frankly, so was I.

"Good morning, Emperor Kadar decided to drop in and attend our meeting," Dean Powell announced. "This meeting isn't going to take long. We just wanted to inform you in person, Aniyas has been expelled from Edgerton and she can never return." Dean Powell had to be joking right now. I waited a few seconds for a laugh, but Dean Powell didn't even crack a smile. He was serious.

"That's not fair! I thought this was a hearing, I didn't even get to plead my case!" I yelled.

Emperor Kadar stood up and said, "Young lady lower your voice and fix your tone right now. It is a privilege that you were even allowed to step foot into Edgerton, and you have the nerve to disobey. Your expulsion is final, and I do not want to hear another word."

I disobeyed again and spoke, "You know what, I don't even care. I never wanted to come to this academia in the first place. I'm not begging or fighting to stay at an institution that has wronged me." I stood up to leave, I was done with all of this!

"Sit down right now!" Emperor Kadar commanded. I didn't listen.

"I said sit!"

"Sit down Aniyas!" my mother said firmly.

"Please sit down," Father pleaded. Mrs. Forte chimed in, as I was still standing.

"Aniyas, I can't imagine how you feel right now, and I do not agree with this decision. I did everything I could to stop this outcome. I fought for you, but it wasn't enough. I am so sorry."

"No need to apologize, I'm over it all," I said, as I ran out of the conference space.

"Come back here right now!" called Mother. I ignored Meesa and ran up to the roof of Edgerton. One day at academia, I was spying on Chase to see if he was the informant. I followed Chase into the stairwell and into one of the doors that said do not enter. The door led to the roof. Chase had no idea he was being followed. I watched as Chase sat on the ledge of the roof and looked out at the sky. Today would be the day I did the same thing; this would be my last memory at Edgerton.

Opening the door to the roof, I was stunned to see Chase and Mara. By the look on their faces, the duo was surprised to see me too.

"What is she doing here? This is supposed to be our spot. How does she know about the roof, Chase?" questioned Mara.

"I have no idea. I've never brought her up here. I promise," Chase reassured her. Okay, what was going on here, because I was baffled.

"Really Chase, how else would she know to come up here?"

"He's not lying Mara; Chase has never brought me up here."

"Just shut up you backstabbing, man stealing, dress stealing liar!" I stood there confused because I had no idea what Mara was referring to.

"What are you talking about Mara?" I asked.

"What am I talking about? I'm talking about the fact you stole the dress I wanted for Allura's party, and even worse, you kissed Chase and you two have been dating behind my back. Chase told me everything!"

I gave Chase the death stare and said, "Mara it's not like that, the kiss was a mistake, and we are not dating. Also, you said you didn't like any of those dresses you tried on for Allura's party, which is the only reason I chose that dress. All you had to do was tell me you didn't want me to wear the dress and I wouldn't have." I stepped closer to Mara.

"Do not come near me!" Mara yelled, as she took a step back. During the heat of the discussion no one realized how close Mara was to the edge of the roof.

"Mara!" I screamed, as I watched her fall over the ledge of the roof.

I had no choice; I used my abilities to save Mara. With my arms outstretched, I harnessed my energy from within to stop Mara from hitting the ground. I engulfed Mara's body with the very same orb I was engulfed in yesterday, and lifted her body back onto the roof. Chase stood there staring at me in amazement. Mara gazed at me as she held her heart and panted.

"Aniyas, how did you just do that? What are you?" questioned Chase. This could not be happening right now; I lowered my head in disbelief.

My cover was blown. What was I going to do?

"Please, please, please, you two can't tell anyone what I just did or what you just saw!" I pleaded. "This must stay between us! Mara, I know you are angry with me, and I understand why, but please don't tell anyone about this. I know you told the guardian patrol about Allura's party, and you told Keir about the kiss, but you must keep this secret to yourself. I am begging you!"

"I know we aren't friends anymore Aniyas, but I'm no informant. I didn't tell the guardian patrol or Keir anything." Well, if she didn't, who did?

My eyes cut towards Chase.

"So, it's you then, you are the informant!"

"I will admit, I did tell Keir about us, but I did not tell the guardian patrol about Allura's party," said Chase.

"Why would you do that? Why would you tell Keir? He wants nothing to do with me now!"

"Maybe I told Keir because I want you to myself. I like you Aniyas. Can't you see that!"

"You know what, you two deserve each other. I appreciate you saving me and all, but I'm done with the both of you. Oh, and Aniyas don't worry your pretty little head off. Your secret is safe with me." Mara stormed off. We both watched her leave.

Chase walked over to me and reached for my hand.

"Do not touch me! Don't even utter another word to me. I will no longer be in the middle of this game you are playing. I'm thankful I was expelled today because that means I'll never have to see your face again!"

"You were expelled today? That's not fair!" Chase yelled.

"Well Chase, I don't have the privilege that you do."

"I know you may not believe me now, but I promise I won't tell anyone what I saw here today, and my dad will get you back in Edgerton. I promise!"

"You know what Chase; I really don't care if you do or don't. It is what it is, and what will be, will be, I'm not going to worry about it." I left Chase standing on the roof alone.

When I arrived back to my dwelling place, Meesa was waiting in the kitchen fuming.

"Where did you go? We looked all over Edgerton for you, it was so embarrassing. Then we come back home, and you weren't here. Where were you?" I didn't respond. Father walked into the kitchen.

"Aniyas, you can't just run off like that." I didn't respond to Adrielle either.

"You know what, I'm tired of this!" Mother raised her hand to strike me, but I blocked her blow.

"Oh, so you think you're grown enough to fight me huh?" Meesa began to swing at me. Father grabbed Mother and held her back.

"Get off me! You are always protecting her! You are always taking her side!" Meesa screamed. Isn't it ironic how Mother felt Adrielle was always protecting me, but I felt like he didn't protect me enough. "I'm over this! Get out Adrielle, take Aniyas with you, and this time I mean it!"

"Meesa where will we go?" Father asked.

"I don't know, you two can be homeless for all I care, just get out!" She didn't have to tell me again; I went to my sleeping chamber to pack.

Mother was still downstairs screaming, and Father was still trying to reason with her. As I continued to randomly throw things into my satchel, I heard Adrielle say, "Fine, I'll leave."

"Good! It's about time! Bye!" Meesa yelled. Seconds later, Father walked into my sleeping chamber and said, "Let's go!"

"Where will we go?" I asked.

"We will talk about it in the car. Get your things and I'll meet you outside in a few minutes," Adrielle replied. I shook my head to let him know I understood. I heard the front door shut, and then I heard the twin's voices. Well, isn't this perfect timing. I was not in the mood to deal with Landon and Landis right now.

As soon as I walked into the living space, Landon approached me screaming and yelling, "I'm tired of you disrespecting my mom!"

"I'm tired of it too!" Landis added. Mind you, the twins were extremely disrespectful to Meesa at times. They have both cursed at my mom, snuck out of our dwelling place, Landis received horrible grades his entire life, and Landon even tried to fight Mother one day. I had never done any of those things to my mother, well except sneak out, but for whatever reason I was the "bad" one.

"Get out of my face!" I yelled. Without any warning, Landon attempted to strike me in my face, and Landis followed right behind him. I bobbed and weaved both punches, while Meesa just stood there and watched. Father entered the room and tried to calm the twins down. This was the last time my mother or the twins would see me. I was never coming back to this dwelling place. I walked out of the front door and got into the car.

It seemed as if I was waiting in the car for an eternity before

Father came out.

"What took so long?"

"I wasn't finished packing the things I needed. I still didn't get everything, but I'll come back tomorrow when things have calmed down."

"Did you get all your belongings?" asked Adrielle. Oh no, I forgot the locket Keir gave me.

"No, I didn't."

"I will get the rest of your things when I come back tomorrow as well."

"I'm coming with you Father." I had to get that locket! "Where are we going? Where will we live?"

"The quarters," Adrielle replied.

"The Abrafo's are allowing us to stay at the training facility." There was a time when I would never want to live in the quarters, but as of right now the quarters was our safe haven. I was grateful for the Abrafo's.

Amid everything that was going on, I was also on bad terms with Keir, and now I had to live with him. I also forgot to tell Father Chase and Mara knew about my abilities. Today was going horribly wrong, so I'll just wait to tell Adrielle more unfortunate news a little later. When we arrived at the Abrafo's they welcomed us with open arms. I wondered would Keir be as inviting when he arrived home from academia. Walking into the training facility, I spotted Allura and her mom. We waved. As the Abrafo's walked us to our sleeping chambers, I began to feel lightheaded. Skipping breakfast this a.m. probably wasn't the best thing to do, another wave of dizziness washed over me. I fainted.

Opening my eyes, the images that surrounded me were blurry.

"Are you okay Aniyas?"

"Aniyas, can you hear me?" There were so many voices asking me questions. I sat up, but I was too weak to stand.

"Just stay there honey. Do not try to move. I will get you a glass of water." That was Ms. Haraka, I recognized her voice. Fear spiraled through my body. Not only was I too weak to stand, my surroundings were still blurry. What was happening to me?

"Here Aniyas, drink this." Ms. Haraka was back with some water. I gulped it down quickly.

"May I have some more please?" After eight glasses of water, my senses and strength returned. My vision was clear, and I was able to stand.

"Go lie down sweetie and get some rest," Adrielle advised. "I'm not asking you; I'm telling you." I did as I was told and followed Mrs. Abrafo to my sleeping chamber.

Shortly after settling in, I was awakened.

"How are you feeling?"

"I'm fine."

"Here's some water."

"Thank you." It was nice of Keir to check on me.

"Wait, what time is it?" I asked.

"It's four-thirty." Wow five hours had gone by. I didn't realize I slept so many hours away.

"Is anyone still here?"

"Yes, everyone is still here. They all wanted to make sure you were okay."

"That was nice of them."

"There are also two new radiant ones here," Keir added.

"Oh yes, today is the day they were coming. I must go meet them," I insisted.

"No, rest Aniyas. I only came in here to make sure you were okay, and to bring you a glass of water."

"I appreciate it Keir, but I'm going to see who these radiant ones are."

"You never listen. You are so headstrong!"

"That I am!"

Unexpectedly my emotions took over me. "I'm sorry Keir. I'm sorry about what happened with Chase. There is no excuse, but it just happened out of nowhere. I don't like Chase in that manner. I like you and I always have. I'm not sure if you will ever like me in that way again, but I don't want to lose you as a friend," I pleaded.

"Let's not talk about that right now. I just want you to get better." Keir reached in to hug me. We embraced. Finally, something went right today. I didn't want to let Keir go.

"I overheard what happened with your mom and brothers today. Well, I heard bits and pieces, but I'm sorry."

"It's okay," I smiled. It really wasn't okay but that's what I told Keir.

"I'm sure you all will work it out, and you will return to your dwelling place."

"There is no working this out, there is no going back to that place. I am done!" I yelled. My vision blurred again, but this time it was from tears. I tried, but I could not hold them back, tears streamed down my face.

"Don't cry Aniyas." Keir embraced me again. It felt strange to cry in front of Keir and be vulnerable. This was something I had never experienced before, I pulled away from Keir's embrace and wiped my eyes.

"Okay, let's go so I can meet these new radiant ones," I said. Hopping out of the bed, I exited the room.

CHAPTER SEVENTEEN

The True Story

"Well, hello there Amanda, I should've known."

"Aniyas, I should've known too." Amanda walked over and we embraced. "Carlos, come over here and meet Aniyas," Amanda said.

"Hi Carlos, I'm Aniyas. Nice to meet you."

"Nice to meet you too." Amanda and Carlos were the two new radiant ones. I didn't personally know Carlos, but I've seen him at chastis. He's an indigent.

"So Aniyas, what are your abilities?" asked Amanda.

"Visions via meditation an orb, jumping, harnessing energy from within to move objects and people, and just recently I was able to engulf myself in the orb. So, I think that is three or four gifts, I'm still working out a few kinks though."

"Wow, that's so amazing!"

"Thank you," I blushed.

"What about you Amanda?"

"I also have the jumping ability, my internal body heat is as hot as an irrupting volcano, so I can shoot lava darts from the palms of my hands. I can also heal people through water, within a certain time frame. The individual's body must be emerged in water, I place my hands into the water, and they heal."

"Amanda that is incredible!" I raved. "Carlos, what are your abilities?"

"I too have the jumping ability, I also harness energy from within, take a deep breath, and push the energy back out through my chest. This creates an extremely powerful force, strong enough to knock down a brick wall."

"Remarkable!" I said. We were all indeed extraordinary!

Once everyone realized I was back up and about, they checked to see how I was doing. Their concern was touching.

"Man, woman, and child illuminated by the sun, we are familia, we are one." Everyone in the training facility repeated after Mr. Abrafo.

"Nice to see you back with us Aniyas. How are you feeling?"

"I'm feeling much better, thank you."

"I see you've met the new radiant ones, Amanda, and Carlos. While you were resting, we introduced them to everyone, showed them around the facility, and explained to them all the things we explained to you when you first arrived. We would like to meet with all the radiant ones and elder indigents in the conference space right now. Combat indigents, please continue training. We will cease training at six. If anyone has questions, please feel free to ask myself or Mrs. Abrafo." These meetings are always interesting, let's see what's in store.

Mr. Abrafo commenced the meeting. "Welcome everyone. First thing on the agenda, our plan of escape. If for some reason this facility is ever sieged we do have a protocol. There is a hidden door with a passageway in the meditation space. The door is located underneath the timer. All you need to do is touch the door with the palm of your hand and it will open. The door recognizes the energy of radiant ones. Once you are inside the passageway, touch the ground closest to the door with the palm of both hands and it will shut. No one can open and shut that door except radiant ones. The door is impenetrable to everyone else. Is everyone still with me?"

"Yes, Mr. Abrafo," we responded.

"Follow the passageway until you come to the next door. This door opens and shuts the exact same way as the first. When this door opens it will lead you to the outdoors. Follow the trail to your left. This trail will lead you into the woods. Keep following the trail until you see two large cherpinal trees. Break the lowest branch on both sides of the trees. Once you do that, and underground passage will open. Go down the stairs. Once the last person is at the bottom of the stairwell, there will be three latches to the left. Click all the latches. This will shut the underground passageway door and open the door to our other underground facility. There is food and water there, enough to last for at least a year." The surprises just keep on coming. I really would like to know who is funding these facilities. I guess only time will tell.

"If for some reason the elder combat indigents or elder radiant ones, including myself don't make it to the second facility, there are instructions under the conference space table on what should be done next. Are there any questions?" asked Mr. Abrafo.

Don't do it Aniyas! Don't you ask that question. I was at war with myself. Aniyas, don't ask! "Who is funding these facilities?" I blurted out.

"In due time all things will be revealed," Mr. Abrafo replied. I nodded in understanding.

"Aniyas, don't press the issue, leave it be," I said to myself. Even though I was still curious, I'll let it go.

"For those that are not familiar with The Book of the Radiant, we would like you to start reading it. Reading the book is a training requirement," Mrs. Abrafo added. "Are there any more questions or concerns?" The room was silent.

Mrs. Abrafo proceeded, "The Extraordinary Assessment of Valor is drawing near. There are four levels that must be completed. The first level is swimming, second is weapons, third will be combat, and the fourth level will only be revealed when an individual has successfully completed the first three levels. Whoever completes the fourth level will be the source bearer. I would like to read a passage from The Book of the Radiant. The source bearer will bear light unto all radiant ones and lead them out of bondage. Their connection to the source will give them power the universe has never seen. The light within, will set the people free." I closed my eyes for a second and meditated on the words Mrs. Abrafo had just read.

"We have been waiting many years for the source bearer, and hopefully he or she is here among us. Emperor Kadar and the regime grow more vicious by the day, and we have no insight into what they truly have planned. They may outnumber us, but with the source bearer, I know we will be able to stand against the regime and their infantry. Hopefully, whatever they may have planned, is after the assessment is completed."

"We don't have to wait! I'm prepared for The Extraordinary Assessment of Valor right now!" Amanda announced.

"Let's go!" yelled Keir. Several radiant ones joined in, expressing their willingness to take the assessment now.

"You all still have a few weeks to train, take that time to prepare," Mrs. Abrafo insisted.

"We are ready!" I shouted.

Adrielle spoke, "Aniyas you just fainted, give yourself some time."

"Father, I said I'm ready! Emperor Kadar and the regime can attack tomorrow for all we know. It's time!"

"The children have spoken. You will attempt The Extraordinary Assessment of Valor tomorrow at dawn," Mr. Abrafo announced. Nervousness rushed throughout my body; abilities, please come back to me!

The conference space was loud with excitement. Allura was jumping up and down.

"Listen everyone, we still have other issues to address. Please be seated so we can continue."

"Yes, Mr. Abrafo," we all said in unison.

"Your body is sacred, so taking care of your body is extremely important. The more fruits and vegetables you consume, the better you will perform. Water is essential for our survival. Ninety percent of our body is composed of water. Aniyas, have you been drinking water?"

"Come to think of it, I have, but only like a glass or two a day." "That's why you fainted. Water and our abilities work hand in hand. Water fuels our bodies. You must intake at least eight glasses of water a day."

"Noted," I replied. I hope this was the reason I was unable to receive a vision. This evening I would be drinking a ton of water.

"Overusing your abilities or using your most powerful abilities back-to-back can also drain your energy." I used my full body orb in the leisure pool yesterday and this a.m. That's what's wrong with me! "Do any of you have any questions or concerns before we move on?" asked Mrs. Abrafo.

"Chase and Mara know about my abilities, well one of them!" I blurted out. Everyone darted their eyes my way. I truly had diarrhea of the mouth today.

"Aniyas, why would you reveal your abilities to outsiders?" Father questioned.

"You know better!"

"Wait, before you chastise me, let me explain. The three of us were on the roof at Edgerton this a.m. Mara stepped too close to the edge of the roof and fell. I couldn't let her die. I had to save her!"

"Mara, Mara Smith?" I recognized the voice from the overhead speaker, but I didn't recognize this woman's face. She appeared to be around my mother's age.

"Yes, Mara Smith," I replied.

"That's my daughter. You saved my baby!" said the woman.

"I'm confused, Mara told me her father was killed when she was a baby, and her mother went missing and was probably dead."

"Unfortunately, I fear her father is dead, and I had to disappear to keep Mara safe, but I am Mrs. Smith." Wow, could this day get any more interesting!

Mrs. Smith continued, "Just like you, Mara's father had abilities, and just like you he exposed those abilities to save a child's life. We were new parents and wanted to get out of our dwelling place for a while. We dropped Mara off at my parent's home and took a ride. After driving around for a while, we ended up at the park. While at the park some guys got into an argument, and they began to shoot. There was a little boy caught in the crossfire. My husband ran to shield the little boy, but there was already a bullet in the direct path of the child. He wouldn't get to the child in time. My husband clapped his hands together, and all the bullets fell to the ground. He clapped his hands again, and the guns fell to the ground. I couldn't believe what I had witness. I had no idea my husband possessed abilities. We also had no idea the guardian patrol was there and saw everything." I stared at Mara's mom in disbelief and continued to listen to her story.

"My husband ran towards me and said, 'Hurry home, look in my information book, and call the number under the name Uncle A. He will tell you what to do. You can trust him. I love you, now go!" Mrs. Smith began to cry. Her pain transferred to my spirit, and tears began to fall from my eyes as well. "I did as he said without a question. As I was running to the car, I looked back. A guardian patroller pulled his gun out on my husband and made him get down on his knees. Why won't he just clap again so the gun would fall out of the patroller's hands? I was confused, but I continued to run to the car, hopped in, and sped home.

"When I arrived at our dwelling place, I was frantic, but I found the number and called Uncle A. I explained who I was, and Uncle A told me to leave everything behind, torch our dwelling place, and come to his home. He gave me directions to his home that I had to memorize, I could not write the address on paper. Luckily, the address was close to our home. When I arrived at the dwelling place, Mr. and Mrs. Abrafo were waiting outside of their door. Mrs. Abrafo had a baby in her hand, it was Keir. I explained to the Abrafo's that I had to get my baby and my husband. Mr. Abrafo informed me I would never be able to return to my parent's home for Mara, and that I would probably never see my husband again. My body went limp, I collapsed to the ground and wailed in agony."

What I was going through at my dwelling place seemed trivial while listening to Mara's mother's story. To be separated from your baby and husband was a pain I couldn't imagine, and looking into her eyes that pain was still there.

"You don't have to finish this story," Mrs. Abrafo advised.

"No, it's okay. I want them to hear it." Mrs. Smith wiped the tears from her face. "The Abrafo's explained that my husband was a radiant one. They also explained if I stayed away from my parents and Mara, they would be safe. I married my husband at the age of eighteen. My husband insisted that Mara be born at home. We used a doula and a mid-wife, so there is no record of Mara's birth. My husband also insisted that I was a stay-at-home mom, so

I never had a job, and my parents aren't my biological parents." This story just keeps getting more intriguing as it goes on. You could hear a pen drop in the conference space. We all continued to listen attentively.

"My god parents had just moved from Cosland to Gardash, they had no family or friends here, and then they met my parents. My birth parents and god parents became extremely close, they became family. When the drug, soar, entered the quarters via the regime, it devasted our entire community. My mom was using while she was pregnant with me. She was so small no one even knew she was pregnant, until she pushed me out in the bathtub one afternoon. The regime would place all mothers whose babies were born on soar in The House of Corrections, and place their babies in the system, so my birth was kept a secret. This was the tragic reality many indigents faced.

"My mother promised she would get sober, but she just couldn't kick the habit. Both of my birth parents were extremely addicted to soar, and they just stop taking care of me. My god parents stepped in and took me in when I was three months old. My biological parents both overdosed within that same year. There was no record of my birth, so my god parents just passed me off as their own. Homeschooling wasn't illegal back then, so they homeschooled me and no one asked any questions. Long story short, there is no true record of me.

"Mr. Abrafo told me to torch our dwelling place, so there would be no signs of a baby ever residing there. He didn't want Emperor Kadar and the regime to go looking for Mara. If her dad was a radiant one, then it was a possibility she could be one too, and Kadar would find Mara and hurt her. As it turns out, Mara is not a radiant one, or she would be here. I was hoping she would be here." Mara's mom paused for a second and looked off into space. "Poor lady," I thought to myself.

"Before they confiscated all the televisions, our story was on the news, well it wasn't our story. The guardian patrol created a false narrative, by saying my husband was a soar dealer that got into a gang war at the park and was killed. They also said a young lady that was a gang affiliated fled the scene, and if anyone had any information about her whereabouts, please call the guardian patrol. My parents knew my husband was no soar dealer, and they knew I was not affiliated with any gang. No one trusted the guardian patrol back then, especially indigents, so no one offered the guardian patrol any information concerning me. I've been with the Abrafo's ever since. I know I was long winded, but I just wanted to say to Aniyas, thank you for saving my child!"

"You're welcome," I replied. Mrs. Smith exited the conference space.

That was intense! Mara's mom was still alive, and her father could possibly still be alive. Keir sure could keep a secret.

"The only people that know Mara's mother is still alive is Mara's grandparents, us, and now you all. We must all keep this information confidential. Mr. Abrafo found a way to tell Mara's grandparents that their daughter was still alive, many years ago. He also told them, they couldn't tell a soul, not even Mara or all their lives would be in danger. You all must vow to do the same. Nothing we say in this facility, leaves this facility. Do you all solemnly vow to keep our secrets?" asked Mrs. Abrafo.

"We solemnly vow," was our response.

"It's time for you all to go home and get some rest for the assessment tomorrow. Rest is also an essential part of keeping your abilities sharp. Remember to drink lots of water to stay hydrated. Miles, please cast the invisible blanket over the quarters so no one can see them leaving, thank you. Have a great evening everyone." Mrs. Abrafo dismissed us.

Mile's invisible blanket was so cool. It wasn't really a blanket but that's what they called it. The invisible blanket wasn't the only precaution we took, no one came or left at the same exact time, and there were several hidden passageways for exit and entry. As we walked out of the conference space, I bumped into my father.

"Did you know about Mara's mother?" I asked.

"No, I didn't. Mara's grandparents moved from the quarters to the conventional area of the province when Mara was a little girl. I was told the same story you were told." For Adrielle to be so nosey, he sure didn't know what was going in Gardash.

"I'm not sure how Mara's grandparents moved up in rank, because it is not easy, but somehow they did."

"You know how to keep some big secrets, just like Keir, so I was just wondering." Adrielle gave me the side-eye.

"Go to bed Aniyas. You have a big day tomorrow, and you had an extremely rough morning."

"I'm headed there now Father." If this were any other time, I probably wouldn't have listened, but I was exhausted. I was going to drink a few glasses of water and go straight to bed. Adrielle gave me a big hug, and we went our separate ways.

CHAPTER EIGHTEEN

The Extraordinary Assessment of Valor

Opening my eyes, I felt refreshed. I stretched my limbs and showered quickly. Dawn was drawing near. As I hurried to the kitchen, I bumped into Keir.

"My apologies," I shouted, as I pressed on towards my destination. No time for small talk, it was time to focus. A light breakfast will do, I grabbed some fruit and water. Allura entered the kitchen.

"How are you feeling, Aniyas?"

"I'm feeling much better, thank you."

"How are you?"

"I'm well, thank you."

"Are you ready for The Extraordinary Assessment of Valor?" I asked.

"Yes, I'm ready. Are you ready?"

"I'm ready!"

"Well, let's go! It's time to start lining up," said Allura. "Aniyas, I'm not sure what this assessment truly entails, but just know if I have to take you down, I will. I love you, but today we are not friends."

"Thanks for the heads up, Allura. We shall see." Winking at Allura, I shuffled ahead of her to line up.

"Grand rising radiant ones. Today you will be attempting The Extraordinary Assessment of Valor. This will be no easy feat. You will be challenged mentally, physically, and emotionally. Only the strong will survive." Did Mrs. Abrafo just say survive, like in someone could die? I slowly raised a finger.

"Yes, Aniyas?"

"When you say only the strong will survive, do you mean like we can die?"

"Though we wish death on none of you, anything is possible during this assessment." I took a large gulp. My eyes darted to Allura, Keir, Amanda, and then to Carlos. They all met my gaze. I signed up for tryouts to be the source bearer, not to be murdered! All the radiant ones looked around at each other and mumbled.

Mrs. Abrafo raised her hand and said, "Silence! Everyone prepare to meet in the swimming space, you have five minutes." So, they were going to try and drown me again, noted! I'm not sure what I originally thought this assessment would be, but it was not this. It was time to prepare my mind for anything.

In the swim space, we were placed into groups. None of my friends were grouped with me and I was relieved. There were three groups of five, and I was in the second group. Allura and Keir were in the first group, and Amanda and Carlos were in the last group.

"You all must swim ten laps in the leisure pool, without stopping."

"That sounds easy," I said to myself.

"Group one, approach the leisure pool. You may start," instructed Mrs. Abrafo.

This was their fourth lap and Allura was in the lead. Maybe this wouldn't be as bad as I imagined. I spoke too soon! What is that? Spikes were shooting out the side of the leisure pool from both ends. Two radiant ones in the pool saw the spikes and jumped out. They were done! Allura's speed made it easy for her to dodge the spikes. She didn't miss a beat. Keir, all though not as fast as Allura, was maneuvering well. The third radiant one left in the pool was having a difficult time avoiding the spikes. Wait, what's happening? He just activated a full body shield. The spikes were bouncing right off him. I assumed Allura was tired of playing, she finished the rest of her laps in lightning speed. Keir finished second, and the human shield was third. We were off to an interesting start.

"Second group, take your places." One of the radiant ones in my group walked out. I guess she quits! The four of us remaining jumped into the leisure pool. We were on our second lap, and I started to prepare myself for the spikes that would be coming during the fourth lap. Three laps in, and two of the radiant ones were already winded. They exited the pool. "Ouch!" I felt something scrap across my right arm. A spike had grazed me, they activated them early!

Focusing, I harnessed my energy from within and with every stroke I made, I forced the spikes away from me. A formidable force in the pool made me look to my left. The radiant one beside me was spiraling her body to dodge the spikes. She looked like an underwater tornado. I was on my last lap, but tornado girl finished before me. Jumping out of the leisure pool, I was upset, and my arm was bleeding.

"That wasn't fair! You activated the spikes early," I complained.

"Early? Expect anything at any time, Aniyas, this universe owes you nothing," said Mrs. Abrafo. Even though I completed the task at hand, I was not happy about it. I lost, and I didn't like to lose. I didn't stick around to watch Amanda and Carlos. I left to clean the blood from my arm.

Walking back into the main training space, I saw Amanda and Carlos.

"How did you all do?" I asked.

"We made it through," said Carlos.

"It was a breeze," Amanda added.

"That's good to hear. How did the others do?"

"Everyone in our group made it, but I see you had a little trouble, Aniyas," Amanda smirked.

"Yeah, I was caught off guard, but it's okay. It won't happen again."

"Will the remaining radiant ones report to the shooting range in five minutes," Mrs. Smith said on the overhead speaker. I walked away from Carlos and Amanda. Amanda should have offered to heal my arm instead of gloating. It is truly every man for himself, no more playing nice.

Mr. Abrafo was waiting for us. "Welcome to level two. You will be split up into two groups of five. There will be five guns placed in front of you: a rifle, shotgun, revolver, pistol, and machine gun. You must load each gun and hit your target with one hundred percent accuracy. You have five minutes to complete this task." Did he just say one hundred percent accuracy and five minutes? "When I call your name please step to the right, this will be the first group." I was in the first group with Keir and Carlos. "Begin!"

Weapons was one of my strengths, and it was showing. I was already firing my pistol. Here we go again! Why do I take the bait every time? I should've known this was too easy! My target was now moving up and down, and side to side. Focus Aniyas, you can do this! I locked in, hit after hit, and finished before everyone else. A trainer handed me my target, after grading it. Yes, one hundred percent accuracy! It felt good to be back at the top.

Exiting the range, I walked back into the main space where the other radiant ones were waiting their turn.

"How did you do, Aniyas?" asked Amanda.

"Bloody arm and all, one hundred percent accuracy, baby!" I winked at Amanda.

"Good stuff!" said Allura.

The rest of my group walked out. Everyone had passed with one hundred percent accuracy. I gave Carlos and Keir a high five.

"Good luck girls!" I said to Allura and Amanda as they headed into the range.

"No luck needed," Amanda winked.

Allura looked back and said, "Thanks Aniyas."

A few minutes later, the second group walked back into the main space. Amanda and Allura passed, the other three radiant ones ran out of time.

"All the remaining radiant ones, report to the weapons room," it was Mara's mom again.

Amanda looked at me and said, "And then there were seven."

We were not split into groups this time. There were seven targets set up. "In front of each of you is a bow with fifty arrows, fifty spears, and fifty javelins. You have four minutes to hit your target with one hundred percent accuracy. You may set your first arrow in place." As I was preparing my arrow, the target started moving further and further away from me. I could barely see it. They were not making this easy. Mrs. Abrafo yelled, "Begin!"

Even though I was moving as fast as I could, I was falling behind. I was still on my spears, while Keir had already moved on to his javelins. "Focus on yourself Aniyas! Pay attention!" I redirected myself. There was now twenty-six seconds left on the timer. Time is moving too fast! I don't think I'm going to make it! Five, four, three, two, my last javelin hit the target. Finishing by the skin of my teeth, I sighed with relief!

"Aniyas, I noticed you had a rough time again," teased Amanda.

"I didn't notice you at all," I smiled. No one was eliminated this round.

We were back on the main floor. "Your final weapons challenge will be with the sword and staff. You must strike your opponent a total of one hundred times, fifty times with the sword and fifty times with the staff." An image of an individual in a red hooded robe appeared, and then six more of these images appeared. "Please find an opponent and stand next to him. You have two minutes, begin!" yelled Mr. Abrafo. Raising my arm, I moved to strike my opponent. Wait, where did he go? Turning around, he was behind me. Whew, this thing is fast, but not faster than me! One hundred strikes in less than two minutes, I passed. Looking around, we all passed. There was still seven of us, standing strong.

"We are moving on to the combat challenge. Please line up in the order your name is called."

"Why was my name called last?" I asked.

"Based on your overall performance thus far, you are in last place," Mr. Abrafo announced. Amanda giggled. Amanda was in second place, behind Keir. Allura was in third place, followed by Carlos, and then there was shield boy, and tornado girl. I've never been last in anything! This was not sitting right with my spirit.

"You will all go into the meditation space one by one. There will be three rounds of combat, which will last for two minutes.

You must win two out of three rounds to move on, and you cannot use your abilities.

"Well, what is the point of having them then," I mumbled. If necessary, you can surrender by waving your right hand.

"Once you are finished with your rounds, please head to the conference space in silence. Keir you may enter." Keir gave his father a nod. Let's see how this turns out.

Keir emerged from the meditation space with a bruised eye, holding his shoulder. He walked past with his head down. That was not a good sign. "Amanda, you may enter," said Mr. Abrafo. One by one my peers exited the meditation space bloody and bruised. It was my turn, and I wasn't looking forward to it. The room was dimly lit. The largest human being I had ever seen emerged from the shadows, I'm not even sure it was human. What have I gotten myself into?

The huge, maybe human, had on a mask, which made it even creepier. I'll just call it gigantor. "Fight!" yelled Mrs. Abrafo. I attacked first. I rushed the gigantor with a power right, then left. He dodged every hit. I was moving quickly, but the gigantor was moving faster. I wasn't expecting something so large to be so swift. The masked creep took ahold of my arm and hurled me into the wall. It took a second, but I was back on my feet. Running, I attacked again. This time I was met by a fist to the lip. My body crashed to the floor. Scrambling to my feet, I felt the blood leaking from my bruised lip. I for sure lost round one.

"Fight!" Mrs. Abrafo yelled again. And just like that, I was lying on the floor once again. Not one single punch had been landed from my end. To win this fight I must be smart. His knees, aim at his knees! I charged, aiming high, but swiftly changed my position and planted a low kick right to his kneecap. His knee buckled. Sensing his vulnerability, I kicked the other kneecap. The gigantor dropped to his knees. While on his knees, I viciously kicked him in the nose. Timber! I chopped gigantor down like a tree. I climbed on top of his thick neck and repeatedly struck gigantor in the face until he waved his right hand.

"Final round, fight!" Feeling confident with aiming at his knees, I tried once more. Big mistake, gigantor was expecting it.

He snatched my foot from under me. Crack! My head hit the floor. Before I could regain my composure, a large foot was descending towards my face. I rolled to the left just in time. Just in time for gigantor to grab my hair and toss me like a doll. At this point he was toying with me. Running full speed, he kicked me in my side. Pain jolted through my body. It was over, I raised my right hand.

Gigantor turned his back and began to walk away. A voice inside of me said, "Do not surrender. You are not defeated!" I raised my hand, but I had not waved yet. Finding strength from within, I hopped to my feet. With a running start I jumped onto his back, placing my arms around his broad neck. Squeezing his neck with every ounce of my strength, gigantor slowly began to lose consciousness. Flipping in front of him, I delivered repeated blows to his throat. Gigantor toppled over. I braced myself for his next move, but he was motionless.

"Aniyas, you are the victor!" It was over! Round three goes to me!

I made my way to the conference space bloody and bruised, but I was victorious. Carlos, Allura, and Keir were seated around the table. They were staring at me like I was insane, but they didn't say a word. That was fine because I wasn't in the mood to answer questions. There was no sign of Amanda, tornado girl, or shield boy. The way Amanda was acting, I hope she was eliminated. Not eliminated like dead, but I hope Amanda was eliminated from the assessment.

Mr. and Mrs. Abrafo entered the room. "How are you all feeling?" asked Mr. Abrafo. Did he not see these bruised and battered bodies? We let out a weak, "fine". My wish did not come true, because in pranced Amanda. She looked at me and burst into laughter. I rolled my eyes. I'm not sure why Amanda was so amused, she was bruised up too, and that made me feel a little better. "You five are moving on to the last level. You will have thirty minutes to compose yourselves. See you all soon," said Mr. Abrafo. I exited the conference space without speaking to anyone and limped to my sleeping chamber.

My arm was still bleeding from the spike encounter. Looking in the mirror, I wiped my swollen and bloody lip. "Aaargh!" I yelled.

A large patch of my beautiful hair was missing! I couldn't believe that gigantor thing snatched my hair out. That's why Amanda was laughing hysterically, and Allura, Carlos, and Keir were looking at me like I was crazy. Ms. Haraka came rushing into my sleeping chamber.

"Aniyas, why are you screaming like that?"

"Look at me! Look at my hair! He snatched out my hair!" I yelled. "What am I going to do? I look horrible!"

"Even though I understand why you are upset, your hair should be the least of your worries right now. You must focus on preparing your mind for the last and final level of the assessment, but bring the comb and sit here. I think I have an idea."

Seated on the floor where Ms. Haraka tapped her hand, she began to comb my hair and hum a sweet tune. She had a beautiful voice. I could listen to her sing all day. Lost in her melody, I closed my eyes.

"Aniyas, Aniyas," called Ms. Haraka. "I'm done, go look." I snapped out of her trance and walked to the mirror. Ms. Haraka had braided one large French braid down the center of my crown. This hairstyle camouflaged the large bald spot on the side of my head.

"I love it! Thank you so much!" I ran over and embraced Ms. Haraka.

Allura walked into my sleeping chamber. "What's going on here?" she asked. I released Ms. Haraka and explained how her mother transformed my hair.

"Oh, that's nice, but it's almost time for our final assessment. Shouldn't you be with me, mom?" If I had to say, Allura might be jealous.

"Honey, I was just helping your friend out, I will be there in a second," Ms. Haraka replied. Allura left my sleeping chamber without speaking another word.

"How are you feeling Aniyas? I know yesterday was rough for you and today has also been a challenge."

"Despite how I look, I'm in good spirits. I'm ready for level four."

"That's great to hear. Hydrate yourself and rest up a little bit, and I will see you in a few. I'm going to check on Allura."

"Okay, thanks again Ms. Haraka. I really appreciate you!" Allura was lucky to have such a great mother.

As I returned to the main space, I ran into Father.

"I was just coming to get you. How are you?" he asked.

"I'm feeling good."

"I see you have a new hairstyle. I like it! Did you do that?"

"No, Ms. Haraka did. Some of my hair was snatched out during the combat level, and Ms. Haraka covered my bald spot for me."

"I'm sorry to hear that moo-moo, but all warriors receive war wounds."

The overhead announcement sounded, "Allura, Keir, Aniyas, Carlos, and Amanda, please report to the main floor."

"The final level of the assessment is at hand, prepare your mind and your body will follow. Are you prepared?" asked Adrielle.

"Yes, I'm ready!"

"Whatever the outcome, know I love you."

"I know Father, and I love you too." I jogged off to the main space.

"You are the final five. You are the strongest, fastest, and bravest of all the radiant ones. It is time for your final test. Hopefully one of you will become the source bearer. Please follow me," said Mr. Abrafo. We followed Mr. Abrafo into the meditation space through the hidden door under the timer into the woods. "This is where your final assessment will take place. I cannot reveal what's in store. You must rely on your instincts and your abilities to see you through. Level four starts now!" We were left standing in the middle of what now looked like a forest. How did the scenery just transform like that? Why is it still so dark? I now knew, we were in for many surprises.

A few minutes had passed, and nothing was happening.

"Okay, what do we do?" asked Allura.

"I'm not sure," I responded.

"Be patient!" scolded Amanda. She was starting to annoy every fiber of my body.

"Shish! Do you all hear that?" asked Keir.

"I'm the one with the mega hearing, and I don't hear a thing," Allura responded. The trees began to rustle. The wind began to howl, and the ground dropped from beneath us.

As we all began to plummet, my instincts kicked in. I had never tried to jump mid free-fall, but now would be the perfect time to start.

"Jump everyone, jump!" I screamed. I harnessed about twenty-five percent of my energy within, and leaped as high as I could. "Ugh!" I clutched onto a large tree branch. I did it! Surveying the forest, everyone was holding on to a tree branch, except Carlos.

"Carlos, where are you?" I yelled.

"Carlos, can you hear me?" screamed Amanda. We all shouted his name, but no response.

"This is an unfortunate situation guys, but we must move on," said Keir.

"Carlos!" I yelled one more time. Sadly, what began as five, was now four.

We leaped from tree to tree. "Aah!" screeched Amanda, as she lost her grip. She was falling! Amanda reached out, grasped onto the side of the tree with both hands, and wrapped both legs around it. She safely recovered. "Whew! I thought I was a goner!" Amanda shouted. As much as I didn't like Amanda, I was happy she was okay.

"It was fun hanging with you slow folks but I'm out of here," Allura said, as she used her mega speed. And just like that, Allura vanished. I had to remind myself it was still every man for himself.

Looking ahead, the ground began to rise. Jumping from a tree, I planted my feet on solid ground. Keir and Amanda did the same. The three of us continued our journey.

"What's that?" I said.

"Something is lurking nearby; I can feel it."

"Stay alert! As you both just witnessed, anything can happen," warned Keir.

I saw a shadow swiftly run behind me. Turning around, I called out, "Allura is that you?"

"Oh my god! It might be fast, but that is not Allura!" whispered Amanda. Turning back around, I almost went into shock. What is that? What is that!

We were face to face with a creature I had never seen before. It had the head of a cheetah, the fangs of a wolf, the body of a lion, the skin of an alligator, the paws of a bear, and the wings of a dragon.

"It's a chewah," said Keir.

"A what?" I replied.

"A chewah, they are described in The Book of the Radiant as fierce and deadly creatures. Don't make any sudden movements and be as quiet as possible. Stay facing the chewah and retreat slowly."

We both followed Keir's instructions. So far, so good, the chewah was still standing in the same place. "Slowly, slowly," I said to myself. Thud! Oh no, Amanda had fallen! The chewah looked her way and charged!

Still on her back, Amanda released lava darts at the beast. The fiery darts had no effect on the chewah. It continued to charge. Keir was running full speed, straight towards the creature. Boom! Keir hit the side of the chewah headfirst. The chewah flew back about six feet, before regaining its footing and charging back towards us. Keir's mega strength bought Amanda time to stand to her feet. She continued shooting darts at the beast. I needed to think of something, and fast!

Keir was preparing to strike the creature again. "Where is a weapon when you need one!" he shouted.

Closing my eyes, I harnessed my energy from deep within. A small orb appeared in my hand. The orb grew as I produced more energy. The chewah was in my direct path and getting closer!

"Amanda, aim your lava darts at my orb!" I yelled.

"What? Why?"

"Just do it!" I yelled louder.

As Amanda aimed her darts at my orb, I directed the orb towards the beast and threw it. The chewah was engulfed in the orb, and the lava darts combusted into flames. The creature screeched in agony, as I tossed what was left of the chewah via my orb. Amanda shouted, "Yes! Aaargh!" In the blink of an eye, a second chewah scooped Amanda up and they were out of sight.

"Amanda, Amanda!" I yelled.

"Aniyas, stop yelling, there may be more," cautioned Keir. I braced myself for more chewahs to arrive.

Some time had passed, and no other beasts had presented themselves. "Maybe there were only two of them," I thought to myself. I felt horrible. We had lost Carlos, Amanda, and where in the world was Allura? I hope she's safe.

"Look, it's a pathway," said Keir, "I wonder where it leads."

"Let's find out," I replied. I sure hoped this path led to a pleasant experience. "We should try to find the others," I suggested.

"As much as I would like to reunite with the others, we are in the middle of an enormous forest. We don't even know which direction to look. There also might be a chance they are dead."

"Why would you say that? Don't say that! They are still out there! Allura is still out there!" I shouted.

"I'm just being realistic, Aniyas. You saw what happened." I dropped my head and continued to walk the path.

The pathway ended at a small cabin surrounded by the forest.

"I have no idea what we are searching for or what are instincts should be leading us to. Maybe there are clues in that cabin."

"There could also be more danger in that cabin, Aniyas."

"Or maybe it is filled with items that can aid us," I countered. Full speed ahead, I ran to the cabin. Keir chased behind me.

"Aniyas, no!" It was too late. I opened the door.

"Hello, is anybody here?" There was no response. "Weapons, weapons, weapons!" There were weapons hanging from the walls. "Look at here, load up Keir! We need these! Food!" I rushed to the kitchen enthusiastically.

"I am starving!" I grabbed a handful of nuts out a bowl.

"No! Do not eat those! You don't know where this food came from, Aniyas!" warned Keir. He might be right, but I was famished.

"After what we just experienced, this seems too good to be true."

"Maybe it's a reward for our effort," I said. Keir gave me the side-eye.

"Fine, I won't eat anything, but I'm definitely taking a weapon or two with me."

I reached for the nine-millimeter. "You would choose that gun," said Keir. I gave a sarcastic smile.

"Where is the washroom? I need to relieve myself," said Keir.

"I need to go too."

"Well let's go."

We walked out of the living space into the hallway. There was a washroom as soon as we turned the corner.

"You can go first," insisted Keir.

"Okay, thanks, I'll make it quick."

"That was fast."

"I told you I was going to make it quick," I giggled.

"I'll make it quick too," said Keir as he walked into the washroom and shut the door. I heard a noise.

"Oh no, not again," I said to myself. There was a door down the hallway that started to creak open at the hinges. I aimed the gun and shouted, "Who's there?" I couldn't believe what came stumbling out the door!

"Allura! You're alive!" I yelled, as I ran to embrace her. Keir rushed out of the washroom.

"What's going on out here?"

"See! I told you she was still out there!"

"That you did, Aniyas! It's great to see you Allura!"

"It's great to see both of you as well," Allura smiled, and then she stumbled to the floor.

"Allura! What's wrong?" I asked while helping her up.

"I'm not sure. I stumbled across this cabin, pun intended," she laughed. "I ate a handful of nuts off the kitchen table. A few seconds later, I was lightheaded. I'm not sure what happened after that. I guess I made my way to the sleeping chamber and took a nap," Allura explained.

Keir looked at me and said, "I told you not to eat those nuts."

"That story does sound creepy. Let's grab some more weapons and get out of here!" I urged.

We were locked and loaded and heading out the door.

"Not so fast children. You come into my home, eat, sleep, use the washroom, and take my weapons without so much as a thank you," a voice said. An older woman with long gray hair emerged from the shadows.

"Where did you come from? Who are you?" I questioned.

"Do you dare question me in my own dwelling place? Who are you, and why are you stealing my belongings?"

"Ma'am we didn't mean any harm. We will be on our way," said Keir.

"Will you?"

The weapons fell from our hands, and the door to the cabin locked. "Why didn't I listen to Keir?" I thought to myself.

"Stay and have dinner, I've prepared all this food. The least you can do is eat," demanded the woman.

"We're not hungry, thanks. Let's go guys," I said, as I swiftly walked to the door. I tried to unlock the door, but it wouldn't budge. I pulled with all my strength, nothing!

"Let me try," said Keir. Keir tugged at the door with no luck. His mega strength couldn't even open it.

"Again I say, come, sit down, and have dinner with me," commanded the woman.

"Again I say, we don't want to," I replied.

"Sit and eat!" she yelled! This was about to get ugly. "Pardon my manners. I got a little upset there. I just want some company. This is the last time I'm going to ask, sit and eat with me," she insisted.

"Keir, get that door opened now!" I urged. He still couldn't open the door, and Allura was still in a daze. She was in no position to help right now.

"Okay, my patience has grown thin." The woman lifted her hands and said, "Come eat and go to sleep, stay with me, and never leave. Come eat and go to sleep, stay with me, and never leave."

"Keir, opened the door!" I yelled.

Before I knew it, we were all involuntarily headed towards the kitchen. I was trying to fight it, but I couldn't stop moving.

"What are you doing? Stop it!" I yelled.

"Now I know what I'm dealing with." Keir raised his hands and said, "The words you say hold no weight, we will leave, we won't stay. The words you say hold no weight, we will leave, we won't stay." We slid backwards towards the door. The woman raised her hands higher and spoke louder. We slid back towards the kitchen table. We were in a real-life tug-of-war.

The forces were so strong in the cabin, the food was levitating, and the weapons were floating.

Keir shouted, "Let us out, but she stays in, and we will never be able to return again. Let us out, but she stays in, and we will never be able to return again." The cabin door swung open. We started sliding backwards towards the front door again.

"They will pay, make them stay, hold them steady in their place. They will pay, make them stay, hold them steady in their place," said what I now assumed was an enchantress. We stopped sliding, but I couldn't move my body.

"Keir, Allura, can you move?" I asked.

"No!" they both shouted. Oh boy, things were not looking good for us.

"Let us soar out the door, never to return anymore! Let us soar, out the door, never to return anymore!" Keir shouted. The entire cabin began to shake. We flew right out the front door and landed on our bottoms.

The enchantress was storming towards the door. Keir bounced up and yelled, "Bring the weapons from within, shut the door and lock her in! Bring the weapons from within, shut the door and lock her in!" All the weapons in the cabin floated to Keir, and then the door slammed shut. The enchantress was locked inside, banging on the window.

"Let's get out of here," said Allura. She didn't have to tell me twice!

"That was amazing, Keir!" I shouted.

"Thank you, Aniyas. That's actually the first time I was able to use my enchantment other than erasing a memory."

"That's wonderful! Your abilities are evolving," I praised.

"Thanks again, but we need to get further away from that cabin. Come on guys, hurry!" Keir commanded. Allura was slower to follow, feeling lightheaded once again.

"I'm trying to keep up, but I still don't feel so well," said Allura.

"I understand but we must keep moving," urged Keir. Allura collapsed. I dropped to her side.

"I need water," she whimpered.

"There's a stream straight ahead." Keir said,

"I'm not sure about that, Aniyas. I don't trust anything in this forest."

"Understandable, but she's too weak to move on. She needs hydration." Keir lifted Allura and carried her to the stream.

Allura scooped the water in her palms and gulped. "This water taste so pure. I really can't describe it."

Thirsty, I gave the water a try, despite Keir's warning. "Wow, it's unlike anything I have ever tasted before," I raved.

Curiosity got the best of Keir, he drunk the water as well. "It is outstanding."

Seconds later Allura hopped to her feet. "I feel exceptionally better!"

"I don't know what it is, but I feel different," I said.

"I feel different too, but in a pleasant way," stated Keir.

"Yeah, I feel faster and more alert," Allura added. She darted off and was back in a flash.

"You are faster," I acknowledged.

"And I'm stronger." Keir lifted me over his head with two fingers.

"Put me down!" I fussed. Keir chuckled. I hoped this wasn't another too good to be true moment.

We continued through the forest. "Where is Amanda?" asked Allura.

"We were attacked by chewahs and one of them snatched her," I explained.

"Oh no, that's horrible!"

"Yeah, it is."

"And I see Carlos hasn't shown back up."

"Nope!"

"Where did you go when you left us?" I questioned.

"Unfortunately, my mega hearing led me straight to that cabin. I was there the entire time."

"I'm just glad that enchantress didn't harm you," I said.

"Something is coming! I can hear it!" Allura shouted abruptly. I didn't hear or see anything, but I heeded her warning, and Keir did too. The ground began to shake beneath us. Boom! Boom! Boom! Boom! To my bewilderment, gigantor was headed our way.

"Not him again!" I thought to myself.

"Keir looked at us and asked, "Are you all ready?"

"Ready!" we yelled. Aiming my nine, I pulled the trigger. Nothing, nothing, there were no bullets in the weapon! Frustrated, I hurled the gun to the ground, and reached across my body with my right hand to draw my sword. I lightly ran my finger across the blade to ensure it was sharp, it was.

"Warning guys, there are no bullets in the guns!" I shouted. With weapons in hand, Allura and Keir stood in fighting stance. Myself on the other hand, I ran, jumped, and sliced gigantor straight down the middle. He fell to the ground split in two. That was easy!

"Alright Aniyas!"

"Way to go!" they cheered. Boom! Boom! Boom! Boom! There I go jumping the gun again. The ground shook violently this time. Four more gigantors had arrived.

We were in full combat mode. Allura used her speed to bounce from tree to tree. The gigantors were fast, but too slow to strike her. Allura threw her spear right between the eyes of a gigantor. Bullseye, and down he went! I'm not sure if these gigantors were weaker than the one we fought earlier, or if we were just stronger. Keir was handling two gigantors with ease, and I slayed another one with a round house kick and a sword across the throat. "Alright seems like you all have this covered, I'm off to become the source bearer." Allura dashed off. I couldn't believe she abandoned us again. We literally just saved her life. Anyway, I rushed over to help Keir, but he didn't need it. Both gigantors were knocked out on the ground.

As we celebrated our victory, we didn't notice that one of the gigantors was still conscious.

He grabbed my sword from my side and sliced Keir in the back. "Aaargh!" shrieked Keir, as he stumbled forward. It was still dark, so we weren't aware of the cliff nearby. Keir fell over the edge.

"No!" I screamed, as the gigantor swung the sword at me. I dodged his attempts to strike me, rolled over to where Allura dropped her spear, and threw it right through the gigantor's heart. He crashed to the ground. I raced back over to the edge of the cliff.

"Keir! Keir! Can you hear me?" I called. "Keir, please, say something!" I shouted. Keir didn't respond. My eyes searched all around, but I didn't see him. I dropped to my knees and sobbed in agony. I couldn't believe Keir was gone.

"Get up, Aniyas! Get up!" the voice inside me said. I struggled to my feet. My heart was heavy, but I continued on. A glowing orb appeared in my hand. No images were materializing, but it was guiding me through the forest.

"Where are you leading me?" I said aloud. After several twists and turns, the orb vanished. "Hey! Come back! I'm still in the middle of nowhere!"

A light began to flicker about twenty feet away. "Keir, is that you?" I ran towards the light. No one was there. The light dimmed. "Hello! Hello!" I called. Suddenly, a luminating spear appeared.

"It's yours for the taking," I heard a voice say.

"Who is that? Who's there?" There was no response. I reached out to grab the spear, but my hand was knocked away.

Why did you just do that?" I questioned Allura.

"Remember I told you, if it came down to it, I would do what needs to be done. I forgot; you don't know much about any of this. That beauty right there, is The Spear of the Source Bearer. If you would've read The Book of the Radiant, you would know that. Now excuse me as I take my rightful place," Allura smirked.

Allura reached out for the spear, but I grabbed her hands and threw her to the ground. Rage filled my heart.

"Do you know Keir is dead because of your selfish ways? Instead of helping us, you left us there, and now Keir is dead!" I screamed.

"I'm sorry about Keir, but we all knew the risk we were taking by coming out here. It wasn't my duty to protect Keir. My one and only purpose is to become the source bearer. So, step aside or prepare to battle." She must still be lightheaded because there was no way I was backing down.

Allura bounced back on her feet, slower than usual. She reached for the spear again, but this time I chopped her hand and struck her in the chest. Surprised, Allura began to throw punches at me. I blocked them and returned the favor. Neither one of us landed a blow. Our defense was strong. Going low, I swiped kicked Allura's ankles. She dropped to the ground. Allura hopped back up, slower than before. Allura swung a powerful right and connected. My head twisted to the side. She extended her hand towards the spear again. I struck her in the side, and she crashed to the ground once more. She jumped back up, even slower than the last time.

"Wait, do you hear that?" Allura turned her head and shouted,

"Keir!" I turned my head in the same direction with excitement, but Keir wasn't there. Turning back towards Allura, she had her hand around the spear. She deceived me.

"That was really low Allura!" I yelled.

"I told you, by any means necessary," she smirked. Allura tugged at the spear, but it didn't budge. She pulled harder, nothing. Concern filled Allura's eyes. I approached her, and she swung at me with her free hand. Dodging the blow, I approached again. Allura grasped the spear with both hands and lifted her body to swing around the rod of the spear. She kicked me to the ground. I hopped back on my feet swiftly. This time I was too fast for Allura. I jumped up and crashed my elbow down violently on Allura's head. She plummeted to the ground, releasing her grip on the spear. I stretched my hand out to grab the spear, but I didn't have to touch it, it came to me. I grasped the spear, and the tip began to glow brighter. Allura looked up at me with defeat in her eyes. I was the Source Bearer!

CHAPTER NINETEEN

Shine Bright

As I stood with spear in hand, Mrs. Abrafo appeared. "Congratulations, Aniyas! You are the one we've been waiting for!" She placed a gold headdress on my head and a bracelet around my wrist.

"Th-thank you," I stuttered. I was in shock. "I'm so sorry about Keir," I sighed.

"Don't be sorry, sometimes our calling requires great sacrifice." I was impressed by Mrs. Abrafo's strength. She continued to speak, "You both fought well, but Allura, let this be a lesson. Never leave your tribe amid a battle, and always remember, you can never stop what is meant for someone else, no matter how hard you try. Allura looked at me and dropped her head.

I wasn't sure if I would ever forgive Allura. Her true colors were revealed, and I no longer trusted her. "Aniyas, this title comes with great responsibility, but I am confident you can manage," assured Mrs. Abrafo. "Shine bright, and never let anything or anyone dim your light!" I shook my head and smiled. "Follow me young ladies. It is time to return to the training facility and present our source bearer."

We were back in the meditation space. How? I wasn't sure.

"Are you ready Aniyas?"

"I'm ready!"

Mrs. Abrafo opened the door and said, "I present to you, the

Source Bearer!" I stepped onto the main floor, with spear in hand. The crowd began to clap, scream, and cheer. Being praised was unfamiliar to me, but I stood there and basked in my glory. Father ran to embrace me.

"I knew it! I knew it moo-moo!" I smiled.

"Aniyas, please make your way to the platform," Mrs. Smith said from the overhead speaker. As I walked through the crowd, they continued to applaud. Mr. Abrafo grabbed my hand and helped me onto the platform. The cheers grew louder. I was honored.

"Man, woman, and child illuminated by the sun, we are familia, we are one." Instantly, the room was silent. Mr. Abrafo continued, "Aniyas, I am proud of your bravery and strength. You went into the fourth level, last on the performance list, but emerged as number one. Let this be a lesson to you all, it's not where you start, but how you finish. You must work hard and never give up! As you lead the indigents to freedom, you have my unwavering support. Whatever you need Aniyas, let me know. At this time, I will meet with all the radiant ones and Aniyas in the conference space. We will return shortly, but right now all hail the Source Bearer! The crowd erupted in cheers and applause.

Tears streamed down my face like a river.

"Keir!" I yelled. I raced into his arms. He embraced me tightly. "I thought you were dead!" I cried. Still wrapped in his embrace, I lifted my head. "Carlos, Amanda, you're alive!" I was elated, and I was even happy to see Amanda. "How, how are you all here?"

"I fell over the cliff onto a ledge below. I hit my head and was knocked unconscious. When I came to, I was back at the training facility in my sleeping chamber," explained Keir.

"I looked over the cliff, but I didn't see you! I would've helped you!"

"It's okay Aniyas, I know you would have. It was dark and difficult to see." We locked eyes and embraced once more.

"Carlos, Amanda, what about you?"

Carlos jumped right in, "I tried to activate my jumping ability, but I couldn't. As I was plummeting to what I thought was my death, I grasped a vine. My strength was depleted, and I didn't understand why, so instead of climbing back up, it was easier to climb down. Fear of the unknown traveled through my body, as I maneuvered down the vines. Finally, my foot reached solid ground. I saw a bright white flash, and I was back at the training facility." I sat there baffled.

"My turn. The chewah took me back to its cave. Why didn't it eat me immediately? I don't know! The chewah fell asleep, and I knew that was my only chance of escaping. Quietly, I tiptoed out of the cave. I saw a bright white flash, and I was back at the training facility."

"Hmm, interesting!" I said.

"Well, Aniyas just beat me fair and square. As you can all see, The Spear of The Source Bearer chose her," Allura chimed in, as she sat in the back far corner with her mom.

"No one asked her!" I thought to myself. "Keir, Carlos, and Amanda, I'm so grateful you are all okay!"

"Thank you, Source Bearer," Amanda giggled. We all stood up to embrace once again.

"You all probably have questions about your time in the forest and how you returned to the facility," said Mr. Abrafo.

"Yes! First off, how did the woods turn into the forest?" I questioned.

"I'll explain everything. Allura and Ms. Haraka already know this information. There is a radiant one we call The Conveyor. He has the ability to transport individuals from one place to another, without them knowing. Once The Conveyor transports an individual, there is only a certain amount of time that individual's mind will allow them to stay in that place before they return to their original location. He can also return a person to their original location. The Conveyor transported you all to a forest right outside of Mathonia. Many people fear traveling the road to Mathonia because of what lies in that forest. You were placed there because that's where The Spear of The Source Bearer would reveal itself, according to The Book of the Radiant. It was no easy feat, but you all made it out alive.

"You all returned for different reasons. Carlos, fear triggered your return. Fear also drains your abilities, that's the reason you could not jump. A radiant one must be fearless to reach their full potential. Keir, being knocked unconscious triggered your return. Also, never turn your back to an enemy, even if you think you have defeated them. Always stay alert! Amanda, it was your capture by the chewah. You had the opportunity to slay the beast while it rested. Never spare your enemy. Allura, I have no explanation why you didn't return when you were enchanted to sleep."

"I'm not surprised!" I blurted out. Everyone glared at me. "Oh, that thought was actually supposed to stay in my head," I said.

"Even though mistakes were made, each one of you survived, and that's what truly matters," added Mrs. Abrafo. I was really growing fond of Keir's mom.

"I have one more imperative piece of information to share. I'm sure you all have noticed, Gardash is always gloomy. The reason, the regime is blocking the sun. The sun enhances the indigents strength and the radiant ones abilities. The massive stone wall surrounding Gardash, is blocking the sun. What was made to look like stone, is an indestructible metal called Chrontum. The wall can only be opened if we unlock the four points of locality. The points are in various areas throughout Gardash and heavily guarded. When the time is right or needed, whichever comes first, we will open that wall."

"I really have to get in the loop. I know nothing," I said to myself.

"Aniyas, this is when your role as the source bearer matters the most, we will discuss that privately. That is all for now, we will continue this discussion in the a.m., but right now we will celebrate Aniyas.

"A celebration for me?"

"Yes, of course! There is a change of garbs in your sleeping chamber." How does Mr. Abrafo know all this information? Why would that thought come to mind at this moment? Let me stop over analyzing and go enjoy this celebration.

Wow, this is beautiful! Placing the dress against my body, I twirled in front of the mirror. Even though it felt like a dream, this was all really happening. I freshened up and donned my gown.

"You look stunning honey!" Father said, as he walked into my sleeping chamber.

"Thank you," I blushed.

"I'm so proud of you!"

"Thank you," I said again. We embraced.

"Now let's go celebrate, everyone is waiting for you."

Walking into the main space, my mouth dropped. The space had been transformed with elaborate decorations fit for a queen. I couldn't believe all this was for me.

"Come Aniyas, sit at the head of the table," directed Mrs. Abrafo. "We have prepared a feast for you." The spread was amazing! Any food you could think of, was probably on the table. I was ready to devour all my vegetarian favorites, and you know it, cherpinals! They even had lava juice! I sat to eat.

"Aniyas, how does it feel to be the source bearer?" Carlos asked.

"I'm honestly not even sure yet, I'm still soaking it all in."

"Understandable, it's a lot to digest!" said Carlos.

"Yeah, but right now, I'm just focused on digesting this food." Everyone at the table chuckled.

"That was delicious! Who prepared this meal?" I asked.

"It was a collective effort by a few of the indigent moms," answered Mrs. Abrafo.

"Thank you all so much, it was absolutely amazing!"

"You're welcome. Now let's have some fun! Hit the music!" yelled Mrs. Abrafo. She hopped up and headed to the dance floor. I glared at Mrs. Abrafo in astonishment. It was nice to see her in this element. I joined her.

After a few minutes, everyone was on the dance floor, even Adrielle. This day has just been full of surprises. Keir shuffled my way and grabbed my hand.

"Are you still upset with me?" I asked.

"Of course not, life is too short to hold grudges."

"Thanks for your forgiveness."

"No prob Bob," laughed Keir. He was so corny, but it was so cute. I felt a tap on my shoulder.

"Excuse me, Aniyas can I talk to you for a second?" asked Allura.

"No!" I continued to dance with Keir.

"Just give me one second, please." I ignored her.

"Aniyas, just give me a chance to explain my actions!" Allura pleaded. I clutched Keir's hand and moved to another area of the dance floor.

Allura was not about to ruin my night. This was not the time or place for that conversation.

"Ooh, this is my favorite line dance! Come do it with me Aniyas!" Amanda shouted.

"I don't know how to do this," I replied.

"Just follow me, it's easy!"

After a few rounds, I had the dance down pat.

"See, you got it!" smiled Amanda. Keir wasn't doing too bad, but Carlos had him beat.

"Carlos, how do you know how to do this line dance so well?" I questioned.

"I have five sisters!"

"Enough said!" We giggled. The song changed, and we all began to jump around. This was the most fun I had ever had! Glancing around, I was ecstatic to be in the presence of my people, my tribe! Everyone looked so beautiful. I wished this night could last forever.

"Hey moo-moo."

"Hey dad!"

"Are you enjoying yourself?" he asked.

"Yes, this is the best time ever!"

"I'm glad to hear that honey. You deserve it!"

"Thanks dad!"

"Okay, now let's boogie!"

"Did you just say boogie?" I chuckled. Poor Adrielle didn't have an ounce of rhythm, but he was enjoying himself, and that's what mattered.

"Bring out the cake!" Mrs. Abrafo shouted. Ms. Haraka and a few other ladies carried out the largest cake I had ever seen. It was a layered cherpinal upside down cake. My favorite! "All hail the Source Bearer. All hail the Source Bearer!" chanted the crowd. Tears of joy collected in my tear ducts. I fought them back. This was like the big birthday party; I never had. I felt so loved!

After four pieces of cake, I forced myself to stop eating and rushed back to the dance floor. We were out there breaking a sweat. I felt another tap on my shoulder, it was Mrs. Smith. She looked stunning. Mrs. Smith is slim and short in stature. She has light skin and long curly hair. Her eyes are large and round, and her nose and lips are thin.

"Congratulations, Aniyas!"

"Thank you, Mrs. Smith!"

"You look gorgeous," she said.

"Thank you, so do you."

Mrs. Smith zoned out for a second. "I really wish Mara was here."

As much as I empathized with her feelings, I didn't wish the same. She looked sad, so I gave Mrs. Smith a big hug. "I needed that," she smiled.

I smiled back. "Dance with me," I said as I grabbed her hands. She smiled again and began to groove with me. This was a special moment and a special night for sure.

It was getting late, so Mr. Abrafo wrapped up the celebration. Everyone said their goodbyes. Allura was still in the corner, where she had been most of the night. She smiled at me. I frowned and walked off.

"What is that all about?" asked Ms. Haraka. She saw our exchange.

"Nothing," I replied.

"Whatever it is, I'm sure you two will work it out." I wasn't so sure about that, but I just smiled.

"Congratulations on your accomplishment!"

"Thank you. I appreciate that!"

"Be wise in all your decisions. Your title holds great responsibility. A great leader puts their people first and remains humble." Her daughter needed this advice more than I did. Ms. Haraka continued, but I listened until she finished. We said our goodbyes, and I hurried to bed before anyone else approached me. I was exhausted!

CHAPTER TWENTY

Rise Up!

I woke up to a glorious smell, which led to the main space. There was an exquisite bouquet of flowers in the center of the table.

"Keir, what is all this?"

"Just wanted to celebrate you once more, so I made breakfast."

"Thank you so much," I blushed.

"Come, sit and eat." He pulled out my chair.

"Such a gentleman and I didn't know you cooked."

"There's a lot you don't know about me."

"You can say that again!" I said as I gave Keir the side-eye.

"Let's not go there," he replied. I rolled my eyes playfully.

"Where are your parents?" I questioned.

"Father went to meet someone, and Mother is cleaning our dwelling place, see." Keir pointed to the screen.

"Your mother is amazing. She's been so kind to me."

"Yeah, she is a great person," he smiled.

"Have you seen my father?" I asked. "He went to your dwelling place to get the rest of your belongings." "Oh, okay. He's really serious about not going back home. I thought he would've folded by now. But anyway, let's enjoy this wonderful meal you have prepared. Let's eat!"

"That was delicious!" "Thank you kindly," Keir responded.

"I need to get dressed for the day. I'll be back."

"Can I come with? I would love to see your spear. It looks so awesome!"

"Sure." I walked into my sleeping chamber after showering. Keir was sitting on the edge of my bed, admiring my spear. I watched and admired him.

"Can I hold it?" he asked.

"Of course, go right ahead."

"Wow, it's heavy!"

"Really? It's as light as a feather when I hold it."

"I bet it is, you are the source bearer."

"Makes sense," I giggled.

"Are you afraid to be the source bearer?"

"No."

"Not even a little?"

"No," I stated again.

"Well, that's good. You've always been fearless," Keir said as he stepped closer to me. He took another step, and another one, until his lips were pressed against mine. I closed my eyes and savored the moment.

A tingling sensation shot through my body, but it wasn't from the kiss. An orb appeared in my hand.

"What is it Aniyas? What do you see?" questioned Keir.

"Your mother is at the front door speaking with two gentlemen. Wait, one of the men is Guardian Patroller Rogers." Another sensation I had never felt before traveled through my body. "This has already happened! We must go now!" We raced to Keir's dwelling place.

"Stay here in the closet Aniyas, this is my home. I don't want to create suspicion by you being here."

"Okay." Keir walked out the closet door.

"No, no!" Keir screamed. I rushed into their living space. Mrs. Abrafo laid in Keir's arms lifeless and bleeding. This could not be happening!

"Mrs. Abrafo, Mrs. Abrafo, get up!" I shouted as I shook her. "What happened? What happened!" I cried.

Without speaking a word, Keir lifted his mother, hit a switch on the closet wall, and carried her into the washroom.

"Amanda! Signal for Amanda! She can heal her!" I shouted.

"I already did," said Keir.

"Good, good then, everything will be okay!" Keir filled the bathtub up with water and placed Mrs. Abrafo in it. Only a few minutes had passed, but it felt like an eternity.

"Come on Amanda, get here!" I thought to myself. This is when I wished we all had Allura's mega speed. There was a knock at the door. She's here! Nope, it was Adrielle, and he was frantic!

"We must go! We must go now!" yelled Father.

"What's wrong?" I questioned. Adrielle spotted the blood on the floor.

"What happened here?" he yelled.

I led him to the washroom.

"Oh no, I'm too late!" he cried.

"You are not too late! Amanda is on the way!" I assured him.

"Oh yes, yes, she has the healing ability. Praise the Leading Light!" he said. Keir remained silent as he stared at his mother.

"Father, why are you so upset? What happened?"

"I returned to our dwelling place, and the door was wide open. The place was trashed! I yelled for your mother. She came rushing down the stairs into my arms, yelling, "Don't let them hurt my baby!" She informed me the guardian patrol had been there looking for you. She told them you weren't there, and they flipped our home upside down. They found a locket in your sleeping chamber. Meesa said once they found the locket, they left. Your mother also said it was odd, because they walked right in like they had the code to our keypad. I had a feeling they were coming here."

"Oh no Father, Keir gave me that locket! His name is engraved in it. That's why they were here, they were looking for me! I also had several visions of the guardian patrol at our door. This is all my fault!"

"It's not your fault, Aniyas! Do not blame yourself!" I began to cry. "Calm down and tell me exactly what happened here," said Adrielle.

"I'm not sure. We will have to look at the video footage." Keir was still silent.

Amanda finally arrived. "What happened!" she shouted.

I filled her in quickly as she prepared to heal Mrs. Abrafo. She closed her eyes, and her hands lit up. They were as red as my eyes when I used to cry all night. Amanda placed her hands in the water, and nothing happened. She tried again, and still nothing happened. Amanda tried once more, and Mrs. Abrafo's body still laid lifeless in the bathtub.

"Why is it not working!" shouted Keir. Amanda slid down the wall to the washroom floor as the tears slid down her face.

"I'm sorry Keir, it's too late, too much time has elapsed. I can't heal her."

"No, no, you just have to try again," encouraged Keir. "Try one more time."

"Yeah, try one more time! You can do it!" I added.

"It's too late guys, I'm so so sorry!" sobbed Amanda. Keir dropped to his knees and wept.

Keir wrapped his mother's body up and transferred her to a back space in the training facility. We went into the viewing space to see what had transpired.

"May I help you?" said Mrs. Abrafo as she opened the door.

"I'm Patroller Rogers and this is Patroller Jackson. May we come in?"

"Sure, come in, have a seat. Now, how may I help you?" she questioned.

"We are looking for Aniyas. Have you seen her?"

"No, I haven't," Mrs. Abrafo lied.

"Interesting," Patroller Rogers said as he flicked a toothpick on the Abrafo's floor. He was ignorant. I despised that man.

"We have reason to believe she might be here."

"Why is that?" "We found a locket in her sleeping chamber that was engraved, From Keir. Isn't that your son's name?"

"Well yes, but I'm sure there is more than one Keir in the province of Gardash," smiled Mrs. Abrafo.

"That might be so, but we have intel that Aniyas has been seen here before."

"I'm not sure where you're getting your information from, but she's not here."

"Well in that case, you wouldn't mind if we take a look around," said Rogers.

"Be my guest." The home was small, so the search was quick.

"I guess she's not here," stated Patroller Rogers. "Wait, what's in this closet?" asked Patroller Jackson. That is when all hell broke loose.

"Just cleaning products," answered Mrs. Abrafo. Jackson pulled on the door handle, but he couldn't open the closet.

"Why can't I open the door?"

"Oh, it gets stuck sometimes," Mrs. Abrafo lied again.

"I think you're pulling our tails. Open that door!" ordered Rogers.

"See, I can't open it either," she said as she tugged on the door.

"Okay, no problem, I'll kick the door down, or better yet just shoot the knob off," threatened Patroller Rogers.

"Please don't destroy my home," Mrs. Abrafo pleaded, as she stepped in front of the closet door.

"I'm going to tell you one time and one time only, move!" shouted Rogers. Mrs. Abrafo stood her ground.

Rogers drew his gun from his holster, and Mrs. Abrafo kicked it across the room. Rogers scrambled after his gun. Jackson also drew his gun, and Mrs. Abrafo kicked his hand and struck him in the nose. The gun flew from Jackson's hand. He crashed to the floor. Pow! Pow! Pow! Rogers shot Mrs. Abrafo in the back. The patrollers tugged on the door once more, kicked it, even shot at it, but the door wouldn't budge. Rogers fired some shots, placed a gun beside Mrs. Abrafo, rushed out of the home, and closed the door behind them.

Keir cried, "I put an enchantment on the closet door this a.m., so we wouldn't be disturbed. I just wanted a little alone time with you Aniyas. If I hadn't done that, the closet door would've opened. My mother would still be alive!"

"Please don't blame yourself Keir! It's not your fault!" I reassured him. Mr. Abrafo, Mr. Edgerton, Chase, and Mara burst into the viewing space. What were they doing here?

"Okay, we aren't too late! You are all here. Wait, where is your mom, Keir?" asked Mr. Abrafo. Keir dropped his head.

Mr. Abrafo looked up at the camera monitors and yelled, "My wife! No, no, not my wife!" Keir grabbed his father and embraced him.

We all walked back where Mrs. Abrafo's body was resting. Mr. Abrafo fell by her side. After a few seconds, he stood to his feet and walked away. We followed him. "Unfortunately, there is no time to mourn or bury my wife. The guardian patrol will be back soon with the guardian infantry. Keir, send out the signal so all the indigents and radiant ones can report here at once.

"Yes, Sir!"

"Hurry back son, you need to hear this!" Keir was back in a flash.

"Someone reported the roof incident at Edgerton. Someone saw you use your abilities, Aniyas," said Mr. Abrafo. I lunged at Mara!

"It was you!" Keir grabbed me.

"It was not me Aniyas! I swear to you, it was not me!" I looked at Chase.

"It wasn't me either!"

"We don't have time for this right now! Be quiet and listen!" shouted Mr. Abrafo. That was the first time I ever heard him raise his voice. We shut our mouths!

"Again, all their forces will be heading here soon. Aniyas, Amanda, and Keir I need you to head to the four points of locality. We must open that wall! I will send a few more radiant ones once they arrive.

"I'm sorry, but why are Mr. Edgerton, Chase, and Mara here?" I questioned.

"I'll take this," said Mr. Edgerton. "I am an indigent," Mr. Edgerton announced. Chase looked shocked. "I am not originally from Gardash. My birthplace is Laythor, where my parents ruled. My marriage to Mrs. Edgerton was arranged by my parents. It was a power move, and taking Mrs. Edgerton's last name was a part of the plan." Again, I was speechless.

"Things were starting to change, and my parents knew if I married into the Edgerton family, I would be safe and could possibly correct the madness that was starting to take place. A few years after our marriage and moving to Gardash, I was informed that my parents had been murdered. My mother and father resisted the new universal command. There would be no ranking system and universal laws under their rule. I vowed to avenge their death and set the indigents free again. I would do that by infiltrating the system.

"The Edgerton's and Kadar are in business together. I earned Kadar's and the Edgerton's respect because I expanded their empire. Their wealth increased ten-fold when I became the CEO of their tech company. Of course, I was paid a nice salary, but I also had access to Mrs. Edgerton's funds. She's always drunk so she never tracks the finances. It was always my goal to build a training facility for the indigents, I just had to find an indigent I trusted. Then one cold day, the universe led me to Mr. Abrafo. We have been working together for many years. Back to Kadar, my wife is having an affair with him, and I'm divorcing Mrs. Edgerton, but that is another story." I looked over at Chase, but that bit of information did not seem to shock him. I'm sure there were more surprises in store. We all continued to listen.

"An ally at the patrol base feeds me intel and tipped me off about the Edgerton roof situation. I was informed Mara was taken in for questioning. That is when I called a meeting with Mr. Abrafo this a.m., and I made sure to get Mara from the patrol base and bring her here. I'm not sure what else they know, so I brought Chase as well to keep him protected. Whatever differences you all have, must be put aside now! We must stick together!"

Mrs. Smith entered the conference space and began to bawl, "My baby! Oh my baby!" She grabbed Mara to embrace her.

"Get your hands off of me lady!" Mara looked at Mrs. Smith like she was insane.

"Honey, I'm your mother!" Chase had that shocked expression on his face again.

"My mother? How? This can't be! My mother is dead!"

"It's true, Mara," Mr. Edgerton chimed in.

"Dad, why didn't you tell me any of this?" questioned Chase.

"I did it to protect you son!" "Please come with me Mara, you too Chase. I have a lot to share with you both," said Mrs. Smith.

"It's okay children. I will come too," said Mr. Edgerton. They left the conference space.

"Aniyas, Amanda, and Keir, you must go now!" commanded Mr. Abrafo. "Keir knows where all the points of locality are and will fill you in on the way. Hurry!" I raced to get my spear.

"Be safe!" yelled Adrielle.

"Wait Aniyas, follow me first, you too Amanda," said Keir. He led us to another area in the back. Keir opened the door, and there were suits hanging on the wall. I was in awe and so was Amanda.

"Find your name and put your gear on. Grab the weapons next to them as well," ordered Keir.

"Where did these come from? They are amazing!" questioned Amanda.

"Mr. Edgerton created them. He also created uniforms for the combat indigents. Now change, Aniyas get your spear, and I'll meet you both in the main space," Keir said. We followed his instructions.

We were all back on the main space floor. Ms. Haraka, Allura, and Carlos had arrived. Allura and Carlos had on their suits already.

"Keir, Aniyas, and Amanda, Allura and Carlos will be going with you," said Mr. Abrafo. I gave Allura the death stare. "Now go!" commanded Mr. Abrafo.

As we walked to the exit Allura approached me and said, "I know we aren't on the best of terms right now, but trust and believe I will have your back out there. During The Extraordinary Assessment of Valor, we had to compete against each other, but this is different. I've been training my entire life to defeat the regime. I will not leave my tribe behind!"

"Okay then, let's go complete this task," I responded. "Keir, wait up!" I jogged off.

"Listen up everyone," said Keir. "We are headed to chastis. That is where the first point of locality is. Its exact location is in Kadar's office. There are five guards guarding the front door, and we will each take one out. Carlos, once inside, I need you to blast through Kadar's office door. The door is made of Chrontum, but it is thin enough to be penetrated if the force is powerful."

"Hey guys, wait up!" yelled The Conveyor. "I can get you all there in a flash!"

I saw a bright white light and the next thing I knew we were across the street from chastis behind some trees.

"I'm sorry guys, I don't know what happened, but this is the closest I can get us," said The Conveyor.

"It's fine, this is close enough. After we get in, just wait by the front door, so you can take us to the next location."

"Okay."

"Are y'all ready?" We all nodded our heads.

"Let's go!" It was time for war, and Keir was leading the charge!

Defeating the guards was a cakewalk. Carlos blasted through Kadar's office door with ease.

"What are we looking for?" I asked.

"There should be a white control switch in here somewhere," Keir explained. We searched the office.

"Here it is!" Allura shouted. The switch was in a file cabinet drawer, enclosed in a glass case. Keir tried to break the glass with his fist, but he couldn't. I aimed my spear at the case, and nothing.

"I'm new to this, still working out a few kinks," I shrugged.

"Stand back!" yelled Carlos. He blasted the cabinet, but the glass case was still intact. Amanda heated her hands and hit the glass with a lava dart. The glass melted right off.

"Victory! Take that losers!" Amanda shouted. Looking at Amanda, I could do nothing but shake my head and laugh.

Keir hit the switch, and we heard the mighty roar of thunder. We ran back outside. The top of the stone wall was opening, and then it stopped about one fourth of the way. A bright light peaked through.

"Omg, it's the sun! yelled Allura. We leaped with excitement!

Keir raised his hands and chanted, "Keep this fissure opened wide. Don't let it close as we break through each time. Keep this fissure opened wide. Don't let it close as we break through each time." Suddenly, we heard the piercing sound of the province alarm, it was time to move and move fast.

The Conveyor flashed us to our next location. He had trouble getting us inside the building again, but he did manage to transport us to the parking lot behind a van. We were at the Edgerton's tech company headquarters.

"This is the second point of locality. The third location is by the river at the old dock, and the fourth location is in the woods. At this current location we will enter via the side door, go to the tenth floor to room 112, and the white control switch will be there."

"Yes Sir!" I whispered loudly. Keir smiled.

" Remember, there are cameras all around, and this building is heavily guarded. There is no way we won't be seen."

"Why didn't we bring Miles with us?" I asked.

"Miles wasn't there when we departed, and we didn't have a second left to spare," replied Keir. "On the count of three we all run to the side door. Allura wait for us though." She giggled. "Carlos, I need you to blast through the door again. Conveyor, we will be right back. One, two, three," Keir counted.

We all ran and bounced back behind the van. We all stared at each other in confusion. "Okay, let's try again, one, two, three," Keir counted once more. We bounced behind the van for a second time. "Something isn't right. Conveyor, take us back to the training facility, now!" ordered Keir.

The Conveyor was able to transport us back to the training facility with no problem.

"Have you completed the mission already?" asked Mr. Abrafo. "We can't see anything from down here. Our cameras and systems have shut down, and as you know the facility is soundproof, so we can't hear anything either. The techs are working on getting everything back up and running."

"Unfortunately, no Father. We were only able to access the first point of locality and hit that switch, but there was some kind of force blocking our path to the tech company headquarters."

"Oh no, they are on to us," said Mr. Abrafo. "We must regroup. They must have some form of a secondary defense. I'm glad you all came back. The guardian infantry would've been waiting for you at the remaining locality points."

Mr. Edgerton rushed into the main space. "I've just been informed that the guardian patrol and the guardian infantry are on their way!"

Mr. Abrafo looked around at all of us and said, "We must find a way to access those points of locality, or we are doomed!"

"Mrs. Smith have everyone meet in the main space!" I ordered. It was time for me to take the lead.

With spear in hand, I stepped onto the platform looking at all the indigents that stood before me. "As you all may know by now, the guardian patrol and infantry are on their way. Our systems are down right now, so I need a combat indigent to stand guard at each entry point of this facility. If you see the enemy approaching, get back here with haste to warn us." A few of the combat indigents ran off to take their positions. "All the children and elderly will be escorted to our second training facility location by Iyana and Malik. Please gather your belongings and follow them. Iyana, take The Book of the Radiant with you and guard it with your life!"

"Yes, Aniyas," said Iyana.

"Everyone else will stay and fight. We can't keep running and hiding forever, now is the time to take a stand. Combat indigents, put on your uniforms and retrieve your weapons of choice. Radiant ones go suit up, and everyone return to the main space swiftly!" They followed my orders.

I spotted Chase, Mr. Edgerton, Mara, and Mrs. Smith on the main space floor.

"I need you all to go with Iyana and Malik," I said.

"I'm staying right here!" Mr. Edgerton replied.

"Me too!" said Chase.

"It's not safe for you all here."

"Not safe?" replied Mr. Edgerton. "I am an indigent. My parents were the rulers of Laythor. I am a trained and skilled fighter. Chase has also been trained in combat. We can help!"

So, Chase had secrets too I see.

"Okay, you two can stay but Mara and Mrs. Smith I need you to line up behind Iyana."

"Aniyas, I've been in this training facility for many years. I have also picked up a skill or two, but we will go help Iyana and Malik."

"Thank you!" I replied.

"Aniyas, please be safe and know that I am proud of you."

"Thanks Mara, and you be safe as well." "Iyana and Malik, it is time for you all to head out. May the creator be with you!" I yelled. Now that our children and elderly were being led to safety, it was time for war!

We waited, and waited, and waited, but there were no signs of the guardian patrol or infantry. What were they up to?

"Mr. Edgerton have you been in contact with any of your allies or informants?" I asked.

"No, my communication device isn't working anymore."

"Okay, thanks. It will be dark soon. We will rotate combat indigents throughout the night to keep guard at every entry point. Can someone please go check with the techs and see if they have made any progress?"

"Got you!" Allura was off in a flash.

"Amanda, go tell the cooks to prepare a meal and only have water available for drinking. We need our strength!"

"Carlos, as we wait for dinner, I need all the radiant ones to meditate. We must be centered, so our abilities can shine through."

"Yes boss, I'll let the others know!"

Allura was back. "Our systems are still completely down, Aniyas."

"Okay, Keir, I need you to go assign night shift watch rotations."

"On it!" Keir replied. This was going to be a long night.

Dinner was over and still no sign of the enemy. We would all sleep on the main space floor, in case of an ambush.

"Everyone, get your rest! We will need it!!" I shouted. Mr. Abrafo had been in the back with his wife. I didn't bother him because he needed that time to grieve. As I was walking around the main space floor, I bumped into Chase.

"Hey, Aniyas."

"Hi, Chase."

"I just want to apologize again, for everything. I'm also ready to fight!"

"No need to apologize, Chase. I'm sure all of this is a lot to digest. I admire your courage to stay here and fight with us."

"Technically, I am us. My dad is an indigent, which makes me half indigent. I am a part of this tribe." I smiled.

"I'm sure you have many questions for me?"

"No, I don't. Mrs. Smith and my dad told me everything I needed to know and gave me a tour of the facility."

"Okay good, because I'm really not in the mood to answer questions right now," we giggled.

"That's what I love about you Aniyas, even in the midst of turmoil, you can make me laugh." Did he just say, that's what I love about you?

"It was nice talking to you Chase, but I must go check on the others," I said as I turned to walk away. Chase gently grabbed my arm.

"Stop running from me Aniyas, stop running from this, stop running from us." We locked eyes, and I was speechless.

"Come, let's go talk in your sleeping chamber for a while," said Chase.

"We can chat in the meditation space, but let me grab a cherpinal from the kitchen first," I replied.

"Cool, lead the way."

"How are you feeling about your parents' divorce?" I asked as we walked.

"I'm not surprised, but I'm still upset. When my father came into the lounge space to show me the divorce papers, I had a tantrum and threw the papers on the floor. The little boy in me still wants a happy family, but that's not going to happen."

"It's okay to be upset, Chase." He looked so sad; I couldn't help but hug him. I knew what it felt like to long for a happy home. As we embraced, Chase went in for a kiss, but I turned my head and his lips planted on my cheek.

"Let's finish this conversation in the meditation space," I said, as I grabbed a cherpinal from the ice chest.

When I opened the meditation space door, Keir was on his knees in the middle of the floor weeping. Looking at Chase, he gave me a nod and walked away. I'm glad Chase recognized and understood the look in my eyes. Rushing to Keir's side, I dropped to my knees and held him. He wept a little louder. My heart was breaking for him. Keir had one of the best mothers in the universe, and she was gone.

"I should've been there to save her, Aniyas. I should've been there. I failed my family!"

"Keir, you can't keep blaming yourself. It is not your fault." I held him a little closer. I'm not sure why, but I began to sing, "Everything is going to be okay. I'm here to wash the pain and tears away. Don't worry, there will be brighter days. Everything is going to be okay. Everything is going to be okay. I'm here to wash the pain and tears away. Don't worry, there will be brighter days. Everything is going to be okay." Keir was no longer crying. He had fallen asleep. Keir was at peace right now, so I didn't want to disturb him. I gently laid his head on the floor, ran to get a blanket, and covered him up.

When I exited the meditation space Chase was standing outside the door.

"How is Keir doing?"

"He's fine right now, just resting."

"Cool, cool," Chase replied.

"How are you?" I asked.

"I'm good."

"That's good to hear. Well, I'm going to get a little rest. I'll be right over there on the main space floor if you need me."

"Cool," Chase said again as he walked away. Lying on the floor, I couldn't stop thinking about Keir or Chase. They were both taking up space in my head, and this was no time for affairs of the heart. Suddenly, another thought popped into my head. I was unable to use my spear today, and my orb vision came after it was too late. That was concerning, I hopped up to drink a few glasses of water.

"Oh, hey there Aniyas," said Allura as I walked into the kitchen. Carlos and Amanda were in the kitchen as well. We exchanged pleasantries.

"What are you all in here doing?" I questioned.

"Just chatting and getting a snack before we call it a night," Amanda responded.

"I'm too anxious to sleep," said Carlos.

"I'm just going to drink a few glasses of water and be on my way," I stated.

"Oh, okay."

"Cool."

"Okay." After four glasses of water, I went to my sleeping chamber.

As I walked, I peeked in on Mr. Abrafo. He was holding his wife, sleeping, poor guy.

"Hey moo-moo. How are you?" Adrielle asked as I turned the corner.

"I'm okay. How are you?"

"I'm good as long as you're okay," said Father. He gave me a bear hug.

"Thank you Father. I really needed that!"

"Try to get some rest, Aniyas."

"I am, I'm just going to my sleeping chamber for a minute."

"Okay, goodnight."

"Goodnight."

Walking into my sleeping chamber, I did something I hadn't done in a while. Dropping to my knees, I raised my hands and said, "Respected Most High, please be with your heir. We have suffered long enough. I beg you to pardon our errors and free us from these fetters. You have favored us with divine abilities and gifts. We were chosen for a purpose. Assist us in banding together and lead us to victory over our enemies. May all my request be granted, gratitude." Before I went back to the main floor, I checked on Keir. He was still sleeping like a baby. Lowering myself to the floor, I closed my eyes.

A tap on my shoulder awakened me. I hopped to my feet.

"It's time to eat, Aniyas," said Ms. Haraka. It was the a.m. already. We were at war, and I slept through the night like a princess. That was unacceptable.

"Forgive me for oversleeping."

"You didn't oversleep, Aniyas. Your body needed that rest. Now go eat and drink plenty of water," smiled Ms. Haraka.

"Yes ma'am," I smiled back.

Everyone was up eating breakfast, including Chase, Mr. Edgerton, Keir, and Mr. Abrafo.

"Glad you could join us Aniyas. How are you?" asked Mr. Edgerton.

"I'm fine, thanks. Any word from your allies?"

"No, not yet. My communication device still isn't working."

"Unfortunate for you, but luckily for us our systems are back up and running," said Mr. Abrafo.

"Good, good," I replied. "How are you Mr. Abrafo?" I asked.

"As good as I can be." I grasped his hand from across the table, and then Keir's.

"Were there any signs of the guardian patrol or infantry last night?" I asked.

"Nothing!" said Keir.

 Ms. Haraka chimed in, "I wonder what they are up to."

"Me too!" I said.

"We are like sitting ducks here. I don't like it," Carlos added.

"You're right Carlos. We must leave. We have no idea what they could be planning for this training facility. Everyone finish your meal quickly, dress, grab your weapons, and meet back in the main space!" I yelled.

We were all back on the main space floor.

"Alright everyone, listen up, we are heading to the woods. We know that terrain. Miles, I need you to activate your blanket. I want it to look as if there are only a few of us in the woods, to draw our enemy out. All the while, we will be surrounding the guardian patrol and infantry as they approach. Mr. Edgerton, keep trying to contact your informants. We need to know what's blocking us from the points of locality. Have our tech guys help you."

"Yes, Aniyas."

"Has anyone seen Carlos, Amanda, and Allura?" I questioned.

"They were just in the kitchen. I'll get them," said Ms. Haraka. They sure liked hanging together in that kitchen.

"Has anyone been in contact with Iyana and Malik?" I asked.

"Yes, they made it safely. No one was harmed!" Mr. Abrafo replied.

"That's great news!" I shouted. "Gratitude to the Highest!"

Over the past couple of days, I picked up The Book of The Radiant a few times. The book referred to The Source as The Highest on several occasions, which were both remarkably similar to the

Leading Light. I was shocked by the similarities. "Get out of your thoughts, Aniyas. Stay on task," I thought to myself.

"Mr. Abrafo, can you please say a few words?"

"Sure, Aniyas. Man, woman, and child, illuminated by the sun, we are familia, we are one. I don't have a lot to say. We all know our purpose. Now let's go claim what is rightfully ours!" The crowd cheered with applause. At that moment, Ms. Haraka walked back into the main space with Allura, Amanda, and Carlos.

"Okay everyone, be as quiet as an inmate trying to escape from The House of Corrections. Indigents let's go! Miles you're on," I said, as I led my tribe into the woods.

Only Keir, Carlos, and Amanda were visible. They were walking behind us. I wished The Conveyor could just flash us to our location, but his ability was limited to five individuals at a time. Looking ahead, the sun was still peeking through the wall. It was a spectacular sight to see. My body began to tingle, but I didn't receive a vision of any sort. "Keep forward to the hill," I said to Miles, as I walked from underneath the blanket.

"What are you doing Aniyas?" questioned Carlos.

"Something is coming, get ready!" I replied. "Carlos, remember, no fear!"

"No fear!" Carlos repeated after me. Swish was the sound of the blade that grazed pass my ear as I ducked from having it sliced off. The guardian infantry had been activated. We were standing face to face with five infantry guards. Where did they suddenly appear from? Keir used his mega strength and threw one of the infantry guards against a tree. The guard's helmet cracked as he crashed to the ground. Boom! Boom! Carlos blasted a hole straight through two guard's chests. Amanda shot her lava darts. One landed right in the eye of a guard and another dart landed in an infantry guard's neck.

"Well thanks guys, I didn't even have to lift a finger!"

"You're welcome, Aniyas," chuckled Carlos. Keir and Amanda smiled.

We were still on the move when an orb appeared in my right hand. A mighty creature appeared. "Chewahs!" I shouted.

Where are they coming from? Running to the front of the pack,

I yelled, "Everyone run to the hill. Mr. Abrafo, please lead the way. Do not leave that spot. If the guardian patrol and infantry get there before we do, fight for your lives! Allura, you stay with us. Now everyone, go and hurry!"

"Let's go!" yelled Mr. Abrafo.

"Be safe, honey!" shouted Adrielle. I gave him a head nod and ran back to Carlos, Amanda, and Keir.

"Two chewahs are near, I can feel them. Stay alert!"

"Growl!" A chewah jumped out and tried to bite Allura's head off. With her mega speed, she ducked to the ground, pulled her sword, and sliced the chewah across its body four times. The beast plummeted to the ground. I threw my spear and there was a crash in the bushes next to Keir. Rushing over, there lied the chewah with my spear in its neck. I raised my hand, and my spear returned to me. The bushes started to rustle. I should've known that was too easy. The chewah I thought I had just slayed, was back on its feet, and so was the chewah Allura had just sliced up.

"Circle formation!" I shouted. We were all standing back-to-back, so the chewahs couldn't sneak us from behind.

"Why are they still alive?" questioned Allura.

"I don't know!" I shouted.

"Remember Aniyas, don't yell. You could be attracting more chewahs," Keir reminded me.

I nodded in understanding. The chewahs were looking for an opportunity to charge. The beasts snapped and snarled at us.

The chewahs looked hungry, and we looked like dinner.

"Okay, so what's the plan? I do not want one of my arms mauled off," said Carlos

"Fire!" yelled Amanda. "Fire! The beast shall be slayed with fire, that's what The Book of The Radiant says. And remember, Aniyas, my lava darts and your orb killed one in the forest. Fire is the only way to kill them!"

"You're right!" I yelled.

"Girls do not listen," whispered Keir.

"Oops, we forgot not to yell," Amanda whispered back. Closing my eyes, I went deep within. An orb appeared in both hands. They grew with each breath I took.

"Now Amanda!" Dang, I yelled again. Amanda launched her lava darts at my orbs, and I released them. The orbs engulfed the chewahs, burst into flames, and disintegrated them.

"Got em!" Amanda shouted.

"Let's head to the hill!" said Keir.

The tip of my spear began to glow. "What's happening, Aniyas?" asked Amanda.

"I'm not sure, but let's keep moving." A powerful force began to lead me in the opposite direction.

"Aniyas, where are you going?" questioned Keir.

"It's not me! It's my spear. It's leading me in this direction. I can't control it!"

"Drop it!" yelled Allura.

"I can't!" I shouted. "You all go on to the hill. I must follow the path and let the spear guide me."

"Are you sure?" asked Carlos.

"Yes, I'm sure the indigents need all of your strength, now go!" They all ran off to the hill, except Keir.

"I'm not leaving you out here by yourself. I'm coming with you!"

"Okay, just stay alert because I have no idea what we are running into!"

We were moving at an extremely fast pace. The spear was basically dragging me, and Keir was having a tough time keeping up.

"Where is it taking us Aniyas?"

"I told you, I don't know, but I do know that hint of sun feels amazing. Wait, that's where it's taking us, to the sun!"

"Well, thank The Source we are almost there because I'm about to pass out!" said Keir. I giggled. The closer we inched to the sun, the stronger I felt. The spear was no longer dragging me.

"We are almost there Keir, hold on!" I shouted. My legs flew from beneath me, and I crashed to the ground. Keir tumbled over me onto his back.

"So, it is you. I always had a feeling something was off about you, indigent!" shouted Guardian Patroller Rogers as he stood over me.

"Where did you just come from Rogers?" I questioned. I

hopped to my feet and so did Keir. Keir had rage in his eyes as he charged Rogers. Rogers picked Keir up and slammed him to the ground. How was that possible? I attacked, and Rogers blocked every blow.

"Aniyas, go!" yelled Keir as he stood to his feet. "I got this!"

"I can't leave you!" I replied.

"Go, now!" Keir shouted.

"Okay!" I yelled, as I ran.

Patroller Rogers leaped in front of me and smiled. I was stunned, Rogers had a jumping ability! Keir jumped and struck Rogers in the face two times. Rogers crashed to the ground. I took off running.

"You are only a few feet away Aniyas!" I said to myself. Looking back, Patroller Rogers was back on his feet.

Rogers shouted, "You're about to die boy, just like your mother, but I'm gone take my time with you!" My heart sank!

Rogers kicked Keir, and Keir slid back a few feet. Keir charged and slammed Rogers to the ground. Positioned on top of Rogers, Keir began to pound Rogers' face. Rogers rolled and lifted Keir off him. The two continued to tussle. Reaching the wall, where the sun was peeking through, I raised my hand. The sun's rays illuminated my spear. My body began to glow brightly. Rogers and Keir stopped in their tracks and stared in awe. After a few seconds, Patroller Rogers could no longer bear my presence or the sun's rays. He shrieked and ran off.

"Keir, don't run after him!" I yelled.

"I have to, he murdered my mother!"

"I know, I know, but he could be leading us into a trap. It's only two of us. We must be smart!" Keir looked back at me with defeat in his eyes.

"We can't let him go Aniyas, we can't!" sobbed Keir.

My heart broke for my friend. "This isn't the right time, but we are going to get him Keir, I promise!" Keir wiped his eyes and nodded his head.

We raced back to the hill. "Whatever just took place back there was amazing! You are still glowing, Aniyas!"

"Thank you!" I blushed. "I now understand why the spear led

me there and what I need to do next." We reached the hill. The indigents erupted in applause when we arrived. Everyone was staring at me in amazement.

"Wow, she's glowing," I heard many voices say.

"Great to see you two!" Father said as he embraced me. "Everyone is here and safe!"

"I'm elated to hear that!" I smiled at Adrielle.

Allura raced towards me. "They are coming! I can hear them!" she yelled.

"How close are they?" I asked.

"We have about ten minutes!"

"Okay," I said as I walked to the peak of the hill.

I reached the peak of the hill and spoke, "Like all of you, I have grown weary of the dire conditions indigents are forced to live in. I am tired of the unjust treatment we have faced, day in and day out for many years. They have hated us since the beginning of time, for no sound reason. We have been divided by rankings, in an unfair power structure. No matter how intelligent we are, how well we behave, how successful some of us may become, it still isn't enough! They will point out the failures of a few, and pin those failures on all indigents, but they individualize our wins and won't praise the great accomplishments of many. Don't let the elites deceive you into hating your own tribe! There are many indigents that love and respect one another!

"Don't go astray like some of the indigents and conventionals that long to be in the elites world. They should be tired of begging, crying, and pleading to be accepted into a power structure, which wasn't made for us in the first place! We are powerful enough to build our own! We must stand together in love and positivity! Emperor Kadar and the regime have been lying to us, to keep us docile, weak, and afraid, but we must be brave! Our true history was stolen and hidden from us, but that is no more. We have awakened! We are not just indigents; we are radiant ones! We are the chosen ones! I stand before you as the Source Bearer, and I will lead you to victory against our enemies! Rise up! Rise up! Rise up!

ABOUT THE AUTHOR

Anece Rochell was born and raised in Cleveland, OH. She is a graduate of the Cleveland Public School System. Two months after graduating from high school, Anece Rochell graduated from nursing school. Her passion for working with children started early, becoming a pediatric nurse at the age of eighteen. Even though nursing has been a rewarding career, writing has always been her first love. She wrote her first song at the age of eight, songs evolved into poems, and poems into books. The Indigent:Book of Aniyas is Ms. Rochell's debut novel. It is Anece's goal to continue writing literature that inspires and positively impacts our youth.

9 781955 228084